I0718869

Ocean's Infiltrator

DEMELZA CARLTON

DEDICATION

This book is dedicated to Michèle

for giving me my first glimpse beneath the surface

of a world I never knew existed.

SIRENA

Help the humans or let them die?

This will not be the first time I choose to be an instrument of death.

The acrid scent of guns and explosives, the staccato of weapon-fire and the screech of stressed steel as a projectile found its mark. Gun-smoke and steam from the ships' boiler-engines wreathed the scene like fog from colder climates. I heard Da-Xia's screams through the murk as she laboured to bring forth her child.

I shooed the sharks toward the ships, away

from my mother, my sister and their patient. I kept to the outer reefs with the other younger girls, fewer in number than they would be in the future. As the ships approached, the other girls fled, tails flicking and fading into deeper, darker water.

I did not. My family stayed, so I remained. They did not fear the danger and I was no less brave than they. Someone had to see to the sharks.

I watched a human dive from his vessel. I shaped a wave and sent it racing across the surface, pushing him back toward his ship to keep him away from my family. He was a German medical officer from the *SS Emden*, I learned later.

"Mother, help me! I am hit!" I heard Healer Duyong scream.

I saw Mother turn to help Duyong. Duty and love warred in her expression, but Mother chose duty, as always. She turned away and dragged the human down deep.

I watched him die, the boom of guns barely background noise to the sound of my sister screaming then gurgling as she drowned in her own blood, riddled with holes torn by the weapons aboard the humans' ships.

Blood blossomed from Mother's arm, but her call was as strong as the voice she gave to me. No shark approached her as she swam to my sister and her charge, only to find she was too late. Da-Xia's death was as quick as the shell that took her head. She never felt the shots that killed the child within her.

To my shame, I raised my voice to sing to the ships over the fire-fight on the surface. My anger was so great that I would have killed every human aboard, shattering their skulls with my song, had I known how. All I could do was fill them with a desire to flee at all cost.

I felt bitter satisfaction at the captain of the closer ship's response. He ran his vessel aground on the reef, the keel screeching and shattering as the waves ground it flat. Smoke rose from the deck of the *Emden* and I remember shaping the waves to skirt the vessel, letting the fire burn without cease.

The second ship's captain found a different focus for his siren-induced recklessness. He'd spotted another ship and moved out of range of Mother to attack more humans instead. His *Sydney* fired on the *Buresk*. Those on board the *Buresk* scuttled their vessel, opening up the seacocks, before they took to the boats. Coal dust spread like a dark cloud of corruption beneath the surface as the *Buresk* descended to the sea floor.

I turned my eyes from the carnage to assist my mother in healing my sister, but we were too late to do anything for Duyong. Once more, Mother dived into the depths, dragging two bleeding bodies with her. The other girls on shark patrol had long since headed home and I was alone. Heartsick, I headed for the beach.

Lit by the fires aboard the vessel I'd wrecked, I shifted to human form and let tears flow as I sobbed on the sand. No eight-year-old child should witness the death of her own sister.

When Mother returned to find me, her face was grave. *"The Council will believe that the humans caused this disaster on their own and that you fled as the other younger girls did. No child in living memory could sink a ship with just her voice - and no lone adult could sink two. You are young to possess such power, yet it will grow greater still as you do. You are my heir now, child. You must do your duty young, for I am not."*

My mouth opened to sob her name, but I swallowed and stood to address her with the respect that was her due. *"Yes, Elder Sephira. I will do as the Council commands me."*

She looked approvingly at the semi-sunken ship. *"You must learn to lead, for you have the power within you to take my place in the Council. But you must learn to control it."*

My anger burned more fiercely than the ship. I wiped my tears away. *"Will I get to kill more humans?"* I tried to control my voice, but it wavered as I thought of my sister. I'd looked up to Duyong so much and her death tore holes in my heart as if the shells had shredded my body and not hers.

Mother smiled. *"First, you must learn to enslave one, so that he cannot resist you. Duty first, then pleasure."*

SIRENA

Mother was mistaken, I know now. There is always duty, but occasionally pleasure is a part of it.

Like now.

I tried to focus purely on the speed, the feeling of air rushing past me as the metal beast between my legs roared his defiance at the road. There were few others around at this early hour and I pushed him harder than I should have.

It was not enough. I felt tears on my face once more at my memories, for my pain dwelt deep. I had not thought of Duyong or Mother for many years, though Mother had survived her oldest child and trained one of mine to take Duyong's place as Healer.

No longer a scared child, as Elder Sirena I had claimed my place on the Council, many years ago now, and I suspected none were as skilled in seduction or song as I. Not a single one of my students showed the promise I had shown – but perhaps they lacked the inspiration. A man who would love a dragon, indeed.

I felt the smile lift my lips as I turned my thoughts to the Council as it was under my mother's guidance and that of her mother before her. She had visited the Atlantic with Grandmother as ambassador in the past. For a moment, I wished I could follow my mother and grandmother to see the only city of our kind. *Mother...*

Movement caught my eye on the street ahead and I reluctantly slowed. Without my sharp eyes, someone might have been hurt. Like my second daughter's father, killed on a wet road whilst riding his old Triumph, with his wife riding pillion behind him. *What a waste. It takes a special kind of man to love a dragon.*

I sat patiently waiting for the mother duck to cross the road with her ducklings, from the river to the pond in the park on the other side. She looked at me for a moment and I gave her a nod of acknowledgement.

She knows what I am. A water dragon on a hog in the pre-dawn light, remembering my own chicks at home. I sighed, missing all three of them, though none were as fluffy and innocent as the ducklings before me.

No, on land I am Vanessa, just another human. I must remember that as the ocean's infiltrator, I am not a dragon or a fish or any other creature — I must think like a human.

Beneath my riding leathers, I concentrated on keeping my skin the same colour as any other human woman. *Oops, I forgot underwear again. I must remember it next time. It causes so much trouble sometimes when I forget…*For a moment, I thought of a time when I had not known about underwear to don beneath my leather clothing. My dragon skin, he'd called it, as he unbuttoned my jacket and slid it off my shoulders, to reveal the pale human skin he'd loved…

My bike snarled beneath me, a sweet sound that I'd missed, so I guided him home.

I reluctantly covered Harley up with his dust sheet in the garage, my riding helmet tucked into the lockbox at the back. I'd considered selling him, as he wouldn't fit with the image I needed to provide in the near future, but sentimentality won out. He reminded me of a certain Scottish engineer who'd had a liking for leather. The man was long dead now, though his legacy lived on. It seemed my life was full of such memories: the highlights that I would never forget amid the farewells that were left unsaid.

I turned out the light in the garage and trudged to the basement, my fair hair fluttering like frayed rope in the light breeze off the river. Stiff locks clicked as I turned keys, stepping into the secure storage room protecting my possessions from prying eyes. The space was filled with furniture – I would need to shift it to the house before I left tomorrow evening. For now, I had a moment to indulge myself.

I knew the bookcases by sight and touch, though it was too dark to discern the words. The books I looked for were as familiar to my fingers as my own skin, for I had caressed the covers many times. They held the history of me and mine. Beneath the books…*ah*.

I dropped to my knees, opening the drawer at the base of the bookcase to pull out the rolled pages my mother had drawn at the end of her life, the colours still bright.

Crossing the room to the light switch, I reflected that I would need more light to see this in the detail I wanted. The light flared briefly, before emitting a sound like an egg cracked on the side of a glass bowl and returning me to darkness.

"Useless human technology," I said aloud as I started up the stairs to where the sunlight streamed in, sitting on the steps with my pages. I made a mental note to have more than one light installed in the basement. Perhaps I would have those little LED down-lights that sparkled so in the lighting shops on Leach Highway.

I unrolled the crackling paper against the bare, white wall beside me, thinking of the envoys I must send on my return.

The first was a map, originally drawn by humans, but marked by Sephira's hand in ink. The city's location, the location of other points she knew and visited, each represented by unlabelled ink dots in the flat blue of the Atlantic Ocean. My chosen envoys faced a long swim.

The second was her drawing of what the city of Atlantis used to look like, when it was on the surface. When our kind were known to humans.

My people taught the Greeks to build as they had, as well as how to rule with a whole people. They had corrupted our governing system as only humans can, but the buildings had not been as poorly constructed as their democracy. Our city had been beautiful, built over and around water, a coral atoll that had sprouted pastel marble which reflected sun and water to perfection. I touched the picture, with its vivid colours. Mother had even drawn in the light in the sky, the glow of the volcano that sent a tsunami over my people's home when only we had survived. What would it have felt like to swim in tsunami waves? The power of it aroused me more than was wise, alone as I was. I took a deep breath to steady myself.

I shifted the coloured page and set it beside the black and white sketch beneath it. Ah, the contrast between the city my people built and the ruin it had become, before I drew my first breath! I toyed with the thought of going in the envoy's stead, but my duty lay here, in my human house in a human city. As I had discussed with Darma, our envoys should be led by Cantrella, for she shared the philosophy of our Atlantic sisters far more than our own.

I drank in the colours, wondering whether Cantrella would be willing to come on land and draw what she had seen for me. I doubted it. Perhaps I should purchase one of the underwater cameras the humans had and ask her to take that instead? I could put digital photographs on my laptop computer, which I would need to replace with the latest model once more.

I lifted my hands, letting the papers crackle and roll up. Practical matters drew my attention more than my memories of the past. I had important decisions to make.

To help the humans or stand by and let them die?

JOE

"Whoever wired up these places either had a death-wish or he was fucking high at the time," I muttered as I found yet another nest of tangled wires under the tin roof. They'd pretty much corroded together. Any insulation on them had disintegrated about the time I was born, I decided. I ripped the mess out and dropped it on the concrete below.

No one in their right mind would have volunteered for this, but I figured I was probably a bit mad in my reasons for it, too.

Skipper and I had come to a business

arrangement. We were going to be partners in a sort of holiday resort during the warmer months at the Abrolhos, to run in between fishing. He'd been sweet-talking all his fishing mates who didn't fish any more to hand over their asbestos shacks to him, so they didn't have to pay a shitload of money to pull them down. I'd been doing a bit of persuasion of my own – calling in every tradie I knew who'd do cash jobs and owed me a favour. When they hesitated, I promised I'd take them fishing when the job was done. Worked like a charm.

Somehow, we'd ended up with about a dozen falling-down fishing shacks on Rat Island and now I was holding up my end of the deal, arranging to get guys out to do the work on them, so the shitholes could become "deluxe holiday villas" or something like that. I didn't know – Skipper's daughter, the travel agent, was writing the press for it.

Now, if I could just get power restored to these stupid sheds we could get the asbestos guys in on their next week off to do some serious renovations. I had the replacement sheeting waiting in a sea container at the harbour, ready to winch aboard the *Dolphin* for the return trip after the first load of asbestos landed in Geraldton for safe disposal. The sooner the asbestos was gone, the better.

I yanked on another stubborn strand of wire and it came slithering across the roof, guarded by a huge spider. I thought the orb spiders were big the first year I was out here, but she was almost as big as my hand. I knew from experience that she wasn't dangerous. I liked the way she and her mates kept the flies and mosquitoes down, so I brushed her off the corroded wiring and dropped it over the eaves.

I figured I'd get this place done before dark and then I'd be finished, a day earlier than expected. Maybe I could spend tomorrow fishing and take some nice fillets home with me. I knew the good fishing spots around Rat now, because I had to know where to take the guys on their fishing trips. I knew the spots that were pretty and not good for fishing, too, though, so we could keep the tourists occupied in trying. Couldn't have them catching their bag limit too quickly – they'd get bored and complain.

I climbed down off the roof and hooked up the outdoor power point on the corner of the house, on one of the frame beams. I plugged in my light and switched the power point on. *Brilliant,* I thought as the globe gave a blinding flash of white before I turned it off again.

I packed everything back in my toolbag and started collecting up the mess of corroded wiring. I dropped the whole lot on my veranda and went into my shack for a beer, a bite to eat and some sleep. I'd need to be up early for the best fish.

SIRENA

I dusted my hands off. I'd finished pushing all the furniture into place. I clicked a pen, writing a list of what I still needed to purchase and arrange for a life on land.

A new vehicle

Clothing and amusements for a child

A new computer

Waterproof camera

Alcohol

I looked down at my list and added another item:

Lightbulbs

Perishable food would wait until my return, for the journey to my home and then back to my land house was not a short one.

I dug out sufficient cash from storage and thought of taking Harley for one more ride before I slid beneath the sea surface in the dark of night.

The engine's vibrations between my leather-clad thighs were irresistible. *How can any man compare to the power of this?* I thought as I roared to the car dealership to purchase something ladylike, shiny and blue.

When the day ended, my new little Mazda sat in the garage, her engine still warm. My sweet Harley was hidden behind the Holden, in the deep darkness at the top of the garage. I'd given him a little service before I'd covered him, lovingly cranking the spanner to make sure he was as tight as I wanted him to be. I felt a wrench that I could not ride him in my role as a responsible, human, suburban, single mother.

I'd already replaced the Edison light globe in the basement, watching it glow in satisfaction before I switched it off. I would call an electrician to add more lighting on my return.

All my new stainless steel appliances were packed into the cupboard beneath the silver hotplate, from the mixer to the pizza cooker. I even had a curved pizza knife tucked into the third drawer.

I sat in the kitchen and opened a chilled Stella. I raised it above my head. "In memory of death and duty," I said quietly, sipping the beer with my eyes closed as my thoughts turned to more recent memories. *Should I pick up my smartphone and call Skipper, to obtain the contact details of his sexy deckhand with the sweet arse?* I shook my head with a smile. *Not tonight. Perhaps one day…*

I drained my drink and threw the empty into my new recycling bin. I looked out the window at the new playground and swing set, hoping they would meet with my youngest daughter's approval when I brought her to land. We would have to drive by a playground full of human children so she would understand its use.

*Marina…*Just the thought of my youngest daughter had me yearning for home. I slipped out of my clothes, throwing them into the hamper beside the new washing machine. I padded across the dining room, snatching up the digital camera on my way to the folding doors that led outside. I closed and locked them behind me, hiding the key behind the mermaid tile on the wall.

I strode across the street and the park to the river in the darkness. I slipped over the side of the ferry terminal jetty and into the dark river water.

On my return, I will truly infiltrate the humans as never before, with my daughter by my side. May heaven help them, if I decide that I will not, I thought as I swam out to sea. *Next landfall is at the Abrolhos, for a slight rest before I head home. If only it were the fishing season, when Skipper's dreamy deckhand might appear on my decking again. Perhaps there is one man who can rival my Harley.* I let my laughter bubble up to the surface as I swept through the water, increasing my speed.

JOE

"Vanessa!" I stepped off the shack's veranda and there she was, like a perfect hallucination. She sat on a chair in the sun, sipping from a steaming cup. More than three years had passed, but she hadn't changed a bit.

I kept my eyes on her as I stumbled closer, scared that I was dreaming and she'd disappear.

She jumped to her feet in surprise. "Joe? What are you doing here?" Her hands and the cup they held started to shake. "The fishing season's over. I didn't think anyone was here."

I smiled. "Maintenance goes on year-round, fishing season or not. Anyway, all that's changed. Fishing is year-round now, too, and we might be allowed to take tourists. Skipper and I have a business plan, buying up some of the old fishing shacks from guys who don't fish any more. I'm here trying to fix them up so they'll have power. Then we can renovate them properly so they look nicer." I frowned. "I didn't hear a plane land." I looked at the jetty. "And you didn't bring the *Siren* over. When did you arrive?"

Her eyes widened in alarm. The cup dropped from her hands and smashed at her feet, but she didn't even glance at it. "Early this morning. You mustn't have heard the plane, you were probably still asleep..." She looked away as her voice faded.

Shit. She didn't take a plane or a boat. She probably swam here while it was still dark. I couldn't keep my eyes off her, drinking her in. In three and a half years, I'd thought of a million questions to ask her and now she was in front of me I was tongue-tied. I'd felt like the world was in black and white and it suddenly burst into colour now I saw her again. I didn't care what she was – I just wanted to hold her again and never let go. *Preferably with as little clothing on as possible...*

She backed away from me. "I just came to pick a few things up and then I'll go again. I'm not going to be here long. I should never have come..." She fumbled for the door handle behind her, not taking her frightened eyes off me. As if she was afraid of me.

I found my voice. "Please, don't go." I sounded desperate.

She dropped her hands to her sides, her back to the door. Her smile was wan. "I have to," she whispered.

"You don't," I told her, grasping her nerveless hands. "Please, stay with me. I can take care of you. I'll never look at another woman again. I'll do anything to make you happy."

"You barely know me," she said.

"I know you're the most beautiful woman I've ever met. I've loved you since the moment I first saw you. You're amazing. You're an expert fisher, you're so smart I can barely follow you sometimes, you kill sharks with a filleting knife, you're incredible in bed and you're a good cook. Your smile and your laugh are like sunshine. I haven't stopped thinking about you since I met you and I don't want to be without you." I took a deep breath. "And your tail is exactly the same colour as your eyes, the most beautiful stormy blue I've ever seen."

She tried to pull her hands away from me, but I held on. "What did you say?" she asked faintly.

"I don't care what you are. You're the most beautiful woman I've ever seen, from top to beautiful blue tail. I love you and I want to stay with you for the rest of my life." I kissed her.

She froze for a moment, before she responded to my kiss, as half-hearted and cold as a dying fish.

"You must be joking," she managed to say when I broke away from her.

I shook my head, my eyes on hers.

"How long have you known?" she said weakly, sliding down the door to sink onto the veranda decking.

I sat on the decking in front of her and pulled out my phone. "Since just after you left. I saw you say goodbye to the island before you swam away with the other two." I started flipping feverishly through the menus on my phone, searching for the video, my only evidence that I hadn't dreamed her. "There." I showed her the grainy video, watching her rise from water, say her goodbye and flip her tail as she swam away. It might have been the millionth time I'd watched it, but a black hole opened up in my heart all the same.

A tear trickled down her cheek. "How many people have you shown this to?" she asked urgently as she wiped it away.

I hesitated. "Just one – Dean saw it before I did. But he didn't believe it was real. He thought it was just a movie."

She managed a weak laugh. "You've had evidence of the existence of my people for three years and you haven't shown it to anyone?"

"I didn't want anyone else to see it," I replied defensively. "You weren't wearing any clothes and it didn't seem right."

Her laughter was stronger. "You could have posted that video on the internet and had humans hunting for us for three years, but you didn't do it. Not because you didn't want people to know what I was, but because you didn't want them to see my breasts?" For the first time, she laughed like I remembered. Then she sobered a little. "Did you make any copies of that?"

"No!" I answered immediately. "I haven't replaced my phone for three years because it has that video on it. I didn't want to share you with anyone."

She closed her eyes. "So if I destroy that video, the only human who knows will be you." She looked as if the knowledge pained her.

I felt an overwhelming sense of loss. "But that's the only thing I have of you. The only memory you left me."

She stared at me in disbelief. "I gave you plenty of pleasant memories, including a parting one that I know you enjoyed. Your electronic memory puts my people in danger."

I struggled to explain. "In three years, even

my best memories fade. A video, or even a picture, helps me to remember."

She held my phone in her hands and frowned at the screen. I reached for it, but she scrambled to her feet and ran out onto the path. "There, deleted," she said in relief before I'd made it down the steps off her veranda. Before I could reach her, she threw my phone out across the anchorage. It smashed against a jetty pylon before it fell into the water in pieces.

"NO!" I gasped.

She held her hands up in a gesture of conciliation. "I will reimburse you for the loss of your phone. It was necessary." She looked at me in concern. "Now, what do I do with you?"

Vanessa just stole, smashed and sank my phone. I felt lightheaded. "Marry me," I told her, with a laugh that sounded slightly hysterical.

She shook her head. "Don't be silly. I'll be gone as soon as it's dark."

"Then spend the day with me. Please," I begged. "Give me a memory to replace the one you just took."

She bit her lip. "What did you have in mind?"

I could think of a million things to do and they all involved taking her clothes off. I voiced the most improbable of the lot. "I'd like to go for a swim with you. I'd like you to show me what you really look like, in daylight. I want to know what it feels like to touch your tail."

She opened her mouth, but couldn't seem to frame the words.

"There's no one else here, just us. No one will see you but me," I promised.

She looked at me for a long moment, before she smiled sadly. "I'll stay with you, just for a swim."

LAILA

"One hundred years ago, the humans were at war with one another. They ventured to sea in vessels which attempted to sink the others. Many vessels were sunk in our ocean, but there is one which stands out. A battle occurred near the Nursery Grounds. A vessel was damaged and many humans were hurt or killed. Three of our kind remained at the Nursery Grounds. Da-Xia was a mother who was due to birth a child. She was labouring as the vessel appeared and the healers could not move her.

"A human from the stricken vessel saw our kind and approached the shore. He was a human healer and *he thought to assist. Healer Duyong stayed with Da-Xia whilst Healer Sephira took hold of the human healer and swam him into deep water, amid metal projectiles fired by the human vessels at one another. She held him there until his breath ran out, but sustained an injury from a piece of metal through her arm. When she returned to Healer Duyong and Da-Xia, she found that metal projectiles had pierced their bodies, also. Both they and the unborn child were lifeless.*

"Sephira carried her own daughter and Da-Xia to deep water, to hide their bodies from the humans. Though injured, she swam home to tell the other elders of the tragedy. Today we have her story to remind us of the dangers of humans, whether they are hostile or well-meaning, and the sacrifices that must be made to ensure our safety."

Teacher Darma spoke further of security and the need for our people to remain hidden from humans, but I turned to Estella to converse quietly. *"Could you do it, Estella? Kill a human in cold blood, to protect our people?"*

Her reply was thoughtful. *"I would not like to. I would hope to blend with humans well enough that death would not be necessary. And you?"*

I did not hesitate. *"My people are here. Humans hurt my mother when she was among them. I could hurt or kill a human to protect myself or my people."*

"How would you do it, Laila? If a human saw you swimming, how could you kill him?" Estella's big, dark eyes were sad.

I closed my eyes and imagined my actions. *"I might try to lure him into the water for a swim with me, then drown him or call sharks to him if it were at night. If he were aboard a vessel, I would shape waves to capsize the vessel and then ensure the human did not survive the wreck."*

Estella shook her head, those big eyes wide. *"I could not swim so close with a human, to pull him down into the depths and drown him. To see the human's face as his air runs out and he realises that you are the instrument of his death. I might be able to shape waves, sink ships or call sharks, but to kill a human with my hands on him? It seems too personal. After all, humans are people, too."*

"But, Estella and Laila, this is what you must do." Teacher Darma's interruption surprised us both. *"It does not matter if the human is unknown to you or if you have joined with him and been as close to the human as our kind can be. We must protect our*

people from humans, at all costs. If the humans catch even one of us, it is death to her and all of our people, for they will hunt us. It is better to die whilst destroying a human witness than to be caught and killed by humans."

Estella turned to Teacher Darma. *"It seems so drastic, Teacher. How often have our kind been called to give their life to kill a human in order to protect our people?"*

Teacher Darma frowned. *"Not in my lifetime, but in legends there are stories of sisters who gave their lives to end humans who knew too much. You must be prepared to act to protect your people, if you are to be permitted on land. That is one reason why we avoid close contact with humans as much as possible. Even Elder Sirena, who has been closest to the humans in her role as human liaison, will not hesitate if a human sees too much. She would take his life and sacrifice her own if necessary, for she is well aware that more than two lives are at stake."*

JOE

Vanessa started north along the path and I followed her automatically. She led me up to the tiny beach at the northern end of the island, where the rusted wreck of a boat lay on the sand. She started peeling off her clothes, folding them carefully in a pile on a rock. Naked, she waded into the water until it licked at her thighs, before she lay back, floating on the surface of the waves.

I swallowed convulsively. *God, she looks good. More perfect than I remember her.* I couldn't help staring.

For the first time, she looked nervous. "No human has ever seen me change before," she admitted.

"It's the first time for me, too," I replied hoarsely.

She touched her heels together and gave a flick with her feet. The movement rippled up her body, before she did it again. It looked like her skin was darkening, or was it just the waves washing over her? Another flick, her feet rising out of the water this time, and I saw the blue wasn't just the water. It was like the skin of her legs had grown together, extending over her feet into curved flukes, as blue as the water. It blended seamlessly up her body, though her torso remained pale.

She turned on her side, her eyes curious. In the skin along her ribs, I saw dark lines that looked like gills. I couldn't take my eyes off her. She'd never looked less human, but I'd never wanted to touch her more. My mouth hung open and I couldn't seem to close it.

"What do you think? Are you disgusted that you slept with a fish?" she asked archly.

My eyes raked her from head to tail. "No.

I'm torn between wanting to touch you to make sure you don't feel like a fish and wanting to sleep with you again."

She smiled properly and laughed. There was an edge to the sound. "Are you coming in, or not?" She twisted, arched and dived down. I caught a glimpse of the darker blue blending with the ocean surface, stretching from her tail flukes to her neck, before she dove too deep to see.

I waded in to my knees, then realised I hadn't brought my boardies or even a towel and these were the only shorts I had with me. If I swam in them now, I'd be working in my undies 'til they dried, possibly the whole day. Or I could take them off and go buck naked now…

Well, it's not like she hasn't seen me naked before, and there's no one else here. I ripped my shorts off and threw them on top of the bushes at the edge of the beach. I plunged into the water after her.

I was painfully reminded of that first day I went out with her on the boat, when I swam with the sea lions. She darted around me with an agility I'd never have. I'd stick my head in the water to see if I could spot her and I'd hear her laughter behind me, feeling the brush of moving water, but she'd be gone by the time I surfaced.

"You said you'd swim with me, not swim circles around me," I complained after about ten minutes.

Almost instantly, she popped up in front of me, maybe an arm's length away. She held out her hand. "Do you really want to swim with me?"

I held onto her hand with grim determination. "For the rest of my life," I told her fervently.

She bit her lip and dived, taking me with her. We swam further, faster and deeper than I'd ever been before. I saw clouds of fish, bright corals and some bigger fish that shied away as we approached. My lungs burned for air, but she didn't seem to notice. I wrapped my arms around her, hanging on so I could bring my face up to hers. I exhaled the air I had left in a small cloud of bubbles and then kissed her, trying to tell her with my eyes what my voice couldn't, down here.

As her lips touched mine, she blew a burst of air into my mouth, then another. The burning in my lungs faded. Her speed didn't slow, even holding me. I felt her body ripple against mine. I held on tightly with my arms, and then hooked my legs around her tail, too. *My God, her skin's soft, softer than any human woman, no matter how many beauty products the human woman used.* I freed up one hand and used it to stroke her side, from her arm to her thigh. *No, from her arm to around the widest curve of her tail.*

I kissed her again and she filled my mouth with breath. I went in for another kiss, the sort that on land would be more for enjoyment than for air, and she responded, her tongue curling around mine even as her tail curled around my leg. Her arms tightened around my back and we'd stopped moving. Not needing to hang on so tightly, I stroked her soft breasts with my hands, letting my hands slide down her sides and across her gills to fasten on her luscious arse. It was somehow even more luscious, with the blue velvet skin covering it.

Half out of my mind with how much I wanted her, I drove my hips hard against hers, even as my hands pushed her closer to me. Shit, if she'd been human that thrust would have slid me inside her, but I met only the soft resistance of her tail. *Fuck, why didn't anyone ever tell me you can't fuck a mermaid?*

I kissed her, over and over, her kisses a mixture of breath and passion. Her hands were everywhere, but so were mine. Her soft skin was cooler than mine, but her hands burned. Suddenly, she tore her lips from mine. The sound that came out was like no language I knew, a squeaky mix of dolphin and whale, but the words were swearing in any language. We spun through the water rapidly, faster than before, so all I could see was a stream of bubbles. My lungs started to burn again. I was ready to let go of her and struggle my way to the surface for a desperate breath, but I realised I didn't know which way was up anymore.

My knees hit sand and I fell over, gasping for breath as my head broke the surface. I should have fallen on the sand, but her body was beneath me, her boobs heaving as she gasped as hard as I did. There were words in her gasping, though, that I struggled to understand.

"Shit, I can't do it. I can't," she said, over and over. I realised that some of the salt water droplets streaming down her cheeks were tears.

"It's okay," I told her.

"No, I didn't mean to lose control like that. I can't," she murmured.

"What's wrong?" I asked, worried. I shifted to the side, so I slid off her onto the sand and coral shingle. *Ow.* I tried to ignore the sharp bit of coral digging into my bum. I reached behind me, grabbed it and threw it across the water with a splash.

"I have a duty to protect my people. I can't let you live, knowing about us," she said, her words fast and forced. "And I can't do it. I tried to pull you into the deep, but I lost control of my tail and I couldn't. I had to take you back to shore. I have a duty to return to my people. I lost control of my tail and I couldn't..." I wasn't sure if she was sobbing or laughing.

Did she just try to drown me? I wondered, thunderstruck. *But she gave me her air, kissed me and felt me up instead, before she carried me to shore. Last time I went swimming with her, she fought off a full-grown tiger shark with nothing but a knife. Like she said, she can't kill me.* I thought about her soft tail, twined around my leg. *It seemed pretty well under her control to me.*

"How can you lose control of your tail?" I blurted out.

"I got turned on and I lost control. I lost my tail and I couldn't breathe…it's never happened to me before. I've heard it could happen, but it never happened to me, or anyone I knew…" she said, wiping her face with one hand.

I was even more confused now. "What do you mean, you lost your tail?"

Her fingers closed over mine, pulling my hand down. "I lost control and lost my tail…" My fingers were warm, wet and inside her before I worked out what she meant. She shifted her legs wider apart, pushing my fingers in deeper.

"You're saying that when you get turned on, your tail disappears and you go back to human?" I guessed. *Well, that explains why you can't fuck a mermaid. You just need get her hot enough to turn human.*

"Yes." She sniffled. "But now I'll have to return to my people and admit I couldn't kill a human who knew about us. I will have to return to try again. I must ensure my people stay hidden from humans."

"So don't go back," I responded, rolling back onto her and pinning her to the sand. I figured she could throw me off fairly easily if she wanted to, but she didn't even try. *She won't hurt me.*

She looked up into my eyes, a wry smile on her face as she shook her head. "I must. I carry vital information my people must have."

She still held my hand between her legs. I stroked her idly with my thumb, hearing her sharp intake of breath. "Stay with me," I murmured. I was rock hard for her and I knew she could feel it.

"I have to return home to my people and tell them of the danger I have placed them in," she replied mechanically, sounding out of breath.

I increased the pressure but not the pace. "Your people are in no danger from me. Who would I tell and who'd believe me? Besides, I want you and all your secrets for myself. Stay with me."

"I can't. I must return."

I looked at her, carefully. Her eyes were closed, her breathing coming in ragged gasps. "But not until dark. You still have all day." I kissed her lightly. "Stay with me for today."

"Yes…" she breathed, arching her back up. She spread her legs wider and my knees hit the sand between them. I pulled my fingers out of her and she didn't stop me. *Half on top of her, half between her legs, in one thrust I'll be inside her, no tail in the way this time.*

"What are you waiting for?" she murmured. "I didn't lose my tail because I wanted you to finger and tease me. Are you having second thoughts about sleeping with a fish?"

"Fish don't have boobs," I managed to say, planting a kiss on hers. "You're not a fish. You're the most beautiful woman I've ever seen."

"But I'm not human," she said softly. "Human women don't have tails."

"Right now, neither do you," I replied as I slid inside her, as easily as she'd slid through the water. *Oh God, she feels good.*

For the first time in my life, I had sex on the beach. Not the sticky cocktail, but the sticky, sandy, salty, orgasmic experience that was nevertheless mindblowing.

Then we headed back to her house and used up all the hot water, washing off the sand that had gotten everywhere.

LAILA

"Elder Cantrella, will you answer the Council's call? Will you be our ambassador to our sisters, the people of the ocean's gift in the Atlantic Ocean?" Elder Darma's words were ceremonial, a formal request and tone that she did not use in her role as teacher.

I waited for Mother's response, though I knew what it would be.

"I would be honoured to answer the Council's call. I request one subordinate to accompany and assist me in this important task. I ask for my daughter, Laila."

Now I understood why my presence was

considered so necessary at this, my first Council meeting. I remained silent until addressed, as was required of me.

Elder Darma glanced at me, but her response was to my mother. "*The girl is old enough to be an adult, but she has not yet done her duty for her people. Can she be trusted to behave as required on a diplomatic mission of such importance?*"

I almost opened my mouth to respond, but managed to control myself.

Mother eyed me seriously before she spoke. "*Laila is my daughter. She will do as she must to protect her people. She will do anything that is required to ensure this mission is a success. I will make sure of it.*"

Elder Nafula lifted her chin, her eyes also on me. "*If the girl does her duty among the humans, she will be an adult, with all the rights of any other adult of our people. She will be able to choose or refuse this mission, as she decides. Child, would you not prefer to do your duty, than such a dangerous mission?*"

I gritted my teeth at being called a child, for it was twenty years since my birth at the Nursery Grounds, but I swallowed my ire. We all knew the penalty for defying the Council, for Sirena had borne years of exile until she complied with their commands. This was the first story we learned as children. I had heard it from Elder Sirena's own lips when she was my teacher, so the story had a poignancy heightened by the bitterness of her tone.

"I will answer the Council's call to any task that is required of me, whether it is duty among humans or a mission among sisters in a distant ocean. I will do as the Council commands me."

I ardently wished to do anything that didn't require contact with humans. After my mother's traumatic experience doing her duty among humans, I would happily remain at the Council's beck and call for the remainder of my life than risk similar pain.

Elder Darma's words took me by surprise. *"Elder Cantrella, the Council agrees to send your daughter to assist you in your diplomatic mission. You may depart once your preparations are complete. The Council wishes you a good and safe voyage. We will eagerly await your return with what tidings you can bring."*

I relaxed in relief. No human would touch me until after my return. No matter how dangerous this diplomatic mission might be, it held no terrors for me. Only humans could fill me with fear.

JOE

The shower, the bedroom, the kitchen table, the sofa bed, back to the bedroom…Shit, I think I'd saved up three years' worth of sex to have in one day, and so had she. By the end of the day, my skin felt like there was a mild electric current running over it and I was going to ache for a week, but fuck, it was good.

Vanessa kissed me one last time on the beach, as the sun set behind her. She held me close and murmured in my ear.

"I will go home to my people. I will explain why I did not kill you and why I believe you should live. I cannot promise that they will not send another of my people for you, but I will return to you and try to prevent it. My people will send me back to land again and I promise I will find you. Until I return, fly home and stay out of the water."

She pulled her dress over her head and handed it to me. I stood transfixed on the beach, watching her run naked into the water, boobs flying, as she dived under a wave. When she surfaced, she turned and blew me a kiss. Then she leapt and twisted, orange light reflecting off her skin as she arced up into another dive. She splashed her tail flukes at me and vanished.

So her people were going to send someone to do me in. I thought of her taking on a tiger shark and decided I'd bet on her over any hitfish her people sent. After all, what could be worse than a tiger shark going in for the kill?

I headed back across the island to my shack. It was a hot night, but it felt cold without Vanessa.

SIRENA

The water on my skin was cool, yet for that long swim home I burned. I was haunted by the sensation of his hands on my skin. This skin, not my human skin. He'd caressed me with such love and such trust, even as I'd tried to drown him. In return, I'd spared his life and trusted him with the secret of my people. *Now I must pay the price for my stupidity.*

The Council convened for my return.

I did not wait for a formal greeting or welcome. For the first time in my life, I was eager to return to land. *"My preparations are complete. I will live among humans in their city called Perth. My house is in readiness for our arrival."*

Elder Darma asked the question as custom demanded. *"I take it that, as always, our secret was preserved? Did any of the humans suspect you were not one of them?"*

I hesitated. *"One human had evidence from three years ago. I destroyed the evidence. There is no risk to us."*

"And what of the human?" Elder Darma voiced the words none of the others had the courage to say.

In any normal meeting, I was expected to answer that the human had also been destroyed. Yet I would not. For the first time, my leadership could be called into question. *Is it time for the tables to turn? Will the Council defy me, mirroring my childhood defiance?*

"He yet lives. I place this human under my protection, for he has assisted me in the past and he will continue to do so into the future. He will not betray our secret, for he will not betray me. If he even thinks to do so, I will call the sharks and watch them devour him alive. I do not forget and I will not forgive."

My statements were accepted without a

murmur. I expected some disagreement, if not outright defiance. I looked for Cantrella, whose hatred of humans should have driven her to demand Joe's death, but she was not present. "*Where is Cantrella?*"

Elder Darma looked as if she welcomed the change of subject. "*Cantrella has been sent on a diplomatic mission to the Atlantic sisters, to obtain information about changes in their ocean. With her she took her daughter, Laila.*"

My relief at their easy acquiescence paled in significance when compared to the risk they had placed the child in. "*You permitted Laila to go on a diplomatic mission to the Atlantic, before she has done her duty? I fear that may have been unwise.*"

Elder Darma was alarmed, but not excessively so. "*The girl did not go alone. Cantrella requested her to assist in the mission. She will ensure the girl's safety and ours.*"

I agreed with their choice of ambassador and was quick to reinforce this. "*Cantrella was a wise choice, for her inclinations match those of our Atlantic sisters. She was not of the Elder Council when their last delegation visited the Indian Ocean, but that may be to her advantage.*"

Elder Darma was surprised. "*Why do you say that?*"

I chose my words carefully. "*I refer to the incident with Alexandre. Cantrella may have forgotten about it.*"

Elder Nafula spoke. "*How could she not be aware of it? Her partner conducted the investigation herself.*"

Elder Indah, ever the healer, entered the discussion in a soft voice. "*Cantrella was still deeply traumatised by her time on land and Laila was not yet weaned. She may not have been as perceptive then as she is now.*"

Elder Darma's confusion was evident. "*What import has history on relations with our sisters today?*"

I tried to keep my words brief, when speaking of an incident that had deeply distressed us all. "*It was twenty years ago. The Atlantic sisters are very traditional. I think it very likely that a similar incident will take place in their own ocean this year. I do not think it wise for Laila to be involved with the Atlantic sisters for such an event.*"

Darma avoided mention of the disaster. "*Cantrella is well able to care for her daughter.*"

Few Elders knew the daughter as well as her mother. I was one of the few, so I tried to explain, "*Cantrella's hatred for humans may overcome her concern for her daughter. Laila fears humans and I fear for her if she is persuaded to take part in their…traditions.*"

Elder Darma's concern was genuine. "*What do you suggest we do?*"

"*If it is too late to recall Laila, then we cannot risk a diplomatic incident in sending another sister to retrieve her.*" I took a deep draught of cool water before I gave my orders. "*I suggest we wait and hope. If my fears are realised, then you must send her to me on land in Australia. In the meantime, we can hope that there is no further trouble.*"

Elder Darma's voice was uncertain. "*Do you think it likely?*"

I delivered my parting commands. "*The Atlantic sisters are nothing if not traditional. It may be their undoing, for in their limited contact with humans they may underestimate the humans' communications technology. I will hear of it among the humans before the news travels to the deeps. When the child returns, send her to me. In fact, send any children for whom it is time to do their duty among humans, starting with*

Laila and Estella. I will be in a position to ensure secrecy is maintained, whilst the girls' safety is assured."

Elder Darma was older than I and today it showed. She was tired. *"It shall be as you decree. Our hopes go with you and the child."*

I acknowledged her good wishes and acquiescence, but it was not my child who occupied my attention. It was poor Laila that my mind dwelt on as I prepared for our departure. I would not have permitted the child to leave.

JOE

I heard the generator start and saw the lights in Vanessa's house as I finished my dinner. *Oh my God, she's back. And somehow I have to say it, before my tongue ties itself in knots again.*

I walked out my front door and onto the path. I stood at the bottom of the steps and looked at the shadow moving across the curtains of her front window. *It's Vanessa. It couldn't be anyone else.*

My head was swimming and it felt like there were fish in it, too. I lifted my foot to the first step and heard the faint sound of her laughter from inside the house.

That's what she'll do when I say it, or if I freeze up

and can't get the words out. I hesitated with one foot in the air.

Shit. I chickened out and headed back to my shack. *I'll try again in the morning.*

In the morning, I dithered in the bathroom, trying to shave as smoothly as possible. I changed shirts twice, determined to look as good as I could. Or at least make sure I wore a clean shirt.

When I couldn't procrastinate any more, I stepped out onto the coral shingle again. I closed my front door as quietly as I could. I stood on the empty path with my eyes closed, taking great big breaths, trying to calm myself down. It felt like my heart was imitating her generator, it was going so fast.

Vanessa, I love you. Please marry me. I repeated the words in my head, hoping they'd come out right. Suddenly, I wished I'd bought a ring I could offer her, something big, impressive and sparkly. *You didn't buy one because you know you don't have a hope in hell of her saying yes. You're only asking her because you'll kick yourself for the rest of your life if you don't ask her. You're fucking talking to yourself, too.*

I forced myself to walk to her steps, then stopped and closed my eyes. I took a huge, deep breath.

"Are you all right, Joe?" Vanessa's soft voice asked.

Shit.

She sat on the veranda, hidden in shadow. She looked concerned as she set her steaming cup down on the table and stood up.

"Yes," I tried to say, but the first time I squeaked. I got the word out on the second try.

Her eyes were wide with curiosity, but she didn't say anything else.

I swallowed and somehow my feet carried me up the steps to the decking. I stood in front of her before I fell to my knees. From this angle, I could only see her eyes over her boobs. *If I talk to her boobs, I can do this.*

"Vanessa, I love you," I began, my eyes intent on the faint outline of her left nipple through her shirt. "I'd do anything to make you happy. Please, marry me, so I can spend the rest of my life making you as happy as you make me," I told her right nipple, more clearly defined than her left.

Vanessa's boobs dipped down, so they almost touched my face. Her hands found mine and she pulled me to my feet as she straightened up. With difficulty, I shifted my gaze to her face.

"Joe, you still barely know me and I won't stay on land all my life. I will return to my people. You'd be better off with a human woman." She smiled fondly.

I shook my head and forced the words out. "I don't want a human woman. I want you. I want to spend the rest of my life with you."

"Joe, I won't be around for the rest of your life. I only spend a small amount of time on land and the rest is among my people, in ocean depths where you can't go. I have a responsibility to my people," she tried to explain.

I voiced my biggest fear. "You have someone else already, don't you? Some Brad Pitt clone with a sexy tail who lives down in the mermaid city, waiting for you to come home." The words came out bitter.

She laughed softly. "No, I have no partner

among my people. Nor do I have one among yours."

I sighed in relief. "Then marry me. You can stay with me whenever you're on land, and when you go back to…the mermaid city…I'll wait for you. I'll always be here for you. We'll get a house near the water and I'll take care of you, every day you're with me. I'll make you happy, Vanessa. I'll do anything for you. I love you." I stumbled over the words, but I managed to get them out.

Movement caught my eye at the front window of her house. I turned, but I only saw the blank window. Vanessa turned to look, too, but there was nothing to see.

"Joe, I'm happy to stay with you whenever I'm on land. You don't need to marry me for that." For the first time, she looked lost for words. "Why do you want to marry me so much?"

I took a deep breath and prayed I could keep my voice steady. "Because I love you. You're the most amazing woman I've ever met, human or otherwise, and I don't want anyone else. Even if I only saw you once a year, and the rest of the time you're off saving the ocean or whatever it is you do, I would still know that you're mine, and I'm yours. Marry me, Vanessa, please."

A small, pale blue streak flew out of Vanessa's open front door and attached itself to Vanessa's leg. "Are you going to mawwy the man, Mummy, and wear a pwitty white dwess? Just like Awiel?" a shrill little voice piped.

I looked down at the little girl clinging to Vanessa's leg. She wore one of Vanessa's light blue t-shirts, which was long enough to be a dress on her. Her hair was light blonde and hung past her shoulders. Her eyes were a shade darker than the shirt.

I dropped to my knees in front of the girl and looked more closely at her eyes. They were the same colour as mine. "How old is she?" I choked out.

"Marina is three years old," Vanessa said softly. "Marina, this is Joe. Joe, this is my daughter, Marina."

I stared at Marina as she turned her spooky blue eyes on me. "Our daughter?" I gasped.

Vanessa blew out a breath. "Our daughter.

Marina, Joe is your Daddy."

Marina clapped her hands and her face lit up with Vanessa's beautiful smile. "I have a Daddy, just like Awiel?"

"Yes, you have a Daddy, sweetheart, just like Ariel. Now you should go inside and eat your breakfast," Vanessa told the little girl gently.

With a, "Yes, Mummy," Marina sprinted back into the house.

I have a daughter. Vanessa and I have a child. I was almost hyperventilating. Then the next thought hit and I blurted it out. "You lied to me, about not being able to get pregnant."

Vanessa closed her eyes. "No, I didn't lie to you. I just didn't tell you."

Something niggled in the back of my brain, but I ignored it. "Now you have to marry me. We can't live in sin if we're bringing up a child together."

Surprised, she laughed. "It really means that much to you?"

"Yes," I told her. "Vanessa, amazing woman who is the mother of my child, marry me."

"Why not?" She smiled. "But you'll have to

make the arrangements. I'll make sure Marina and I wear pretty dresses."

My heart sang – probably as off-key as drunken karaoke, but a song all the same. It was too good to be true. I was going to marry the perfect woman, the mother of my child.

LAILA

"Keep the pace up and we will be there sooner than you think," Mother instructed, though she seemed to struggle more with the long swim than I did. *"We will leave the Indian Ocean within a week, skirt the south of Africa and head north-west, to find the ruined city where our people began. Their last delegation visited us when you were only a baby, but I still stand in awe of what they did to Alexandre. The Elder Council condemned it, of course, but I have always longed to meet our sisters who were there..."*

Mother had plenty to say but her voice grew dull and I did not listen for long. Her excitement in visiting the Atlantic Ocean and our sisters there was evident. That was all I needed to know.

The background behind her glee I knew, too. She was going to see the city even her idol, Elder Sirena, had never visited. For once in her life, she could claim a slight superiority over the Elder she admired so much to the point of obsession. Sometimes I wondered if Mother had partnered with Elder Sirena's daughter, Maria, because the Elder herself would take no partner.

Maria was as different from her daughter Estella as she was from her mother Sirena. When I'd told my best friend Estella of the journey I must take and bid her farewell, she had hugged me tightly and made me promise to come home safely. She had not wanted to let go of me, insisting that I tell her all the stories about the city of our ancestors. I wished she could have accompanied me, but she was to remain home. She could not leave without her matriarch's permission and Elder Sirena was on land, engaged in some important mission among humans.

Our people had come from the city originally in search of a new ocean and new humans, to start a new society that broke with the traditions of the Atlantic – this I knew, too. There were stories Elder Sirena told us as children, of the beautiful marble city where we had once lived both above and below the surface, but the surface city had been swept away by a tsunami and only the water city remained, peopled by our sisters who lived there still.

As a little girl, I'd dreamed of the city and what it was like to live in a palace like the humans did, wishing and wondering. We all had, including Elder Sirena. She said that her mother Sephira had seen it, carved marble offset by beautiful soft corals of every hue, but the splendour was less now than it had been then, when Atlantis stood on the surface. She said there were pictures of Atlantis drawn by those who remembered it and painstakingly copied many times through history. The present pictures were carefully preserved on land and she spoke of them with longing, for she had seen them. Perhaps one day I would venture on land to see them, to compare what I would soon see with the glory it had held in the past.

But to venture on land, I would need to have contact with humans. Likely, the contact would be closer than I could bear. I shuddered at even the thought of touching a human, or permitting him to touch me.

"Are you well?" Mother asked, looking at me in some concern.

"Of course," I assured her. *"Just a bit tired. I hope our stay in the Atlantic is extended, so that I have plenty of rest before we need to attempt such a journey again. It is a long swim."*

She smiled at me. *"It is. Even I find it a strain, swimming against the currents where we must. I will extend our stay as long as I can. But do not allow yourself to become too tired. You must appear fit and well when we arrive to meet the Council in Atlantis."*

I wondered why my health was so important, but I knew Mother cared for me, though her emotions were often hidden deep. After all, she had insisted I accompany her, to keep me from contact with humans in her absence. She always had my best interests at heart.

JOE

I used Vanessa's old laptop to arrange flights home for the three of us. Marina fell asleep in the little six-seater plane as we flew over the Geelvink Channel to the mainland. My eyes not leaving my drowsy daughter, I offered both ladies a lift to their accommodation in my ute, parked in the Perth Airport long-term car park. Vanessa happily accepted.

I spent the whole plane trip home wishing I'd bitten the bullet and bought a house now that I had the money, but I'd kept delaying it, hoping something better would come up. It would have been perfect to be able to ask Vanessa and Marina to come and live with me in my own house, but as I still lived with my parents that wasn't going to happen.

Still, now Vanessa could help me choose our home. I brightened at the thought.

"Where would you like to live?" I asked Vanessa as she helped Marina into the back seat of my dual-cab Hilux ute.

"Hmm?" Vanessa pulled her head out of the car and closed the door. We both climbed into the front.

"Where would you like to live?" I repeated. "I have the money to buy a house now, but I hadn't decided where. Where would you like to start looking?"

Her face lit up. "I know exactly where I'd like to live. Can I show you?"

I shrugged. "Sure." I turned the key in the engine and put the ute into reverse. "Okay, so tell me where to go."

The stereo kicked in and *Bittersweet Symphony* blared out of the speakers. I reluctantly turned it down.

Vanessa sounded eager. "Tuckfield Street,

East Fremantle."

I drew a blank. "And I get there…how?"

Vanessa laughed. "Just get onto Canning Highway, I can direct you from there."

With her directions, we pulled up alongside a beautifully renovated old two-storey house overlooking the river in East Fremantle by the time the CD had made it to Jebediah's *Leaving Home*. I looked up and down the street, but I didn't see a single For Sale sign. Even if I did, I figured they'd be "Price on Application" and I couldn't afford them. This was seriously expensive real estate.

"Vanessa," I began. "These are expensive houses. I might not have enough money to buy one of these…"

She laughed and got out of the car, walking to the gate of the nearest house. Before I could stop her, she'd opened the gate and crossed the front garden, vanishing around the back of the house.

"Vanessa!" I hissed. "You can't do that. This house isn't for sale. It's someone's home, you can't just barge in like that…"

She didn't return, so I assumed she hadn't

heard me. I sat in the car, worrying. I glanced at Marina, but she'd fallen asleep in the back seat, so I went back to worrying.

The front door of the house swung open, to my dread, and Vanessa stood in the doorway, beckoning to me.

"Quick, close the door and get back in the car, before someone sees you!" I hissed, terrified someone was going to arrest her. "What if the owners come home and find you in their house?"

Vanessa laughed louder this time. "Welcome to my home, Joe. Can you bring Marina in? I put her clothes in the front bedroom, overlooking the pool. Her bed's made up, so she should be able to sleep for as long as she needs to." She disappeared back into the house.

Fuck. This place must be worth three million dollars, at least. There's no way I can afford the mortgage on this, I thought as I carried my sleeping daughter into one of the house's many bedrooms. Marina didn't stir as I tucked her into the frilly single bed, so I headed deeper into the house in search of Vanessa.

She stood in the kitchen, a pen in her hand and a notebook in front of her on the bench. She looked up and smiled when she saw me. "What do you think?"

I tried to find the words. "It's a beautiful house, Vanessa, but I can't afford the rent on something like this."

Vanessa shook her head. "I won't charge you rent, Joe. The real estate agent shifted the tenants out when I told her I was coming home. I own it."

I tried again. "I can't afford the mortgage repayments on it, either."

She looked puzzled. "What's a mortgage? This is my house. Look, I even had them put in a children's playground for Marina." She took my arm and pulled me to the glass doors that led outside, pointing. A new playground stood in the garden, with rubber matting beneath it. Behind it was a big white outbuilding.

"What's in there?" I asked, nodding at the outbuilding.

"That's the garage," Vanessa replied. "That's where my cars are."

It took me a minute to absorb this. "Cars? You own more than one car?"

Vanessa laughed. "Of course! Come and see." She slid open the glass doors, which folded up like a fan against the wall, and led the way outside. She took a key and opened the outbuilding door. She stepped inside, clicking on a light, before spreading her arms wide. "My cars."

If I'd expected an Aston Martin, a Maserati or even a Porsche, I was sadly disappointed.

Why wasn't I surprised? Every car was blue. Some classic old Holden with "Special" in a chrome badge on its aqua-blue paint; a perfectly preserved, light blue Kingswood; a Corolla in a shade of dark blue that reminded me of grapes; and a brand-new Mazda in metallic blue.

Vanessa pointed to the bay next to the Mazda. "There's space for your ute and a couple of other cars, if you like, Joe."

A couple of other cars? Does she seriously think I have a car collection?

She opened the back door of the old Holden. "Have you ever done it in the back of one of these?" she asked over her shoulder.

"Done what?" I replied, before I realised. "Shit, no." I paused. "Have you?"

Vanessa shook her head. "Would you like to?"

Does she need an answer to that? I crossed the garage to better investigate the old car.

Within five minutes, we were stiff, bruised and unsatisfied and we'd agreed never to attempt to have sex in the back seat of a Holden again. Or any car, for that matter.

I stretched as I put my clothes back on, noticing some dust-sheet-shrouded mounds between the bonnet of the uncomfortable Holden and the garage wall. "What's that?" I asked, pointing at the nearest one.

Vanessa laughed. She hadn't dressed, so she had my full attention as she moved to touch the sheet. "This is Harley. Want to see him?"

"You keep another man in your garage?" I asked doubtfully.

Another laugh. Vanessa whipped the sheet from the object beneath it, revealing a big, shiny motorcycle. "What do you think?"

I looked at it, imagining every bikie gang in

Perth and wondering which one he belonged to. "I think I don't want to meet the man who owns that. Why didn't you tell me you were a bikie's girl?"

"No man owns me or mine," Vanessa said softly. She climbed onto the motorcycle and I found myself staring at a living, breathing fantasy out of a magazine. She stroked the metal and I almost drooled. "This is my Harley. Would you like a ride with me, Joe?" Her eyes were wicked as they looked up at me.

I was so turned on it hurt. "Yeah," I managed to say. "But can we start in your bedroom first?" If she said no, I was ready to drop to my knees on the concrete.

She laughed softly as she dismounted from her Harley Davidson. I only now noticed the badge that had been hidden by the curve of her boobs. "You're offering me a better ride than my Harley, Joe?"

My tongue felt like it was wrapped in electrical tape. *She's the most beautiful woman in the world, but she's agreed to marry me and she's naked for me right now. Just say it.* I let my eyes lift from her boobs to meet her enticing gaze. "Yeah. I think I can make you happier than any machine. Even that beast."

Her smile grew wider and she didn't laugh. I'd never seen her look so excited. "Let's go upstairs then." She led the way back into the house, leaving her clothes in the garage. I stumbled after, my eyes on her bare arse.

LAILA

Mother summoned dolphins and whales, singing them up and telling them of our presence. *"Ambassador Cantrella and Laila, come from the Indian Ocean to confer with our sisters in the Atlantic,"* she repeated to one and all, speeding them on to announce our arrival.

The water rang with crisscrossing voices, as distant creatures took up her song and broadcast it throughout the Atlantic. It was a peculiar harmony that heralded our approach.

Waters became warmer and their colours lighter, the seabed rising to form a continental shelf. The fish were unfamiliar, the seagrasses, algae and corals even more so. I felt afraid, so far from home and all things familiar.

Mother ordered me to swim on and swim I did, obedient to her authority. I could not forget that I was a child and hers to command. She was hard, but circumstances in her past had made her so. She loved me and cared for me in her own way. She would not order me to do anything that would place me in harm's way, for if I were lost she would be forced to touch another human to beget another child. That was an ordeal she could not face and one I did not wish to, either. This she knew well.

I reminded myself that as long as I was assigned to the Ambassador in the Atlantic, I was safe from any human's touch. My apprehension did not lessen, but started to take form. At least I did not have humans to dread today.

I began to see shaped stone on the sea floor. The stone looked like human structures, or what had once been structures, now encrusted in coral as everything became in time at this depth. I pointed these out to my mother.

"Atlantis, the first city of our people," she responded with satisfaction. *"This is where our people first lived before the humans began to hunt us. Even Elder Sirena has not beheld its splendour."* She lifted her head with pride. *"We are close now."*

I felt resentment at how casually she dismissed the Elder who had been my greatest teacher, but I knew Mother's admiration for Sirena knew no bounds. She envied the woman her power and her charisma, craving Sirena's approval more than she would admit. Arguments between Mother and Sirena in Council meetings had been spun into legends, but it was always Sirena who prevailed in her human-friendly policy. Mother lived for the day when Sirena might defer to her, if only for a moment. That day had not yet come.

I looked around at the coralline city, missing the splendour Mother saw in it. I saw only stone and decay.

Between two encrusted columns I saw a tail that was neither fish nor dolphin. Then another on the other side.

The voices heralding our arrival became more musical, spinning the song with their own variations of curiosity and welcome.

Our Atlantic sisters began to appear in more than fleeting glimpses, accompanying us but at a distance.

As the water shallowed still more, the structures seemed in better repair. I saw intact arches and columns supporting beams and roofs, though the coral was ever-present, in more colours than I had ever imagined.

We headed for a large structure that must have been part of a palace above the water, the pitted steps a fitting backdrop for the five Elders lined up in front of the building.

Mother stopped in front of them and I slowed to float behind her with my head slightly bowed.

"I am Ambassador Cantrella of the Black line, Elder and Watcher of the Indian Ocean and this is my daughter, Laila. I come to consult with you on matters important to the Council of the Indian Ocean." Mother's majesty was modelled on that of Sirena, but her voice shook a little and spoiled the image for me. Her voice lacked volume and did not carry further than the few clustered before us. Mother was no less

nervous than I.

The middle Atlantic sister flicked her tail and moved a little forward, closer to us. Her voice rang out to easily encompass all her assembled people. *"Ambassador Cantrella of the Black, it is an honour to welcome you to the Atlantic Ocean. And you bring a child..."*

Voices hissed in whispers throughout the crowd, the words too quiet for me to discern, though the wide eyes on the expressions of all were enough for me to feel a frisson of fear. What had we done?

JOE

"Shit. Vanessa!" I called, starting to panic.

She came running. "You shouldn't use that kind of language around Marina. What is it?"

"She's…she's…" I stammered. It was my first time helping Marina wash herself in the bath.

Vanessa walked into the bathroom, looking worried. "What's happened?"

I pointed wordlessly at the bath, where Marina giggled under the water.

Vanessa marched up to the bathtub. "Now, Marina, I told you not to show your tail in front of humans."

Marina squeaked something and giggled again.

"English. We speak English when there's humans around," Vanessa said.

Marina popped her head out of the water. "But Mummy, I asked Daddy if he wanted to see me swim. He said yes!"

I'd agreed to it like any father who wanted to see his little girl show off. I didn't expect her to splash me with a silvery tail where her legs had been and stay under the surface of the bath indefinitely.

Vanessa's arm around me was steady. I realised that I was shaking. "Marina, your Daddy is a very special human. He's allowed to see your tail and mine. But even your Daddy isn't used to seeing tails in his bathtub. I'd like you not to show your tail unless I'm showing mine, please. "

Marina pouted. "Yes, Mummy." She screwed her little face up in concentration. The silvery skin seemed to retract around her legs as it returned to a more normal colour. Within a few moments, I had a normal little girl with skinny little legs in the bathtub again.

Together, we dried her off, dressed her in a pair of pyjamas and put her to bed.

"Goodnight, Daddy," Marina said as she gave me a kiss on the cheek. "Did you like my swimming?"

"Yes, sweetheart," I replied. "And you have a very pretty tail. As pretty as Mummy's."

"Do you have a tail, Daddy?" she asked.

"No, Marina, I'm a human. Humans don't have tails," I told her. "Good night."

I sat with Vanessa on the sofa, still not entirely calm from my panic earlier.

"I'm sorry, Joe," Vanessa said softly. "Marina's only a little girl and she forgets."

I tried to smile. "Yeah, one minute I'm bathing a little girl, the next minute there's a snapper in the bath." I tried to voice one of the questions swirling through my head. "Why is her tail silver? Aren't they all the same colour as yours?"

"No, we're all different," Vanessa responded. "I think Marina's will darken as she gets older, probably to the pale ice blue of her eyes."

"So mermaid tails are all different shades of blue?" I asked.

"No. Maria's is dark blue, but Belinda's is gold. Her daughter, Zerafina, has an orange tail. If you see her quickly, she looks like a giant goldfish." Vanessa smiled at some memory of Belinda's goldfish daughter.

"Belinda has kids?" I couldn't imagine the ice queen condescending to sleep with anyone.

"Just one. Zerafina is almost nine years old, now."

I cleared my throat. "What about your other deckie?"

She laughed. "Maria was a deckie for three months. That hardly makes it her chosen career path." She turned serious. "Maria's daughter is around sixteen, now. Maybe seventeen. She's almost ready to be an adult."

I couldn't wrap my head around it. "Maria has a teenage daughter? She must have gotten pregnant really young."

Vanessa frowned. "She was older than I was, when I had my first child."

"She's older than you? Wow, you both look the same age. Do all of your people only have one child?" I asked her.

She smiled again. "Most of us do. One is enough to maintain the population. We don't need to have any more."

What I'd give for her to get pregnant with more of my children. To see her tummy swell and know we'd created a new life together...

"Don't you want to have more children?" I blurted out.

"I think I have as much as I can handle already," Vanessa said shortly. She stood up, starting to smile. "But if this is your roundabout way of suggesting we go to bed and practice making another child, I'm definitely up for it." She led the way to the bedroom.

I had other questions, but the burning one now was: *What colour underwear is she wearing and how soon will she take it off?*

LAILA

"You must be tired after your long journey, Ambassador Cantrella," the Atlantic Elder said smoothly, *"I am Zelia, Facilitator of the Elder Council of the Atlantic. Permit me to escort you to the Black palace, so you may rest."* She moved to Mother's side and beckoned for her to follow.

Mother graciously swam with Elder Zelia away from the assembled people. Ignored and insecure, I followed behind as closely as I dared. The two Elders' undulations were both stately and slow, leaving me ample time to look at the people who flanked us.

Perhaps it was their expressions, but I found their faces and bodies unattractive. *Does their seeming hostility and my fear cloud my perception?* I reflected. It was not a matter of colour, for they were as many colours as my own people, but of shape. One had an overly large nose, one had crooked features and one had a particularly short tail. One appeared to have no chin whilst the one beside her had a jaw so large it dwarfed the rest of her face.

I had not noticed that our people were particularly favoured in both feature and figure until I saw the contrast presented by the sisters of the Atlantic. Both Sirena and Darma had told us many times that it was important for our survival that both we and our progeny were pleasing to the eyes. We were commanded to join only with humans who inspired feelings of attraction within us, so that our children might have similar attraction in the future.

I wondered what the Atlantic sisters bred for in their children. Were the humans around their ocean so ugly that they held only minimal attraction? Or did the Atlantic sisters breed for different qualities altogether? It did not appear from those I saw that they bred for beauty.

I longed for my friend and for my teachers, so that I might ask them my questions. I missed Estella's sweet insight, where she could see to the heart of a matter and explain it patiently to me. The thought of my friend's face and round form made me ache to see her again, though she was an ocean away.

I shook myself from my sadness. I was a child ambassador to a foreign people and I must learn as much as I could, so that I could bring back stories to make Estella's eyes shine with excitement and the Council bow to me, as they waived the need for me to join with a human in honour of my courage in doing a different duty. I knew I dreamed of what could never come to pass, but even I dared to hope it would be.

Angry, I began to look around me. The Atlantic sisters were fewer in number now, as we approached a part of the city that was more ruined than the palace we had come from. The palace we proceeded toward was dark and empty.

"…we have had limited time to prepare for your arrival, so I hope you will forgive your accommodations. The Black palace has been in disarray since the last of your line died. We have prepared the two largest sleeping quarters for you and your daughter. Should you require any assistance, please do not hesitate to ask. Once you are rested, we shall summon the Council to formally welcome an honoured visitor from so far…" Elder Zelia continued without cease, with Mother nodding in response. Mother seemed too tired to speak and her movements betrayed some pain. Perhaps her years had started to catch up with her, though she was only twice my age, far younger than her partner or the other Elders on the Council.

I did not dare to interrupt and followed my elders into the dark of the Black palace, hoping that the morning would improve my impression of this gloomy place.

JOE

I arrived at my parents' house first. Vanessa and Marina would arrive a little later, in her car. She'd laughed when I said she should stay away for her own safety, but she didn't know my mother and I did.

"Hi, Mum," I said, kissing her as I went into the house.

"I thought you'd be back before the weekend, Giuseppe. Was it such a difficult job this time?" Mum was making lunch and it smelled good.

No one calls me Giuseppe except Mum. Now she's

going to flip out...

"Mum, can you sit down a minute? I need to tell you something." I felt like a five-year-old who'd broken her heirloom vase throwing a football around the lounge room. No, I felt like the five-year-old who'd broken an even more valuable vase after getting in trouble for breaking the first one.

"Have you met a girl? Are you finally going to give me grandchildren?" Mum sat down, suddenly excited.

I thought of Marina swimming in the bath last night and closed my eyes, trying to keep calm.

I took a deep breath and tried to get the words out slowly. "Actually, I met this girl almost four years ago. I haven't seen her for a while, but I saw her again recently and she's agreed to marry me."

"Why would she stay away from you so long?" Mum frowned.

I hesitated. *Because she's not human and she was living in the depths of the ocean, in the mermaid city.* "Um, she's a teacher, and she's been teaching at remote places overseas. It's been hard to stay in contact, until she came back to Australia."

"So, when do plan on marrying this girl?" Mum asked, suspiciously.

I smiled. *Tomorrow, if I could.* "As soon as I can."

"What's the hurry? Is she pregnant?" Mum demanded.

I heard a car engine in the driveway and a door slamming. *Oh thank God, she's here.*

I opened the front door to let Vanessa in. Marina clung to her legs, hidden behind Vanessa.

"Mum, this is Vanessa, the woman I'm going to marry," I said proudly.

Vanessa stepped inside cautiously, but she was smiling.

I turned to look at Mum. She shoved away from the table and strode toward Vanessa. I'd never seen my mother look short before, but she did in front of Vanessa.

"Are you after my boy's money? Did you get pregnant so you could catch my boy?" Mum demanded of Vanessa. "He's a good boy with a good job and he's about to buy a house. Don't you think you can seduce that out of him."

Vanessa looked puzzled, but her smile didn't falter. "Mrs Fisher, I have a lovely house of my own in East Fremantle, down near the water. I also have a house on Rat Island, up at the Houtman Abrolhos, and a fishing boat that can comfortably house my family. I think you'll find that Joe's money or property is the last thing I'm interested in."

Mum didn't ease up. "You're not showing yet. Are you sure you're pregnant?"

I cleared my throat. "Actually, Mum, we're not planning a baby at the moment."

"Then why the rush to get married?" Mum demanded.

"I have no reason to wait, and it's important to Joe if we're going to live together. He'd like us to be married, and so I agreed," Vanessa said calmly.

Marina picked this moment to peer out from behind Vanessa. "Who's the gwumpy lady, Mummy?"

Vanessa shushed her, as Mum launched a fresh onslaught.

"You're trying to get my Giuseppe to take

care of some kid whose father left you?" Mum's voice rose to a screech.

I opened my mouth but no words came out, because I had no idea how to even start explaining to Mum about Marina. While I did my best fish impression, ironically it was Vanessa who seemed more human.

Her voice was cool with steel. "Joe has expressed a wish to take care of *his own* child, and we have agreed that he should have the opportunity to do so."

Oh shit. Mum turned on me. "You got a girl pregnant three years ago and didn't tell me? You just left her?"

Vanessa stepped between my mother and I. "I didn't tell him about it. Marina was born while I was away and communication was difficult. Joe only met our daughter last week, when we were visiting the Abrolhos for some camp maintenance."

Mum was struggling for words now. "You…"

Marina detached herself from Vanessa's leg and planted her feet firmly on the floor, looking up at her grandmother. "Don't you yell at my Mummy and Daddy. That's not nice."

Oh my God. It's volcanic Vanessa, mixed with my mother at her maddest. In miniature.

Silence and statues in Mum's kitchen. Vanessa seemed to be smothering laughter, but her small smile said plenty; I choked down rising panic as Mum looked like she was fighting something for sure. Still, Mum was the first of us to move.

She stiffly dropped down into a crouch, so she was on a level with Marina. "I'm your Daddy's Mummy, and it's my job to tell him off if he does something wrong. Doesn't your Mummy tell you off sometimes, too?"

Marina pouted. "Not when I'm a good girl."

Mum laughed. "Are you going to be a good girl?"

"I am a good girl," Marina insisted.

"Then you can have a biscuit, if you like," Mum told her, smiling, as she climbed laboriously to her feet. She went over to the fridge and pulled down the biscuit tin. She pulled off the lid and held it out to Marina.

Marina looked at Vanessa instead of the tin.

Vanessa nodded. "You may eat one of your

grandmother's biscuits, but remember your manners."

Marina took a biscuit. "Thank you, gwandmother," she mumbled around the biscuit.

"Nonna," Mum corrected her. "I am your Nonna, Marina."

I breathed again.

SIRENA

"Don't touch that!" an angry female voice shouted, followed by the appearance of the woman herself.

Marina glared at the angry woman, ready to reply in kind, but I shook my head and she subsided.

The woman's expression shifted from angry to condescending. "Do you have an appointment?"

I forced myself to smile, despite my distaste. "No, we've just arrived in Perth. We've been out of mobile range…"

"Then you'll have to make an appointment before we'll see you," she interrupted, to my annoyance.

"You see me now," I replied. "I just wanted to try on a couple of dresses to check my size and leave with one…"

She laughed unpleasantly. "You make an appointment like everyone else, so we have time to assist you properly, then you can place your order and collect it in three months when it's ready." She looked me up and down with distaste. "That's how it works, dear."

I stood up and gestured to Marina to take my hand. "I will not make an appointment, for I don't believe you're capable of assisting me at all. If I wanted to wait three months, I'd contract a designer like Leona Edmiston to do me a custom dress." I swept out of the shop, trying not to laugh at the shocked look on the rude woman's face.

I was thoroughly sick of wedding dress shopping and I'd only ventured into one shop.

The next shop on my list was considerably smaller, with a pink façade. "Designs by Michèle" was written in white script across the bright pink.

Michèle had staff who were far more polite and I agreed to try on a pretty white dress that reminded me of the distant past. Far from my future as Joe's wife, the first of my people in the Indian Ocean to marry a human. I breathed deeply, steadying myself, as I stepped out of the changing room and in front of the mirrors.

"Just like Ariel, Mummy," Marina breathed in awe.

The shop assistant smiled as I struggled to take the three steps to the mirror. The enormous skirt on this dress made those steps more difficult than walking through water. I looked lovely in the mirror, of course, if I ignored my pained expression.

"Let's try it with a veil," the shop assistant suggested, reaching for something filmy and white that she draped over my head.

I felt like a corpse, shrouded in white sailcloth, about to be buried at sea. I thought of Giuseppe, lost to the waters so many years ago, and shook my head. I pulled the veil off. "No," I replied. "I want something different, without such a huge skirt. Something simpler."

I struggled back to the change room and my own clothes, so I could stroll through the shop and look at other options.

"A water dress, Mummy!" Marina shouted from across the shop and I followed the sound of her voice to the garment she pointed at.

The dress was placed beside something enormous and white, with a big veil that was partially draped over it. I lifted the filmy white fabric, then dropped it again, admiring the effect.

"That one," I said to the shop assistant, pointing at the half-hidden dress.

"But that's a bridesmaid dress…" she began.

I smiled. "Not on my wedding day, it won't be."

I slid easily from my casual clothes and into silk, stepping out of the change room with less discomfort than before. The lighter dress permitted me more freedom of movement, though not as much as I liked. I turned before the mirror, admiring the style as I thought of what I might change.

"It's very pretty, Mummy," Marina said.

"Can I have a dress like that when I'm grown up?"

I laughed. "Sweetheart, you'll have a dress like this in a few weeks, the same as me."

The shop assistant looked hesitant. "Ma'am, it takes up to ten weeks to get dresses made to your measurements…"

My smile was tight. "Is Michèle here today?"

She hesitated and I knew the answer already.

"Where is she?" I asked.

"She's in the office, doing the quarterly accounts," the woman admitted. "I'll see if she has a moment."

I smiled to myself and sat down, smoothing the silk beneath my fingers.

"Can I help you?" The woman who looked enquiringly at me was as gold as the ring I'd wear the day I married Joe. Her hair and skin were the same shade, as if she spent much of her spare time in the sun.

I turned my beaming smile on Michèle as I stood up. "I'd like you to use this as a base for a design I have in mind."

She looked from me to Marina. "For yourself and the little girl?"

I felt my smile widen. "That's right."

She eyed me, her mouth moving as if she were still adding up figures in the office behind her. "It will be very expensive and take eight weeks."

I met her eyes. "Four weeks."

Michèle's eyes were more calculating still. "Do you know what jewellery you will wear with this?"

I pulled the box from my bag. "Pearls," I replied.

She pursed her lips. "Pearls are somewhat old-fashioned. Are you sure?"

I opened the box of black pearls so that she could see the contents. Her sharp intake of breath told me she would design my dress.

"Once we've finished the design, I need to take these to Kailis, to arrange the jewellery. I would aim for classic, more than old-fashioned," I replied.

She couldn't hide her smile. "It will be a pleasure." She held out her hand, as delicately as I had been taught to as a child. "I am Michèle."

I took her hand. "Vanessa Wood-Jones,

soon to be Vanessa Fisher."

JOE

When Vanessa and Marina returned from dress shopping, Vanessa seemed distracted. She suggested we order pizza for dinner, but she barely ate more than Marina. Once we'd managed to get Marina bathed, brushed and in bed, I slid an arm around Vanessa before she could slip away.

"What's wrong?" I asked softly.

She looked at me with a rueful smile. "Wedding dress shopping is harder than I thought. Do I have to wear a dress?"

I hesitated. "It's the normal thing to do, so

I'd say, yes, you do. The less you wear, the happier I'll be, but my family want all the traditional things. A church wedding, a restaurant reception, dancing, suits, speeches, flowers, cake…and they want you to make the decisions on all of it." I smiled to soften the words.

For the first time, she looked lost. "I've never been married before – none of my kind have, not in living memory! I know less than you do about weddings and such things. I like blue and I like seafood. Tell your mother…tell her…that I think she should plan what she thinks best and I'll pay for it." She looked at me. "I don't know – you tell me what we should do."

I laughed. "I haven't been married before, either. It'll look strange if I plan our wedding – usually the women in the family take care of it." I stopped laughing when I saw this didn't cheer her up much. "Look, Mum's coming over tomorrow to ask you questions about the wedding. I'm sure she'd be delighted to deal with all the wedding details – I'm the first of her kids to get married. She has so many ideas about how it must be and what has to happen…if you want her to plan the whole thing, all you'll have to do is tell her that and she will. You'll be her favourite daughter-in-law forever."

"Thank you," Vanessa replied, coming in closer for a kiss.

Some time later, when we were wearing a lot less, I asked the question in the back of my mind. "Why did you come ashore again? And how long will you stay this time?"

She turned to face me in the dark, running her hand lightly up and down my chest. "Like last time, I came ashore to perform a vital task for my people and I will return to the depths once it is complete. When another such task arises, I will return to shore again." Vanessa's words were calm and cautious.

"But what are you actually doing? What is your vital task? How long will it take?" I swallowed. "I want to know when you'll leave me."

"I am the best at blending in with humans, so I am the ocean's infiltrator, living among you to obtain information. As for the time…I will be here for as long as it takes. Months, perhaps, or years, maybe. I don't know." She moved again, her lips on my cheek before she found my mouth. Several kisses later, she continued. "The less you know, the safer you are. My people have many secrets and our existence is just one of them. How much do you really want to know, Joe? I don't want you in any more danger than you are already, simply in knowing what I am."

"I don't know," I admitted. I'd seen too many movies not to ask it, though. "You're not trying to take over the world, are you?"

Vanessa's boobs shook with laughter in my appreciative hands. "No. We're not trying to take over the world – merely survive it."

I thought for a long moment before I replied. "Then…I guess I don't want to know about them, or why they sent you here. I just want to know everything about you, that's all. And…when I ask, I'd like to know you're being honest and not lying to protect me. I'd also like some advance warning of when you're leaving so I can say goodbye." I could feel that black hole yawning wide inside me at the thought of her first goodbye, when I hadn't had a chance to reply, but I tried to ignore it. It wasn't hard. After all, Vanessa was right beside me, her skin warm against mine.

"I will tell you if you're asking something I feel you'd prefer not to know the answer to and I'll give you plenty of time to say goodbye. But it's much too soon to be thinking about such things now. I would prefer…oh, hello…" Vanessa shifted in bed, poised to make me a very happy man.

"I love you, Nessa," I said blissfully, as her wordless reply left me in no doubt that she loved me, too.

LAILA

The Elder Council did not assemble on the structure steps as they had for our arrival. They were inside the structure, enclosed in walls and a roof that I found as strange as the buildings they had assigned us as sleeping quarters. I was not accustomed to sleeping in still water and my sleep had been restless. Mother did not appear well-rested, either, though her eyes were bright with eager excitement.

"You are welcome, Ambassador Cantrella. You are the first of the Black line to enter this chamber for almost fifty years," Elder Zelia said with a bow to

Mother.

Mother looked intrigued. *"For that long? The Black line is thin among the blood of our people, but I did not realise it ran thin here, too."*

A look was exchanged between Elder Zelia and a tall Elder with hair as dark as mine. The tall one approached Mother.

"I am Elder Nadie." She and Mother exchanged deep nods. *"I am the historian of our people. I keep our records and knowledge. What do you know of dragons?"*

Mother looked suspicious. *"Dragons? Imaginary creatures. Stories told to children."* She dismissed dragons with a flick of her fingers.

Elder Nadie smiled thinly. *"Stories told to children here, too, of when we were a whole people — male and female, or dragon and mermaid, as the humans called us. The dragons of the Black line were the strongest and among those with the most courage, so they were the most hunted by humans. The last of these was Dubhan. Only a child, Dubhan fled. Humans from Holland, England and Portugal pursued him in their wooden sailing ships. We believe Dubhan headed for your ocean, for your people travelled there in search of the last Black dragon, but we heard nothing of dragons after Dubhan departed the Atlantic. Dubhan was very young, unable to defend against the humans. It is my hope that Dubhan died with honour, as was customary for those of the Black line.*

"*The Black line turned its energies to fighting the humans, at the price of progeny. They had few daughters, for the more powerful of their number did not dally long enough to produce children. The last daughter was Raimunda, who died almost fifty years ago. Her only child was killed when she became trapped in a human vessel. Raimunda herself died attempting to save the child. Her palace has remained empty since, home only to eels and octopi.*"

Elder Nadie's eyes darted eagerly to Mother's face. "*Did your people find Dubhan? Are you descended from the last Black dragon?*"

Mother shook her head. "*There are no dragons in the Indian Ocean, nor have there ever been. We are only the people of the ocean's gift, as my ancestress was when she arrived in the Indian Ocean. Many have searched for these mythical dragons, but none have found. If there were dragons in the past, there are none now. I had wondered if they existed at all, or whether it was only a legend.*"

Elder Nadie's smile seemed to grow thinner

still. *"Though they have not been seen in living memory, dragons are well documented in historic accounts. I assure you the creatures the humans hunted as dragons did exist, even if they do not today. Now, if they were..."*

Elder Zelia cut across the softer-spoken Elder. *"I have more questions for the Ambassador, so your historic accounts can wait. Please, Ambassador, can you tell us more of your people? Most of us have not visited your ocean. How do you..."*

They interrogated Mother incessantly, asking about her life and our home. I felt myself drowse, curling up unnoticed in a dark corner where soft corals had colonised the colonnade.

"Child! The Council does not wait with patience for one as insignificant as you!" The shout brought me back to consciousness. An insistent hand pulled on my arm, dragging me through the water from darkness to light. *"Show some respect, child,"* the same voice instructed reproachfully, in a quieter tone.

I tried to draw myself up as I would at home, but I felt exposed and uncertain in the scrutiny I saw. The Elders, my mother included, formed a circle around me, inspecting me minutely and I did not know why. I wanted to curl up and hide.

"Can she breed? Is she fertile?"

A hand with sharp nails poked my breast. *"Why has she not done her duty? She seems to have developed correctly."* The hand crept around the back of my tail to touch me intimately and I squirmed away, scared.

"Is she disobedient? Does she dare to refuse to do her duty?" This voice was suspicious and hinted at consequences she would like to inflict upon me.

I shivered, curling up smaller than I had in repose.

Mother permitted herself a tiny smile. *"She is as docile as any other child, who approaches the age of adulthood. When the time comes, she will do as she is told."* Her eyes on me held a warning.

Wanting to scream and swim, I held still as hands crawled over me like curious crabs. I felt violated. I *was* violated.

"You have done well to bring her with you. She will be put to use." Elder Zelia smiled at me in a way that I did not like, then turned her attention

elsewhere. *"What is it you came to investigate?"* Her eyes travelled to Mother and the Council moved away from me.

I let the cool water flow over my skin, cowering beneath the creepy remembered sensation of so many strangers touching me. They paid me no attention, though they had not dismissed me, so I felt forced to stay.

"The fires and shifts on the sea floor. We have noticed more movement of late and we wish to know if you have experienced similar changes to your seabed in the Atlantic Ocean." Mother's words sounded rehearsed. She had not seen the sites where the seabed glowed red and orange, the waters hot and full of dark vapours. I had and I did not like such places.

Elder nodded and gestured toward one of the other Elders. *"Elder Sophia?"*

The indicated Elder gave a sharp nod. *"The fields of fire are more active than any other time in living memory. From our histories, it seems that they are more active now than in the time when the humans in our city were wiped out as the waters reclaimed it."* Elder Sophia shook her head. *"The humans study this, too, and their vessels may be found nearby on occasion. It is dangerous to approach, but I can take you so that you may see the magma flows."*

Mother gave a nod of acquiescence before she replied. *"Then you will take the child with you to observe the fiery phenomena. She will report to me on her return."* She did not even look at me as she ordered me into dangerous, human-infested waters.

Aghast, I opened my mouth to protest, but remembered myself in time. As at home, I was a voiceless child in the Elder Council. Though my head felt heavy as I performed it, my bow of obeisance held as much respect as I could muster.

Mother, what are you doing? Do not sacrifice me in fear for yourself. My fear is greater than yours. I thought the words but I did not say them. I was thankful that my eyes did not cry beneath the water, for I would have cried my body dry and only my fear would have remained.

JOE

Mum and my sisters put the wedding together, not me. They asked Vanessa to help, but all she'd said was that she had no family to invite, few friends as she travelled so much and it was mostly my family there. Vanessa told them it should be planned for those who would be there. When Mum managed to interrogate her long enough, Vanessa said the same things she'd told me - she'd like the colours to be mostly blue and white, she wanted seafood served at the reception and that would work well with an ocean theme.

My sisters wanted to be bridesmaids, but Vanessa balked at dressing five girls instead of just herself and Marina. Her dress and Marina's were a secret not even my mother knew about.

The morning of the wedding dawned. Vanessa kissed my cheek and whispered goodbye as the sun was just coming up. "We'll see you later, Sleeping Beauty," she said softly.

By the time I managed to open my eyes, she'd already gone.

Mum and Dad arrived a couple of hours later. Mum wore a dark blue dress and Dad had come for his suit. We'd hired dark blue ones instead of black, to keep with Vanessa's choice of blue and white.

Mum made breakfast and we sat around, talking about the weather. It was a perfect day, not too hot and not too cold, with a cloudless sky. I wondered idly if mermaids could control the weather. Vanessa had said something about them controlling the waves…

I heard a car pull up and Marina's piping voice.

Vanessa and Marina walked in, looking beautiful in very casual clothes. Both of them wore their hair loose, arranged in curls that I'd never seen on either before. Vanessa wore some makeup, her lips a glistening pink, and it looked like Marina had something on her lips as well.

Vanessa smiled at me, her whole face lit up, but Mum got between us and hustled my daughter and my soon-to-be wife upstairs before I could get up. My eyes followed them up the stairs.

"She's a real beauty," Dad said softly. "I didn't know they had pearls like that up at the Abrolhos."

I laughed. "Dad, there's pearl farms up there. Abrolhos pearls are as beautiful and expensive as they come."

"I meant Vanessa. You were lucky to catch her, Joe."

The luckiest fisherman in the world. "Yeah, I know," I replied fervently.

He climbed laboriously to his feet. "I guess if the girls are getting dressed, it's time we put on some fancy clothes, too. I hate suits."

I'd never worn one. But I'd wear anything Vanessa wanted, if by the end of the day she'd agree to be mine. I nodded and followed him into the downstairs bedroom where our suits were laid out.

When we were all trussed up in suits, ties, waistcoats and shiny shoes, we wandered outside to have photos by the water with the photographer Mum had hired. By the time we were done, I was sick of the uncomfortable suit and wishing we'd decided to get married on a beach.

As I walked back into the house, Marina came flying down the stairs, like a dolphin riding a wave. Her dress was in two layers. The top layer was made of something white and almost transparent, with a shimmery fabric underneath that shone different shades of blue as it caught the light. It varied from the pale blue-green of the shallows to the deeper colour of the blue holes in the reef, right down to the dark blue of the deep ocean. In here, out of the sun, I even caught a glimpse of the stormy blue in Vanessa's eyes.

A strand of light blue pearls clung to Marina's neck, matching her eyes. Her shoes were the same colour.

"You look beautiful, sweetheart," I told her.

"Mummy has more pearls than me." Marina pouted.

I laughed softly. "When you get married, sweetheart, I'll make sure you have as many pearls as Mummy."

The photographer hurried in and took up a position at the bottom of the stairs. He started snapping pictures in quick succession. Both Marina and I looked up, and there she was.

Vanessa stepped slowly down the stairs, wearing a dress made of the same fabric as Marina's. That's where the similarity ended, though. Vanessa's dress highlighted every perfect curve, falling just short of the toes of her sparkly sandals.

Her pearls were more numerous than Marina's, but they were very different. Hers were every shade of blue, from pale silver to deep ocean, just like the dress. They went from her neck to the neckline of her dress, spaced out across her smooth skin by an almost invisible web of chain. It looked like she wore a whole season's harvest of Abrolhos black pearls, and it probably cost as much as I earned in a year. *Well, Mum's never going to accuse her of going after my money again.*

I wondered how much the rest of the wedding had cost, but I knew I'd never find out, for Vanessa's finances were yet another mystery to me. A mystery I didn't need to solve, as long as I had her.

I think that's when it finally hit me. Staring at this vision in a blue dress, I realised that the most beautiful woman in the world was going to be my wife. *Oh, thank you God.* I couldn't look away and I couldn't breathe. *Shit, how will I be able to say my vows when I'm speechless just looking at her?*

Vanessa reached the bottom of the stairs and held out a hand to me. Mine shook as I took it. For the first time, I saw her nails were painted in a shade of iridescent blue that matched her dress. My mouth gaped open as I stared at her, less than an arm's length from me. She took the last step that placed her up against me. She slid her arms around me and leaned forward to put her lips to my ear. "Breathe, Joe. I'm the one tied into a dress. I'll need your help to take it off later."

I looked down at the design of woven strands across her bare back, tied into an ornate bow just above the curve of her bottom. *Oh God, sex with my beautiful wife on our wedding night.* "Just say the word," I managed to say.

Her voice lowered to a barely audible whisper. "Remember, Joe, whatever we have to do today, that at the end of it we'll be alone and I will say the word. All day, all I want is you."

She laughed softly and pulled away from me so I could see her smiling face. I forced myself to take a shaking breath as my suit felt tighter than ever. She pressed her glistening pink lips to mine.

Marina rushed in through the front door. "There's a white car and it has a pussy cat on the front!" she squealed in excitement.

Vanessa stretched her hand out once more. "Come on, Joe. Your family is waiting to see us get married. It's time to go to the church."

I took her hand without hesitation and all three of us walked out to the waiting Jaguar.

LAILA

Elder Sophia seized my arm the moment the meeting was over, dragging me outside before the others moved. She gestured imperiously with her free hand to two sisters outside. *"Come. We will take the child to the fields of fire."*

The two girls nodded and followed without question.

"Move your tail, child. We will get there faster," Elder Sophia grumbled and I swam, obedient to her wishes. After a few minutes, she released my arm.

I thought of breaking away from her and

her companions, but I did not dare to defy her orders or those of my mother. We swam in silence until the city was far behind us and the waters were dark and deep once more.

I felt tired, but I did not slow or stop as long as the Atlantic sisters continued. Until I dropped, I was honour-bound to show them that a child of the Indian Ocean had as much stamina as any of theirs.

After an interminable swim that lasted 'til the sun set, Elder Sophia called a halt.

I felt bone weary and glad to rest.

The Elder's voice was gentle for the first time. *"What is your name, child? I do not remember."*

"Laila," I replied dully. Even my tongue felt exhausted. *"Child of the Black line, daughter of Elder Cantrella of the Indian Ocean Council..."*

"Laila," she said with a smile. *"I know the rest, child. Perhaps more than you. I will tell you as much as I dare whilst I have you. I am Elder Sophia and these are my daughters, Priscilla and Salina."* Each girl nodded at the sound of her name. Both had dark hair like mine, but Priscilla was smaller than I, whilst Salina was the same height, though rounder in the tail. All three

had a silvery cast to their tails, marking them as descendants of the Silver line.

"*I am honoured, but I do not understand…*" I began, hesitantly. In strange waters with strange sisters, my words stuck in my throat. I was afraid to say something wrong.

Elder Sophia patted my arm and I shrank back, still shaken at the memory of so many Elders touching me whilst I was forced to stay still. "*I will help you to understand, Laila, but I cannot change your fate.*" She looked sad.

"*We are far enough away that we may rest properly until it is light. Salina, will you watch?*" Elder Sophia did not wait for an answer. She swam to the surface and spread herself out between the waves.

Salina smiled at me and pointed upward. "*Sleep, Laila. I will watch so no harm comes to you.*"

Still I hesitated. "*I have trained as a Watcher. I should…*"

Salina's smile grew broader. "*And I am not a Watcher, but I will watch for you and you will be safe. Rest.*"

Reluctantly I complied.

When I woke in the morning, the sunlight

shone full on my face, reflecting off waves and the occasional flying fish.

"Good morning," Priscilla greeted me. *"We must be under way."*

And we were.

We followed the currents to the north, 'til the swirl of the sea drew us to shallower waters where steam rose from the seabed.

"The fields of fire, a ridge that runs the length of our ocean," Elder Sophia explained, pointing from north to south. *"They spew more rock now than ever in living memory or historic record. We fear the worst, but if it means great change, the humans will suffer more than we. When our city sank beneath the waves, it was the humans who died, not the people of the ocean's gift. When their cities sink, we will emerge stronger still."* She smiled, not the slightest bit sad at the thought. She looked at me. *"Do you like humans, Laila?"*

I shook my head as quickly as I could, my eyes on the red and orange flow beneath me. *"No. No, I don't like humans at all. I've never met one and I don't want to..."* I broke off before I could speak of my desire for disobedience.

"Nor do I," Elder Sophia said softly. *"They*

have killed too many of my friends."

She swam away from the steamy waters, heading still further north. I followed her, with her daughters trailing behind me.

At a place that seemed no different to any other, she stopped and pointed down. *"There they lie, on the seabed."*

Together, we dived deep, until I could discern human artefacts strewn across the sand.

"The humans killed my friends and I will not lightly forgive their treachery." Elder Sophia's eyes blazed in the deep water.

I could not fathom how humans had done such a thing, given the secrecy that shrouded our people. *"I don't understand,"* I whispered. *"How could humans have killed our sisters? They do not know of us…"*

Salina approached. *"Did the Council tell you what happened to the last of the Black line here?"*

Elder Sophia shook her head before I could answer. *"No, they were vague and did not say. The Black line challenged the humans and died for their pride. I survived, but at a price."* She looked at the debris below us with bitterness.

"How?" I asked.

Elder Sophia gently curled an arm around my shoulders and I did not shake her off. *"Have you heard of submarines, child? I have sunk two in my lifetime and I hope never to see a third..."*

I listened.

JOE

The wedding was a blur. I stumbled down the aisle beside Vanessa to the altar, I stammered through my vows and I didn't let go of her hand until I had to put a ring on her finger. The fog in my head lifted a little when the priest told me I could kiss her and I felt her cool lips on mine. Then the priest said something about Giuseppe and Vanessa Fisher, everyone clapped and cheered, and we had to walk back out of the church. *We did it. Beautiful Vanessa is my wife.* I couldn't keep the beaming smile from my face. I must have looked like an idiot.

My family came up, hugged, kissed and congratulated us both. I couldn't tell you what any of them said.

I remember hearing Vanessa humming at the edge of hearing and I turned to find out why. Dean stood there, looking stunned as he gave Vanessa a hug. I heard her whisper, "Mermaids don't exist and you will not remember me."

Mermaids don't exist. For a moment, I believed it, but one glance at Vanessa told me otherwise. *How can I ever forget my wife with her sexy tail?*

Dean's eyes grew huge and blank, but Nessa smiled and laughed as if it was nothing, before turning to one of my cousins, who was next in line.

Dean shook my hand, for the first time in his life lost for words. "Shit mate, where did you find her? She's hot!" he managed to get out, before stumbling off.

We went to a beach for photos and it wasn't as hard as the photos before the wedding. All I had to do was look at my new wife and I couldn't keep the smile off my face. When it was late afternoon, the classic Jaguar we'd hired for the day took us to a reception place right on the water, the sunset lighting up the windows as they served pre-dinner drinks.

I barely tasted the food and grinned like an idiot at whatever my family had to say. There were speeches, there was food, and at some point I ended up on the dance floor with Vanessa. *How does a mermaid learn to dance?* I wondered as I stumbled around the dance floor with her.

Marina fell asleep under the bridal table, her head pillowed on a stuffed fish. Mum and Dad took her home and the other guests started to say goodbye and leave, too. Vanessa guided me out of the reception venue to the hotel.

A blur of check-in counter, key card, short lift ride, carpeted corridors and a plush hotel room with a huge bed.

The door closed. All was quiet and we were alone. Husband and wife.

LAILA

"Raimunda was always reckless, epitomising the Black spirit more than most. So when the humans started venturing deeper beneath the water, she was furious. How dare they invade our domain? She took the submarines as a personal affront, an attempt on their part to seek and destroy us. She was a Diver, one of those who looked for human technology beneath the surface and attempted to understand its function. The humans destroyed many submarine and surface vessels in their wars and it was several years before she felt she could destroy her own submarine vessel.

"I climbed aboard the first one with her, under cover

of night. The vessel Thresher was cramped inside, so we hid in the rooms where the humans stored their weapons and power generation devices. The vessel ventured beneath the waves with us aboard. Each night, we took a human to join with, singing him to a state where he would not remember us.

"When the vessel attempted to reach the surface, Raimunda put her knowledge of its inner workings into practice, damaging some of the power generation equipment so that the vessel was destroyed. When water flooded in, we made our escape.

"She was not fertile, but I was and I gave birth to Priscilla nine months following. She agreed to wait for another raid, assembling a team of younger girls whose time it was to do their duty and those who, like her, craved a challenge. Her anger spun through the water like coral spawn in the current and from the youngest child to the Facilitator of the Elder Council, we all wished to show the humans that we would NOT have our territory invaded by them again, for they could not survive beneath the surface.

"When Priscilla was weaned, we struck again.

"Raimunda's strike team this time consisted of her own daughter, Onyxia, and a child of the Gold, Ava. They boarded the vessel by night as it lay on the surface in a human port in the Mediterranean. Ava was to sing the humans into submission and let the rest of us aboard once she had control.

"She was a powerful singer, as all of the Gold line are, and her control was complete. She called us aboard and we chose our human companions. Onyxia favoured a human who worked with the larger weapons and she plied him with questions on how such weapons worked.

"She placed one such weapon in a firing tube, in readiness to fire, then joined with the human on the engine room floor. She laughed as she told me she wanted the humans to go out with a bang, as was fitting.

"The weapon exploded within the vessel without warning and it flooded quickly. I swam out, for I was close to a breach whilst not near the explosion, but I was the only one. No others emerged. I waited and called, but I did not even hear their voices. My friends and so many children…dead, because of the humans. I searched and I called, but none had survived. Only I and the new child I carried.

"The Scorpion was the end of the Black line, for it took Raimunda and Onyxia, little Ava and so many others. So much sorrow for what was supposed to be a breeding event. It was almost thirty years before enough *of our younger children were old enough to breed, and we went looking for dragons to renew the Black line."*

Elder Sophia lapsed into silence, her head bowed as if under a great weight of water.

"Dragons?" I ventured. *"Are there dragons still?"*

Priscilla and Salina laughed.

Elder Sophia's smile was sad. *"We found none, though we searched all oceans including your own."* She gave a sigh. *"How much do you know of your own ocean, child?"*

I shook my head. *"Nothing of dragons."*

She touched my arm, reassuring once more. *"Then I must tell you this, too."*

JOE

We looked at each other for a second and then Vanessa was in my arms. I didn't care if I kissed off all her lipstick or messed up her hair.

I unfastened her pearls and dropped the intricate net on the table by the door. I pressed my lips to her neck, struggling out of my jacket and loosening my tie.

"Um, Joe?" She sounded apologetic. "Can you please help me out of this dress? And please, please, don't ever ask me to wear a long dress again. There's nothing I hate more than long skirts. I feel like I'm drowning with every step, and I'm not even in the water. I've worn it all day for you, but now I want nothing more than to get out of it."

I stared at her, almost lost for words. "You hate long dresses and you still wore one today, just for me?" I dropped the jacket and tie on the floor.

She laughed. "You're the only person in the world I'd do this for. I'd rather have gone naked all day than wear this."

I closed my eyes, mesmerised by the thought of marrying her naked. We couldn't have done it in front of my family, or a priest. There would have been heart attacks all round. I opened my eyes again. Nope, she wasn't any less beautiful clothed.

"You looked so beautiful today. Hell, you still do." I just looked at her and drank her in. *How can she look so perfect, all day and all night?*

Her breath hissed through her teeth. "I bought new underwear in the hope that I might still look beautiful with the damn dress off. Now, can you please let me out of it so I can show you?"

I kissed her again, letting my hands slide

down her back. She guided my hands this time, to the complicated knot just above her bottom. "It's a bow, on top of a double knot," she murmured.

The bow came undone easily, but the knot was tighter and harder to deal with. In the end, I had to get down on the floor behind her so I could see what I was doing. Once the first knot was undone, the second was easy. She tugged on the strands a few times, before the whole dress slid down into a puddle at her feet.

Instead of the filmy blue and white fabric, I came face to face with a small strip of blue lace bisecting Vanessa's sweet arse.

I stood up slowly and she turned on the spot to face me. Vanessa was wearing what looked like a lace swimsuit, with no straps on her shoulders and cut very low in the back. I'd never seen a woman wear anything like this in real life – this was like something out of a porn film or a men's magazine. Or an explicit fantasy. Her smile was wicked. "Do you like this more than the dress?"

"Oh God yes," I breathed. I wanted to touch her, everywhere, and kiss her again. I wasn't going to last more than five seconds if I didn't take this slow.

Her lips firm on mine, she started undoing the buttons on my waistcoat, then my shirt. She slid them down my shoulders and my arms, so I had to let go of her to drop them on the floor. When I held her this time, her lacy boobs pressed against my bare chest. She started to undo my pants.

"I bought new underwear, too," I told her shyly.

Before I knew it, she had my pants around my ankles and I kicked them away. Her hands were warm on my arse through the black silk of my boxer shorts.

"Where do we start?" she murmured.

I reached down and slid my fingers under the blue lace and inside her. My other arm held her close to me. "I want you to come first, so you'll be really wet," I told her.

It felt like no time at all until she gave a shudder in my arms and a wordless cry, muffled by the fierce kisses I gave her. When she finished, she started pushing me toward the bed, before tipping me over onto my back.

My shorts were gone and she undid some buttons low on her tummy. She dropped something lacy on the floor and crept onto the bed on top of me. The touch of smooth, wet skin against my groin was all I needed to understand. I plunged deep inside her as her hips ground against mine.

That night, I came inside my wife for the first time and I lost count of how many times she came for me. Hell, by dawn I'd lost count of the number of times I'd had sex with my wife and I didn't care.

Life doesn't come any better than this.

LAILA

"When my daughters came of age to do their duty, I led them and the other children on an expedition to find the last Black dragon, if Dubhan still lived. Our party searched our own ocean, but we then headed to yours, around Africa the way the humans' ships had travelled in pursuit. History held that dragons could live far longer than the rest of us and we held out hope..."

I found myself laughing. *"We told stories as children about dragons. That they could change the colour of all of their skin, live for centuries, fight off a hundred humans and they were legendary lovers. Dragons don't exist, my teachers told me. They were just what humans called our kind when they saw us...*"

Elder Sophia looked sad. "*Our histories tell us there were dragons and even their names, but the legends may have been written by the dragons themselves, so who can say how much was elaborated? Perhaps we wished to idolise them, too, embellishing them into legends when they were just like us. I read them all and followed the tales to the Indian Ocean, around the south of Africa and into the Roaring Forties, where the sailing ships had gone.*

"*But there was no sign of dragons, though the bones of ships lay on the seabed, broken and scattered. We followed the shipping route east and north.*

"*We searched the small islands and called to whales and dolphins, singing Dubhan's name so the waters rang with it. Our delegation visited the Indian Ocean Elder Council, requesting permission to continue the search and it was granted. Your mother was not part of it then — the Council was led by a powerful woman of the Gold line named Sirena. The Black line would still survive in our ocean, had our Council the strength of a single Elder like Sirena. I believe all the stories about the power of dragons in a heartbeat after one look at her.*"

I felt a smile lift my lips. *"Elder Sirena leads our Council still. She frightens even my mother. But she can't be a dragon — she can't change colour. She is always the shimmering shades of shallow water on sand."*

Elder Sophia's eyes were narrowed. *"And yet she permitted you to accompany your mother here, as the only members of the Black line."*

"Elder Sirena would not have permitted it. Mother made her request for me when Elder Sirena was on land, passing for human as she lived among them." I closed my eyes, wishing Mother had waited. *"We left before she returned."*

"Ah." Elder Sophia's single word of reply held a great depth of feeling. She stayed silent for several minutes before she spoke again. *"Did she warn you about Alexandre?"*

I shook my head. *"No, I do not know that name."*

Her eyes were sad. *"We searched for the Black dragon. Every island, reef and undersea cave. Our girls were eager to be adults and we had all but given up hope of finding the Black dragon when we crossed the path of the Alexandre. A large ship with humans aboard over deep water — it was as if the Indian Ocean had granted us a gift, to make up for swallowing our dragon. We boarded the ship and the girls joined with the crew.*

"As dawn approached, the girls were tired and they had exhausted the humans. I ventured into the engine room of the vessel and used my knowledge of their technology to ensure all evidence of our visit was destroyed. I took to the water after the girls just as an explosion sank the ship. We were lucky."

I wanted to ask more about the ship and the explosion, but the two girls approached and Sophia's eyes went to them instead of me.

"Did you tell her what the Council will command her to do?" Priscilla asked.

Elder Sophia's eyes were closed as she shook her head.

"What?" I asked, looking from one to the other. *"What will they make me do?"*

"You must breed, as we did in your ocean. Our Council will command you to provide them with children, to ensure the future of the Black line in the Atlantic Ocean." Salina sounded sad.

I felt my mouth open and not close. *"You mean I must do my duty here? Join with humans, here?"*

Priscilla nodded. *"Do not worry. We will help you."*

I summoned a stunted smile as I thanked them for their consideration and assistance, but I felt sick. Not only would the Atlantic Elders violate my body, they would permit a human to violate me, too. And I would have no choice but to submit.

JOE

We'd been married two months before the fishing season started. I volunteered to go alone, as I'd originally planned, dreading the thought of the cold, lonely nights without Vanessa, but she wouldn't let me.

She made her arrangements and, instead of flying over, we took the *Siren*. The first night the *Siren* floated in the fishing boat harbour at Geraldton, we slept aboard instead of in a hotel. The fridge and freezers were full of supplies, the icebox was surrounded by foam eskies full of more and Marina fell asleep in

Belinda's old bunk, surrounded by stuffed toys.

Sitting at the dining table, sharing a beer with Vanessa, I looked around the cabin of the *Siren*. I never thought I'd see it again, but I'd also never get the memory of that kitchen bench out of my mind. I turned to Vanessa to say something, but the look in her eye said she was thinking the same thing.

"We never did try out that bench without a condom," I started to say.

"There's plenty of raspberries in the freezer," Vanessa replied.

We got reacquainted with the bench, the dining table and the bunks in the lower cabin before we fell asleep, exhausted, in each other's arms, the taste of raspberry still on my tongue.

When I woke up the next morning, we were already underway, more than halfway to the Abrolhos. Marina's toy killer whales had declared war on the stuffed dolphins and fish on the dining table. I made myself some toast and went up top to the fly bridge to spell Vanessa at the controls.

I draped my arms around her and kissed her neck. She smiled and wished me a good morning, but kept her eyes on the screens and the ocean in front of her. I offered to drive, but she shook her head.

"Not seasick today?" I asked her.

"No, I don't get seasick," she replied absently. Then she stood up, pointing. "There! The Easter Group!"

I looked and saw waves breaking on the horizon and nothing else. It could have been the sun on the water. I said as much.

"No, it's Suomi. Here, take the binoculars and look," Vanessa insisted, passing them to me.

I looked through them. On the horizon was a white sand island with brown things scattered along it. The waves were breaking between us and the sand.

"Your eyes are better than mine, to see that," I told her, amazed.

She shrugged. "Of course. My eyes are better than a human's because they have to be. It's dark in the deep water and visibility can be low sometimes."

Shit. I forget that she's not human. After last night, it wouldn't surprise me if she's part angel.

To cover my embarrassment, I said, "I'll go down and get Marina. She might want to come up and see, too. If she can negotiate a ceasefire between the dolphins, fish and orcas."

Marina left her toys in apparent peace and I helped her scale the ladder. She frowned as she looked into the binoculars. "Oh look, Mummy, sea lions!" she exclaimed, pointing.

"Where?" I asked, looking through the binoculars. I could still only see the sandy island.

"On the beach, Daddy!" She laughed like she thought I was joking.

Vanessa's voice was gentle. "Daddy can't see as well as you can, Marina. You have very good eyes. Can you count the sea lions for me?"

Marina snatched the binoculars from me. "One, two, three, four, five, six!" she shouted. I caught the binoculars before she dropped them.

I looked again, but all I could see was the sandy beach. I counted the brown things and came up with six. At this distance, they didn't look like sea lions or anything alive, except maybe slugs.

Eventually, we got close enough for me to identify them as sea lions, before we turned the *Siren* north, to follow the best approach into the anchorage. I saw some boats tied up at jetties, but there were less than last year, particularly at Rat. Skipper's *Dolphin* was tied up at his jetty, but quite a few were empty. Well, it wasn't Easter yet. Maybe they weren't going to start 'til later in the season.

Vanessa tied up with minimal help from me and started unloading boxes onto the jetty. I went up the jetty in search of a wheelbarrow or a trailer to help bring them up to her house. Our house, now.

Marina stood on the deck, watching us unload the boat, until she decided she wanted a ride in the wheelbarrow. She helped me push the load up the jetty to the house, then rode back in the wheelbarrow, her giggles frightening the Pacific and silver gulls into flight from the jetties on either side of ours.

Marina picked out a bunk in the house's bunkroom. Vanessa made up her bed with the special Ariel quilt cover Marina had chosen. We unpacked the food and put it away in the house kitchen while Marina built a castle in the lounge from the foam eskies. We cooked some frozen pizza for dinner and I barely had the energy to wrap my arms around Vanessa in our bed before we were both asleep.

LAILA

I sang up fish with Priscilla and Salina. I liked the little ones, but they preferred the reef sharks, tasty morsels the length of my arm that were a meal in themselves. Both of them knocked theirs out with a quick blow on the edge of the reef, but I carefully broke the necks of each of mine before I swallowed them whole.

When we had all caught and eaten our fill, the two sisters escorted me back to the Black palace where I was expected to sleep. *"Where do you sleep?"* I asked petulantly.

Salina laughed. *"In the Silver palace, of course. There are more of us and Priscilla snores a stream of bubbles all night."*

Priscilla smacked her sister on the tail. *"I do not make any noises in my sleep. I am sure it is Mother, who is entitled to make any sounds she pleases in her advanced age."*

"I find it very hard to sleep in somewhere as dark and still as the palace," I confessed. I didn't want them to go and leave me alone with Mother.

"You do not sleep in a structure in the Indian Ocean? Is that possible?" Priscilla asked, laughing.

"No," I answered. *"We sleep in shallow waters between the reefs, in hammocks made of kelp that shift in the currents."*

Salina shook her head at her sister. *"You should not make fun of the child. We have seen how the Indian Ocean sisters live and it is quite primitive. They have no buildings and make do with little. It is not her fault she is not used to civilisation."*

I curled in on myself, embarrassed. *"I did not know you were joking."* Now I wished to go inside the palace and hide.

The girls exchanged a glance and bade me goodnight, swimming away quickly.

I headed inside. In the darkness, I found my seagrass hammock and climbed in, my eyes closed as I faced the dark ceiling. I wrapped my arms around my chest, trying to compress the ache of loneliness and fear.

I missed Estella. I wanted to go home.

JOE

I woke up to hammering outside. I reached over, to find cold cotton sheets telling me Vanessa was already up. I could hear Marina playing with her toys somewhere else in the house. *Oh well, another morning at the Abrolhos. At least it's daylight. Today I'll put the solar panels up.*

I put on some clothes and headed to the kitchen for some coffee. Marina was barricaded under the kitchen table. War had broken out between the marine mammals again and it looked like the seals were winning, because they had the high ground on top of the eskies.

I heard Vanessa say, "I'll go see if he's up," before she opened the front door. Her face lit up at the sight of me in the kitchen.

"Skipper's looking for you," she said softly.

I squeezed past her out onto the veranda, my coffee tightly clenched in one hand. Vanessa's green tea steamed on the veranda table beside a book.

Skipper stood out on the coral path, his mouth open in surprise.

"Morning, Skipper," I said easily. "Vanessa gave me a lift over in the *Siren*. I'm going to put up her solar panels today." I touched the boxes on the veranda with my foot.

"Oh, that would be wonderful." Vanessa's voice came from right behind me. Her arms wrapped around me and her cool lips kissed my cheek. "Thanks, Joe."

I think Skipper's jaw hit his chest, it dropped so low.

"Now you're up, I'll put some of those croissants in the oven. Did you want to stay for breakfast, Skipper?" Vanessa asked, turning.

He hesitated. "Sure," he said, sounding scared.

Vanessa stepped lightly back into the house.

Skipper's eyes on my face were hard. "You're playing with fire, mate. You take one wrong step with her and you'll fall off a cliff, or your boat won't come back one day. Don't you remember how cut up you were when she left last time? She's not one who'll settle down with anyone."

He means well, I reminded myself. *She scared the shit out of him and with good reason, but he doesn't know her as well as I do. I wouldn't be alive today if it weren't for her.*

I kept my voice low, so Vanessa might not hear me. "I remember how cut up I was when she left. I blew through more than four cases of beer in a couple of days. The next time I saw her, I proposed and eventually she agreed. I married her." I held up my hand, the morning sun glinting on the new gold ring. "Shit, I'd rather swim with sharks than live without her. We have a little girl now. Marina."

Vanessa's hearing was as good as her vision, it seemed. She appeared beside me before

Skipper could say another word. "Did Joe tell you?" she asked excitedly. When she held out her hand, the diamond caught the light of dawn more spectacularly then my plain gold band.

"Mummy! Mummy! There's a cheeky lizard in the kitchen!" Marina squealed, running out onto the veranda. A king skink followed her, as long as her arm, moving more slowly and quietly.

Skipper stared at Marina, as she fastened herself around my leg.

"There he is!" Marina shouted, pointing at the skink. "Look!"

The lizard hurried between the decking to hide beneath the house. I didn't blame him.

Marina tried to climb up my leg, realising the lizard could be underneath her. I lifted her up to my hip. She looked at Skipper and so did I.

"Who's the man, Daddy?" Marina asked, opening her big, blue eyes wide.

"This is Skipper, sweetheart. He's a fisherman. He catches lobsters," I told her, trying not to smile.

She stuck out her little hand. "Pleased to meet you, Skipper. How do you catch a lobster? Do you swim after him?"

I fought to keep from laughing. *If Skipper had to swim after lobsters, he wouldn't catch many.*

Skipper came up the steps to the veranda and shook Marina's hand carefully. He looked from my face to hers and I knew he could see the similarities. He started counting under his breath.

He managed a smile for Marina. "Well, I put a big box in the water with some lobster food inside and wait for him to come and get his dinner. He eats the lobster food until he's too fat to get out of the box and I come and get the box with my boat. Then I catch him in the box."

Marina clapped her hands in delight. "I want to see the lobster in the box!"

"You can come fishing with us next week, sweetheart," Vanessa told her.

"Yay!" Marina squealed, sliding down my leg and running into the house. I heard the killer whales launch an attack on the seals. Apparently now they were fighting over lobsters.

The kitchen timer went off. Vanessa excused herself and went inside.

"How old is Marina?" Skipper asked me, urgently.

"She's three and a half," I told him, knowing what the next question was going to be.

"Shit, you move fast. Why didn't you tell me you slept with Vanessa on your first season out here?" His voice dropped so low I barely heard it.

Because I didn't believe it myself. I still can't believe I'm married to her. "Would you have believed me?" I said instead.

We both laughed.

"No," he admitted. He looked grumpy then. "I said she'd try to steal you from me. You're the best deckie I ever had."

I spoke without thinking. "That's what she said, too." *Oh shit. I know she heard that.*

Skipper's laugh was short. "You've changed," he said shrewdly.

I was thoughtful. "Yeah, I have. I got lucky and married an incredible woman I don't deserve. I just hope my luck holds and she doesn't find out."

"Croissants are ready!" Vanessa called from the kitchen with a smile. Her eyes were on me and they were filled with love.

Oh God, please don't let her find out. I don't ever want to lose her.

SIRENA

I watched Marina in the water from the deck. Joe gripped the side of the boat, ready to spring to her aid at the slightest suggestion she needed him, but I only smiled. She could swim better than he could.

"Watch this, Daddy!" I heard her call and looked around to see what she had summoned. I saw the shadow before Joe did, crossing the deck to stop him, but I was too slow.

"No, Marina! Watch out!" Joe shouted, leaping over the side and into the water.

The hammerhead changed course.

Marina screamed a command at it, but Joe didn't understand what she said. He headed toward the shark, as she screamed again.

"Shit," I muttered as I vaulted over the side after him. I felt my shorts rip as I shifted to my tail, but that didn't matter. I wrapped myself around Joe, pulling him back toward the boat, as I sent the shark away from him and I.

"NO!" Joe shouted again, struggling to get away from me.

Marina looked at me. "Keep my Daddy safe, Mummy," she said, her face pale with fright. She called the shark again, her voice stronger and clearer now.

He fought me but I held on grimly, keeping his head above the surface. "Watch, Joe. Or I'll sing you into paralysis and leave you on the deck. She wasn't in danger until you jumped in the water and distracted the shark."

He relaxed a little, but his voice came out through gritted teeth. "How can I watch while a shark attacks my little girl?"

I pressed my lips to the back of his neck. "Watch what your little girl can do, Joe. She wants to show you."

Marina called the hammerhead one more time, guiding him to swim past her, and she caught hold of him. Giggling, she rode that shark for a good hundred metres up the channel, before ordering him to take her back.

I pushed Joe up the ladder, not taking my eyes from my clever girl, until she returned to me.

She was breathless with excitement. "Can I ride on Ham again tomorrow?" she asked, as she dismissed the shark back to the depths.

I looked at Joe. He was hyperventilating on the deck, his head between his knees. His eyes were bulging and I felt sorry for him.

"Maybe another day, sweetheart," I told her. "Better stick to dolphins when Daddy's around. I think he's a little bit scared of sharks."

She crept over to Joe and gave him a hug. "Don't worry, Daddy. I'll protect you from sharks. I won't let them hurt you," she said.

He put his shaking arms around her, hugging her more tightly than necessary.

JOE

The first morning fishing I struggled to get up. "Your coffee's on the sink. Take it on board. Marina's asleep on the bunk below," Vanessa told me quietly as she shook me awake. "We need to be back before Skipper heads out."

I sat on the deck with my coffee, as she cast off and pulled out into the anchorage without my help. I drank the coffee as quickly as I could, because the pots weren't far out.

I was useless at spotting the buoys, but she didn't ask me to help with that. We took it in turns to hook the ropes up to the winch and empty the pots into the tubs.

Her pots had pink bow-shaped plastic tags on them now, not a pink ribbon to be seen. They were still full of old fat lobsters, all of them alive.

"What happened to the ribbons?" I asked.

"They perished. Belinda ordered these to replace them," Vanessa said.

My head was starting to wake up. "Do the old lobsters seriously like pink?"

She hesitated. "No," she admitted, not looking at me.

Well, I thought it was stupid then, too.

"Then why the pink tags?" I pressed.

She took a deep breath, still not looking at me. "The ribbons and the tags help to identify my pots under the water. So the girls could put the lobsters in the right ones."

I whistled. "You mean your deckies stocked your pots and then pulled them up full? Where'd you get that many big lobsters?"

She looked fearfully at me. "They sing them up from the deeps. They aren't in the pots long enough to die, or eat each other. I don't bait them, either."

"Who filled your pots last night?" I asked.

"Two of my sisters are here for the week. They will be replaced by two others next week, if they grow bored. We will catch our quota more quickly than before." Vanessa said this in a low voice, her eyes on the deck.

"You told my mother you didn't have any family," I said slowly.

She looked up. "My mother and blood sister died a long time ago. These sisters are two of my people, that's all. We are all sisters to each other. Sister is just a title among my people, like Mr, Miss or Mrs among yours." She looked at me, curiously.

I took my chance. Looking deep into her eyes, I asked her the most important question. "Why did you tell me that pink ribbons work for big lobsters?"

She bit her lip, but she didn't look away. "Because I owed you a favour and I thought improving your catch would be appropriate payment. I didn't know the girls would swamp your boat while they were filling the pots, or that they left you on a rock and in danger. My attempt at payment only placed me deeper in your debt." Her eyes filled with tears. "I'm sorry."

Shit, I'm confused. I don't get how she's responsible for me getting my dinghy stuck on a rock. But she's crying and I know what to do about that. I walked up to her and put my arms around her. "It's okay," I told her, with no idea what I was talking about.

Clack. Something clamped on my foot and left me in agonising pain. "Fuck!" I shouted, trying to shake the fat bastard off my foot. *I like Skipper's little lobsters better than these fat bastards. His only break one toe, but this one's breaking my whole foot.*

Vanessa said something in the mermaid language, all squeaky. The lobster let go of me and went and hid back behind the tub. She picked him up and squeaked something else, then dropped him back over the side of the boat into the water.

She knelt on the deck and examined my foot with cool hands. "Are you okay?" she asked with a sniffle.

I flexed my toes. "Yeah, I guess," I replied.

She stood up and smiled ruefully. "I just

seem to get deeper in your debt. Maybe one day I'll find a way to repay you what I owe."

Just stay with me. Stay, and don't ever leave me. I stared back at her, but didn't dare say the words.

She looked away. "We better get moving, if we want to be back before Skipper heads out. I'll never hear the end of it if I deprive him of his best deckie for the start of the season." She eyed me thoughtfully. "You know I won't let you in the house if you smell of rotten lobster. Make sure you stay out of the way when he's throwing them."

I was indignant. "I haven't caught a dead lobster since my first season out," I protested.

She dropped the pot over the side. Over her shoulder, she said, "You are the best deckie I ever had." Her eyes were on the pot sinking into the depths.

"How many deckies have you slept with, then?" I blurted out, instantly regretting it. *Don't tell me. I don't want to know.*

"Two," she said quickly, before she hurried into the cabin to shift the boat to the next buoy.

Shit. So she did get raped by Skipper's last bastard of a deckie. I'm going to hunt him down and kill him slowly.

"What happened to the other one?" I asked cautiously.

She glanced at me, then looked away. "He drowned, a long time ago," she said shortly, hooking up the next pot to the winch. She didn't say any more.

I felt a sudden chill. I didn't need to kill him. She already had.

Shit. That's what I get for opening my stupid mouth. Answers I don't want to hear.

LAILA

"It is time for a breeding event. Would you like to take part?" Elder Zelia addressed Mother.

Mother stated her reply gravely. *"I have borne my child for my people, at great cost. I will not willingly choose to bear another."*

The Elder turned to me. *"How about your daughter?"*

"I have not yet been called to do my duty for my people..." I began before I realised the question had not been directed at me. I had spoken out of turn in a Council meeting.

I had angered all of the Elders by my

outburst, I saw clearly, and Mother in particular. Mother was the diplomat, the Elder. Answering difficult questions such as this were her province, not mine, and I was going to pay dearly for my words in disrespect. *"Then you may do it for the people of the Atlantic, in preparation for doing your duty for your own people at home."*

I opened my mouth in horror – no one had ever been called to do their duty twice, except Elder Sirena. Her bitterness had known no bounds. I did not have the courage to seduce humans twice in my lifetime. Mother's warning look silenced me, for I knew she had it in her power to order me to bear a dozen children, if she chose, for my disobedience. I curled up in consternation at the very thought of such repeated violation of my body by those I feared most.

Elder Zelia smiled, pleased that I was going to join them in what I was certain was my worst nightmare, a nightmare my own mother had promised to make a recurring one. *"Then you must join us now. We hold to traditional ways in this, for they are still necessary."*

Mother could feel the tension in the water

and even her sympathy for me would be sacrificed to diplomacy. "*I am sure that my daughter would be honoured to do her duty alongside her sisters in the Atlantic. It will differ so much from my own experience. When I was called to do my duty, I was alone and overwhelmed. I was forced by a number of humans, without my consent. I am pleased that my daughter will not be alone, when facing such dangers.*"

Elder Zelia laughed. "*She faces few dangers in our ways. The humans will be sung into submission, before the breeding sisters are close enough to touch. I am surprised that you did not use a song to similar purpose.*"

Mother frowned, as she always did when thinking of humans. "*The humans forced me to close my mouth and damaged my throat, so I could make little sound, let alone construct a powerful song.*"

Elder Zelia looked thoughtful. "*Perhaps you would like to accompany the breeding sisters, including your daughter. Many of us will be needed to assist once breeding is complete. We are very traditional in this respect.*"

Mother smiled, which was a frightening thing to see. "*I would be delighted to assist. It is a pity my people are not similarly thorough in ensuring our safety."*

Elder Zelia clasped her hands. "*I will send one of our teachers to instruct your daughter in behaviour during a breeding event. Whilst she is trained, I would like to hear more of your people and their modern breeding. How is it possible that your people venture on shore?"*

Elder Zelia led Mother away and I was approached by another Atlantic sister.

"*If I am to train you before the event in two days, you must listen to every word I say. Two days is hardly enough to train a girl...*" she said, gesturing for me to follow her.

In two days, my worst nightmare would be realised. I would be required to join with a human, or risk a diplomatic incident. I resolved to sing the human to sleep and inform the Atlantic elders that the man could not be roused so I could not join with him.

In my mind, I envisioned this happy outcome, yet I dreaded the worst, for I would be required to repeat this until I had conceived and borne two children for my people. It was enough to make me want to remain a child forever, but a child could be ordered to obey in this.

The sooner I birthed my first child, the sooner I could refuse to come into further contact with humans, after I had conceived the second. If only Mother did not insist on more than two children between now and the birth. I resolved to ensure my behaviour was impeccable, from this moment on.

If it felt intrusive to be examined by Elders who had the right to do so, how much harder would it be for me to permit a human inside me? Or even two? I shrank in fear at the very thought.

When the time came, I did not know where I would find the courage to do my duty and I dreaded the day.

JOE

I woke up in shock, my body still curved around Vanessa's in sleep. It sounded like some fuckwit had cranked his stereo up real loud at the wrong time. I waited a moment, hoping he'd realise his mistake and turn the shit down, once it had woken Vanessa up. Then maybe she'd agree to…

"What is that?" Nessa asked, sitting up and pulling away from me.

Her boobs were suddenly out of reach. *Fuck.* "The 'Gurge," I mumbled. "Fucking plumber."

Vanessa stood up and crossed the room to the window. "The what?"

"Regurgitator," I replied, getting up and looking for some shorts to pull on. "I'm going to fucking kill him before someone else gets to him first."

"What?" Vanessa sounded confused.

"It's Dean," I said grimly. "He's finally come to fix the plumbing and he's the only person stupid enough to play Regurgitator that loud when there's fishers asleep."

Vanessa had my toolbag in her hands. "Fine, I'm going to go kill his power." She pulled out my biggest hammer.

Shit no. I just fixed the power in Skipper's deckie camp. I don't want Vanessa to pound the shit out of it so I have to do it all again. Gently, I tried to pry the hammer from her fingers. "Let me do it. I won't have to spend as much time fixing it if I break it." *Especially not if I just flip the master switch off.*

I marched outside and found the switchboard, killing the power with one stroke of my finger. Then I headed back to my veranda to watch.

"Shit!" came Dean's voice from inside the dark shack I used to live in. He threw the back door open and barrelled out the back toward the generator. Then he let out the most unearthly, high-pitched scream I'd ever heard. He stopped for breath. Then he did it again.

He slapped at his face and shoulders as he ran blindly toward our place. He raced up the steps and sounded desperate, his voice still helium-high. "Joe! You gotta help me, mate. The power's gone out."

He was out of breath and his eyes bugged out of his head. A shredded veil of spider web clung to him. The orb spider herself sat calmly on his chest. She looked like the huge one Marina had named Charlotte.

I shook my head. "Maybe in the morning, mate, after I'm done fishing." I jerked my head toward the house. "Vanessa's waiting for me inside."

Dean managed a smirk. "You mean that hot chick I saw you with yesterday? I'll fuck her for you while you fix my generator. She's got the biggest fucking tits I ever saw…"

I decided not to tell him about the spider.

The words I did say came more easily than I'd expected. "Fuck off, Dean. That's my wife you're talking about. You can think what you like, but you say anything like that about her again and I'll hold you down so she can rip your balls off and feed them to the sharks."

I turned my back on the bastard and started to walk away.

"Not game to take me yourself, mate?" Dean taunted.

I turned. "Nah, mate. I just don't want to touch your balls and I wouldn't want to deprive my wife of the pleasure of tearing them off."

I strode back inside, locking the door loudly behind me.

I had my lips and my hands on Vanessa's beautiful breasts, to her evident enjoyment and mine, when I heard another scream from outside.

"Isn't that your friend? Aren't you going to help him?" she murmured, moving closer to me.

I let her nipple pop out of my mouth so I could reply. "He can sleep with Charlotte tonight and scream 'til he loses his voice. Stuff him."

She laughed, which sent her boobs moving. "Poor Charlotte. Well, now we're up, would you prefer sex or sleep, Joe?"

I didn't hesitate. "Both, in that order?"

"Sure," she whispered, moving closer still. *Oh, yes...*

SIRENA

Fishing at the Abrolhos was over too soon. Before I felt truly ready for it, we returned to Perth. It was time for me to commence my work in earnest.

Joe wished me luck as I headed off to my first day at work. I'd signed up to teach at the Ocean Discovery Centre, the public bit of the State Fish Research department. I'd be in the same office as the researchers who studied changing ocean currents and the sea floor. I would be working with a combination of sea creatures and children – things I was very familiar with. Or so I thought.

I reported to the front desk, which was also the counter for a gift shop full of t-shirts and toys. There was a huge, stuffed, albino lobster mounted on the wall behind the desk. I wondered how old he was before he became stuffed.

"Can I help you?" The woman before me looked cheerful so I returned her smile.

"I'm Vanessa Fisher – I work here, as of today?" I made my answer its own question, hinting at a request.

"Oh, we've been waiting for you! Wait 'til I tell Fleur." The woman leapt up from her seat and dashed into a darkened room to the left of the counter. "Fleur," she called.

A tired-looking young woman wearing a smile on her face appeared from the darkness. "You must be Vanessa. I'm Fleur. You'll be shadowing me today, helping me out with a school group." She held out her hand to shake mine and I took it.

"Leave your handbag with Sue here and come have a look," she said, heading back into the darkened room. I left my bag with the lady at the counter and followed Fleur.

The room turned out to be a museum gallery of information, pictures, words, videos and exhibits. I saw an old pearl diver's helmet and wondered about it, before another stuffed lobster caught my eye. "Plenty of lobsters around," I commented, touching the plastic housing around the large crustacean.

Fleur laughed. "With the rock lobster industry making more money than any other fishery in Western Australia, you'd hope so."

"Really? We make that much money? Good to know," I replied. It had not been the case when I started fishing for them, many years in the past before my husband was even born, but times had changed, as I had noticed when the lobsters we caught at the Abrolhos were sold this year. "Maybe I can afford a new TV up at the Abrolhos next season."

Fleur looked impressed. "You have a fishing camp up at the Abrolhos? You must be rich."

I felt uncomfortable discussing this, so I changed the subject. "What will we do with the school children?"

Fleur smiled. "We usually do some activities

with them in the activity room and take them in small groups through to the touch pool. Here, let me show you." She unlocked a blue door set in an equally blue wall and let me into a small laboratory. In the centre of the room was a waist-high pond with a large number of sea cucumbers and sea stars, some marine plants and a sea urchin.

The algae moved. "Oh, a bamboo shark! Isn't he sweet," I couldn't help saying, reaching out to touch the tiny shark's tail.

I heard the noise of lots of children outside, but Fleur didn't seem to notice it yet.

"You just need to get all the kids to wash their hands and make sure they don't kill anything," Fleur instructed. She turned her head as she, too, heard the noise. "Oh hell, they're here. Good luck!" She vanished.

The first group of children were small, loud and didn't listen. They washed their hands and kept lifting the sea stars and sea cucumbers out of the water. The sea cucumbers screamed shrilly, making me wince, but the children didn't seem to notice. Perhaps it was outside their range of hearing.

The second group were no better.

The third group contained all small boys. Two of them began throwing the sea cucumbers across the pool to each other. I was ready to cry at the screaming, but the children didn't seem to notice. I managed to get them to put all of the creatures back in the water eventually, except for one sea cucumber that had landed on the floor. I dismissed the children quickly and searched for the lost one. By the time I reached it, the poor creature was piping in exhaustion, but even that sound died with it. I felt tears slip down my cheeks at the senseless loss.

Fleur came in behind me. "Time to clean up in here and then we break for lunch. So, what's the damage? How many sea cucumbers did we lose today?"

I held out the casualty I'd cried over. "Just one."

She whistled. "You're a miracle worker. I've never had so many survive a morning full of little shits like those ones. You're on touch pool duty all day!"

I gave a sad smile.

"Come on, time for lunch. I'll introduce you to the researchers." She led the way out of the darkened gallery and up some stairs, using a security pass to gain entry to a bright lunchroom.

She introduced me to the researchers in a blur, though I tried to remember names. Some I had met and corresponded with in the past, so these I smiled at with feeling. These were the people I needed to interrogate for information. Once I knew all they did, I would use my influence to ensure their research followed the path I chose.

After a half-hour conversation with the familiar researchers, I learned that they had done little more in three years. They lacked funding, they lacked interest and they lacked any inclination to follow my gentle persuasion to do more research in my area of interest. I felt dejected and it was time to watch children kill sea cucumbers again.

I sighed as I followed Fleur out to the room with the sea creatures. I vowed to try and save them all from the horrid children.

But, of course, I did not succeed. The little

shits had more energy and desire for mischief in the afternoon. One tried to stuff a screaming sea cucumber into another child's pants. The screaming child was less traumatised than the creature, but the child's teacher cooed in sympathy to the child as the group exited my domain.

I leaned on the side of the touch pool, exhausted, after the last of the children had left. I could still hear the poor creatures screaming in my head, though they had all survived. Just.

Partly to calm myself, but more to comfort the stressed sea creatures, I started to sing as quietly as I could. Fleur came in with a mop and a terribly stressed expression as she started to deal with the water on the floor, but she said nothing so I kept singing, too low for her to hear.

I saw the little shark start to swim, then the sea stars relax, before the stressed trepang started to calm. I finished my song as I saw the last one start to feed.

Fleur finished with the mop. She dropped it in the bucket and looked up at me. I was surprised to see her expression now held a smile, for mine felt far from it.

"I'm really glad that's over. I felt like I was going to cry, those kids were so horrible – spoilt little brats. Then I came in here to mop the floor and suddenly I feel better. It must be you." Her smile beamed at me. "See you tomorrow, for more of the same."

I made myself smile in reply. "See you tomorrow."

I collected my things and returned to my car for the long drive home. I wondered if my singing or my presence had really had any effect on the woman, or if she was just being polite. After the little control I had over the horrible children, I suspected the latter.

"How was work?" Joe asked me anxiously when I got home.

I looked at him and felt my heart lift. No matter how badly my work had gone, how little I had affected the human researchers, this delightful man would love me and offer comfort. The smile I felt on my face was his doing and not mine.

"Fine," I replied lightly. "What would you

and Marina like for dinner?"

Thinking about my heavy task and how I dreaded making another attempt on the morrow to change the behaviour of both bratty children and stubborn researchers, I missed Joe's reply.

"What?" I asked, shaking the sad thoughts from my head.

"Let's get takeaway pizza," Joe said with a smile.

I heartily agreed.

JOE

I woke up in the dark, alone. I could hear the storm raging outside. Heavy rain or hail clattered on the tin roof. The fierce wind rattled the windows and whistled around the house. The thunder cracked and rolled, while the lightning made the curtains glow.

"Nessa?" I said softly. I got up and checked the ensuite, but she wasn't in there. I went downstairs, but there were no lights on in the house at all. The storm was louder down here.

I headed to the kitchen for a drink. The front door was wide open to the storm.

Horrified, I rushed to close it, but I saw movement outside.

"Nessa?" I called again, loud enough to be heard over the storm.

"I'm here," came the response from the deluge outside.

"Are you okay?" I asked, worried, rushing outside with my shirt over my head to keep the rain off.

She stood in the front yard, her face turned up to the downpour. She gave a big sniffle. "I don't know," she said, her voice cracking. She turned her face to me, crumpled with tears that blended with the rain streaming down her face. *She looks like she's taking a shower with her clothes on.* Her satin nightdress was soaked, clinging to her body like a second skin.

"What's wrong?" I asked immediately. "What can I do?" *What did I do this time, more like.*

"It just feels so hopeless," she said sadly, her arms out as if she was asking for something. "Week after week of work and I'm useless. How can I influence your people when I can't stop them from killing the sea cucumbers? Do they deserve to die? I can't…I can't make that call. Your people are too many for one of me. It feels like I have nothing left, and to save them will take more than I can give."

Oh God, please, no. She's going to go back to the mermaid city and leave me. "Even at home, with me? Is there anything I can do to help?" *Please, please let me help. I'll do anything.*

She smiled sadly. "Not tonight. I want to swim." She turned away from me to face the river at the bottom of the hill. Storm-tossed waves broke over the road.

"No, it's too dangerous," I blurted out, striding towards her.

She didn't turn to look at me. Instead, she ran down the hill and into the flooded road. I watched her dive over a wave and into the water. I waited and waited, but I didn't see her come up.

A big gust of wind caught my wet clothes and I shivered. Crossing my arms over my chest, I retreated to the house.

I grabbed some old towels from the laundry and took them to the lounge room. Huddled in a towel on the couch, I waited for Vanessa to return or exhaustion to claim me. Whatever came first.

SIRENA

The water felt cool and familiar on my skin. The stormy waves were a faint reminder of the strong swells I enjoyed so much in the ocean. The only human comparison I had was standing under the trickling stream from a water-saving showerhead, closing my eyes and remembering the pounding sensation of a waterfall.

It didn't matter. Even in this light current it felt good to swim again as Sirena and not the human Vanessa. At this early hour of the morning in such a storm, I took a risk I would not normally have done.

I removed my chemise and tied it around the base of a mooring rope. The current caressed my skin as I focussed on it, feeling the shift of my skin as it covered my legs and feet to form my tail.

I flexed my tail flukes, following the river bottom to the deepest part of the river channel. The remains of river and fishing boats littered the mud in the murky water. I wondered how many humans had died here, over time.

How many more would die here, if I failed? *Does it matter?*

I pushed on, upstream instead of down. Though it was the taste of the salt water of the sea that I craved most, my curiosity drove me to follow the current to the waters nearer the city.

I swam carefully under the Narrows Bridge, keeping as close to the riverbed as I could until I was far from its lights.

In the middle of Perth Water, between the city and the high rise apartments in South Perth, I surfaced. I looked up at the tall buildings, glowing hazily in the driving rain.

I am here as an infiltrator, to be part of the human society in order to glean their knowledge and influence their actions, but I feel more like a traitor. Am I a traitor to my people, staying with Joe where I am happy, whilst my task goes unfinished? Am I a traitor to his people, if I fail to save any of them? Would this world be better, without humans?

The rain fell faster, almost hiding the buildings completely. *Is this what the world should be? The humans and their edifices gone?*

Something bumped against me in the water. The bump was hard, but the object was soft.

I ducked beneath the surface, searching.

I was bumped again, from the other side. This time I saw the small bull shark before he darted away in the murky water. There was a small group of them in the water, swimming around me. I was reminded of obnoxious human children, crowding around the touch pool, killing the sea cucumbers with their lack of consideration. I itched to slap one of them. Perhaps all of them.

One shark darted in closer, ready to bump me.

This one is but a child, younger than the humans. He is no bigger than Marina and he understands far less. He does not deserve violence. Particularly where violence is not necessary.

I raised my voice, not in anger but in song. The little sharks approached me. I began to swim slowly, so that they could keep up. They surrounded me like a school and swam with me. I changed direction without warning. Some of them stayed with me, whilst others overshot and swam hard to return to me. Once the school surrounded me, I continued, taking darting turns until they all learned to keep pace with me.

For the first time in my life, I played with sharks. More surprising still, I enjoyed it. As a token of my thanks, I guided them to a small school of fish before I departed.

As I headed back downstream against the waves and currents, I wished that the human children were as easy to control. How much easier my task would be if humans were as susceptible to song as sharks!

Like Fleur had been. I felt stupid to have missed such an obvious solution. I swam home as fast as I could.

JOE

I heard dripping on the wooden floor and jerked awake. It was still dark, but the storm had died down a little. The lightning and thunder were more distant and the wind didn't sound like it was going to blow the second storey away. The rain still drummed on the metal roof, but it was the water raining inside that had me worried. *Is the roof leaking?*

I uncurled from my towel nest on the couch and stumbled across the floor to the light switch.

Nessa stood in a puddle in the middle of the

floor, her eyes lit up brighter than the light above her head. Her nightie was still soaked through and clinging to her.

I stared, I swallowed and finally I spoke. "Are you okay?"

She looked surprised, then thoughtful. The faintest of smiles touched her lips. "Yes." Her smile grew clearer. "I played with some sharks and looked at the lights through the storm."

I felt my jaw drop. *Sharks? She swam out to sea? So she did almost leave me and not return.* Her words slowly sank in. *She floated at the surface and looked at lights, where someone could have seen her? Isn't secrecy everything to her?*

I pulled the towel from around my neck and held it out wide for her, like I did when Marina climbed out of the bath.

She took a tentative step closer to me. I held my arms out and she stepped right into them, so I could hold her close, wrapping the towel around her wet clothes. I started to rub her dry.

There was something rough and hard under my fingers. I reached under the towel for the lump and it came away in my hand. I held it up to the light.

"A seashell?" I asked, my heart sinking further. "You went swimming in your nightie?"

Delicately, she took the spiralled grey cone between her finger and thumb. "No, I tied it to a mooring rope and swam naked."

At first, I was consumed with the thought of Vanessa swimming naked. Somewhere in my head I knew this should scare me, not turn me on. *Swimming naked with sharks in a storm isn't normal.* But then, there was nothing normal about Nessa. I pressed on. "And collected seashells?"

She turned the shell in her fingers, looking closely at it. "No, I think it stowed away on my nightie. It must have been on the mooring rope. It's a mud whelk."

Where does she come up with these things? "A what?" I blurted out, feeling stupid all over again.

Nessa smiled. "A mud whelk. A kind of sea snail."

She swam out to sea. Without me. Away from me. I swallowed, not sure how to ask her. "You swam out to sea?" I stammered.

Her eyes lifted from the snail to my face. "No, I swam to the city, under the Narrows Bridge to Perth Water. Through the storm, I could barely see the buildings from the water."

"And…the sharks?" I couldn't work out what to ask about them.

Her tone was calm. "Juvenile bull sharks, near the South Perth foreshore. They wanted to play and I found I did, too."

Somehow I wasn't reassured. "I'm trying to understand how you could swim naked in the Swan River, right outside the city, in a really fierce storm. Then, you played with a pack of dangerous sharks. What if you'd been bitten or someone had seen you?"

Nessa laughed. "I wasn't on the surface for very long, Joe. If anyone saw me in the storm, I'm sure they thought they just saw a dolphin. There are dolphins in the Swan River, too."

Oh shit. If she looked like a dolphin then she didn't swim as a human.

She looked mischievous. "There's never been a story about mermaids in the Swan River, Joe, and there isn't going to be one any time soon." She smiled. "I swim deep and the visibility is close to zero." Nessa held out her hand. "Come on, the sun will be up soon and Marina with it. I'd like to get a little sleep before she wakes."

Maybe I was imagining things, but she seemed more exhilarated than tired. *Maybe that means I'll get some sex,* I thought hopefully, as I followed her up to bed.

LAILA

We boarded a vessel in the middle of the night, when the surface seemed as dark as the depths. This vessel had large metal boxes on board, stacked up high on the deck. I heard the scratch of claws on metal and saw a crab scuttle between two of the boxes. I looked more closely, to find the boxes were alive with crabs, like some human-made artificial reef.

I pointed them out to one of the Atlantic sisters. *"How do they survive, so far from the water?"*

She smiled in the dark as the spray of a stormy wave splashed over us both on the deck, wetting our bare skin and the metal boxes. *"Not so far from the water,"* she replied.

I followed her deeper inside the ship, to where the humans lay, sleeping and unsuspecting.

All but two were asleep in their beds, each to a separate room. There were only eight humans on board the vessel, but there were four of us. We chose the sleeping humans first, for their isolation worked to our advantage.

My human had hair on his face and breathed noisily as he slept. I lifted the covers from the man and he did not wake. He slept with no clothing, so it was plain to see that the man was already aroused. My heart sank as I realised my plan would not work. I would have to let this human inside me.

Filled with dread, I crept onto the bed, astride the human. With my eyes tightly shut, I began to lower myself onto the engorged appendage. I felt a sting of pain and cried out. I lowered myself further, only to find the pain increased. I heard my voice cry out, longer and louder this time.

I cannot do this, I told myself. I felt a trickle of

water track down my cheek.

I tried to lift myself off the sleeping human, but there were suddenly hands on my hips, holding me down. I opened my eyes, to find the human looking up at me. My voice died in my throat, all the songs I knew unsung.

His expression was not hostile, just wondering. He sat up and pressed his open lips to mine, so I could feel his hot breath in my mouth. He put his arms across my back. In one swift movement, he rolled with me. I found my head resting on the pillow. The human was still between my legs, but now he was on top of me instead of I on him.

I opened my mouth, desperate to salvage this situation, but the human put one finger across my lips. He pressed his lips to my cheek and pushed his appendage between my legs, so that the complete length was inside me. Pain burned, but not as bad as before. He almost pulled it out again, before pushing it back in. In, out, in, out...he continued doing this for perhaps a few minutes, before he paused for a few seconds whilst all the way in. He pulled himself out of me completely, his appendage less engorged. Then he moved off me, lay beside me and returned to sleep.

I moved off the bed, standing up. Blood and white fluid ran down the inside of my leg. I ached inside as I left the room and returned to the passage outside. My heart swelled with relief.

I have done my duty. It is over!

In the passage, an Atlantic sister waited. She pointed at a room across the passage. *"We are not wasteful. We use the humans as many times as we can before we discard them. The success of a breeding event depends on as many joinings as possible."*

I entered the room, to find the human also asleep. This human was not aroused, so I took his floppy appendage in my mouth until he was. When I lowered myself onto this human, there was less resistance, though there was still some pain. I moved my hips as I had been instructed to by the Atlantic sister, falling into a rhythm.

I began to find the sensation almost pleasurable, so that I did not feel pain. Instead, I felt a pleasant heat spreading from between my legs to the rest of my body, in a sudden rush that left me breathless. I kept up the rhythm until I felt a hot spurt from the human. I hoped to feel the rush of heat again, but it did not happen.

I left the sleeping human and returned to the corridor. The skin between both my legs was now considerably sticky.

The Atlantic sister was still there. She pointed to the front of the vessel now. "*The sleeping humans are all taken. Next you must take one of the awake ones on watch.*"

I went out onto the deck of the vessel, walking around to the control room. In this room, a human sat looking at screens. He did not hear me, for there was loud noise emanating from a black box on the console in front of him and he moved his head in time with a rhythm in the noise. He looked up as I entered the room and I immediately began to sing, the sound of my voice clashing horribly with the noise from the box. I sang the human a song of control, singing until his nodding head slowly stopped moving and he sat still at the chair behind the screens, his only movement the in-and-out motion of his chest as he breathed. In and out. I swallowed, steeling myself to join with yet another human.

I moved closer to the man. This one wore clothing. I struggled to remove the clothing on his lower body, until his hands moved slowly to assist me. He removed this clothing himself. I could clearly see this man was aroused, but he was not lying down.

After a moment, I lifted one leg across his so that I sat astride him on his chair, both of my legs dangling down on either side. Awkwardly, I took his appendage in my hands to guide it inside me.

At this point, the human's hands were on my hips and he began to push as the first man had. After a few moments, he lifted me to sit on the surface where the control screens were, rising to his feet so he remained inside me. The surface vibrated beneath me with the noise from the black box, making the skin of my bottom tingle. Then he, too, continued with the in and out pattern of the first man, pumping his hips with the rhythmic music from the box. His lips moved to mouth the words I heard in the noise and once I thought

I heard my name. I dismissed the thought. The human did not and could not know me.

When this human's appendage sent a hot spurt of liquid up inside me, he pulled out quickly, leaving a sticky mess on the control screens. He resumed his seat as if nothing had happened and I slid down to the floor. My hips now aching too, I walked stiffly to the door.

Please, let this be enough.

The Atlantic sister was in the corridor.

She pointed at a different room. *"Now you must try the humans a second time. This time will be longer than the first."*

Aching and sticky, I entered another room.

Diplomacy be damned. I turned to walk back out of the room and met Mother.

"You must do your duty." Her voice held finality.

I returned to the room to do my duty.

JOE

"I want to see penguins, Daddy," Marina announced one morning, her mouth full of cereal. "They're birds that fly through the water."

I swallowed my coffee before I spoke. "Penguins live in Antarctica, sweetheart. It's a long way south of here."

Vanessa walked in, looking perfect in her nightie with her hair tangled like some fantasy mermaid's. She looked sexier than any fictional mermaid, though, probably because I knew what we'd been doing to get her hair so tangled. "Why are we going south?"

Marina jumped up and clapped her hands. "We're going to see penguins fly through the water!"

Vanessa pulled a tub of yoghurt out of the fridge. "Sure, we could do that today, if you like. Joe, can you pack some swim gear, towels and some bottled water into a backpack, please?" She lifted a large spoon of pink and white yoghurt into her mouth.

She kissed Marina on her way through. "I'm going in the shower, sweetheart. Eat up all your breakfast and we can go see the penguins."

When Vanessa emerged in a breathtaking bikini, I immediately held up the sunscreen with an eager offer on my lips.

She laughed. "I don't need any and nor does Marina, but you make sure you don't get burned."

My face fell, but my spirits quickly lifted when she leaned over to look at the contents of the bag on the floor in front of me. "Another towel, some more water and we can grab something for lunch on the way."

Vanessa straightened up and turned to smile at me. "If you get the extra things, I'll get some clothes on and we can go." She started down the hallway. "Marina! Are you ready?"

Marina came barrelling down the hallway, dodging past Nessa. "Yes, Mummy!" She wore her bathers already.

Nessa tied something that looked like a big, filmy scarf around her waist like a skirt. "Right, me too. Ready, Joe?"

Beautiful. I can still see everything.

"Wake up, Daddy! Time to go to the penguins!" Marina giggled, pulling on my shirt. I tore my eyes away from my beautiful wife's arse to look at my equally beautiful daughter's face.

"Sure," I replied. I lifted my eyes to Vanessa's face. *What was it I wanted to ask again?* "Where are we actually going?"

Vanessa laughed. "Penguin Island, after a stop at the bakery for supplies."

She drove her little Mazda down to Rockingham, as if she knew precisely where she was going and didn't need to check a map.

"Daddy, have you ever seen a penguin?"

Marina asked me from the back seat.

"No," I replied. "Have you?"

Marina giggled. "No. But today I'm going to catch one for you so you can see it, Daddy!"

I smiled all the way to Shoalwater, where Vanessa parked near some sand dunes.

"Okay let's go get tickets for the ferry," Vanessa said, headed for the nearest building, but it wasn't open yet. "Maybe we can walk over." She looked out across the beach.

"Walk over?" I squawked as I looked at the island across the water. It must have been at least two ks away – I couldn't swim that far and I definitely couldn't walk on water.

"Sure. It's low tide – the sand bar is out." Nessa pointed at the sand spit at one end of the island and I saw it ran pretty much all the way back to the beach where we stood. "We'll be fine."

I looked at the signs, full of warnings. "*This sandbar is dangerous. Lives have been lost*," I read aloud. "Are you sure?"

Vanessa dismissed my worries. "They couldn't swim. We'll be fine." She led the way down the beach with Marina, leaving me to carry the backpack.

The going was pretty easy. It was damp, soft sand like the beach on the mainland. There were terns and pelicans on it, but they moved out of the way pretty quickly. Suddenly Marina stopped. "I need to take my shoes off!" she announced, handing her sandy thongs to Vanessa, who passed them to me.

The sandbar was a little under the water here, so she didn't want to get her feet wet, I figured, sticking the thongs into my backpack.

I heard a high-pitched little scream and looked up. Marina was gone. Vanessa dove into the water away from me.

"No, wait!" I shouted, struggling out of my pack.

Vanessa surfaced. "Stay there, Joe. I'll get her." She went under again.

I stood on the water's edge, feeling stupid and useless. I looked around, but I couldn't see either of them in the water between the island and the mainland. I looked desperately at the mainland, where the lifeguards on duty were already headed out toward me.

When the lifeguards reached me, there was

still no sign of them.

"The lady and the little girl, right?" one asked me. "Can you see them?"

"No," I replied, annoyed. "When I do, I'll definitely make sure you know."

"Can they swim?" a female voice asked. I turned and realised that one of the lifeguards was female. Her boobs weren't anywhere near as impressive as Vanessa's, so it wasn't hard to look at her face instead.

"Yep. They're both pretty good swimmers," I replied. *You have no idea how good…* I kept scanning the water, looking for them. I knew they'd come up, because they had to.

"You really shouldn't have tried the sandbar today. You should have waited for the ferry, especially with such a little girl," she began.

"Look, can you help me look for them instead of lecturing me on what I should have done, now it's too late to do anything else?" I snapped. "My wife said the sandbar so we took the sandbar. When you find them, then we'll take the boat."

She shut up then, thank God, hopped on her jetski and headed off in the direction that

Vanessa had gone.

The male lifeguard had some binoculars, scanning the water with them.

I waited for what felt like forever. It was Vanessa and the tiger shark all over again, except this time I knew she had to come up. She had to. I couldn't lose her now. And I couldn't lose Marina, my daughter, EVER.

Shit, where are they?

LAILA

This human had been sung into docility by an Atlantic sister with a powerful song. He lay on his back like he was asleep, but his eyes were open. I sucked on the human until he was ready to join. He tasted strangely unpleasant. Once he was ready, I slid down onto him and began rocking.

This took considerable time, but I didn't dare stop. The human was so slow to respond that I felt the rush sensation again during this joining. Curious, I wondered what it would take to bring it on deliberately. Once again, the joining was complete before I could work this out.

When I returned to the corridor, the Atlantic sister was nowhere to be seen. Wearily, I turned to enter the next room.

This room was already occupied by Salina and a human. She lay on the bed with her head on the pillow, whilst the man's head was between her legs. A look of intense joy crossed her face for almost a minute, her soundless smile speaking for her. Her smile faded to a frown and she directed an order at the human. "Now give me a strong child."

The human head rose and he lifted his body so that his torso was above hers. The remainder of his body, from his hips down, was between her legs. He began pushing in and out of her, as two humans had done to me.

I gave voice to my question, not expecting her to reply. *"How do you make them do this? I ache from the efforts I must make in joining with them."*

Salina turned to me, heedless of the human inside her. *"You must sing them a powerful song of control, then give them orders. I order them to give me pleasure, then to give me a child."*

I stared at her. *"I did not know that joining could be enjoyed, nor that the humans could be made to do the work."*

Her voice was kind. *"You have not been educated in all the facets of a successful breeding event. When the human gives a breeder pleasure, it makes her more fertile and receptive to the child he can create. As for making the humans exert themselves, you must understand them. These humans are more like animals than we are. The desire to join with a female is so strong, that when reduced to their most simple state by our song, they react instinctively to a naked female who expresses an invitation to join. I find all that is necessary is a few words of guidance and the human male will make joining quite an enjoyable experience. We never lack for volunteers for breeding events. I suggest that you try it."*

I turned away from the sight of the human man pumping between her legs, though she did not seem concerned, and left the room. I hurried to the next, which was occupied only by a sung human.

I lay on the bed, beside the somnolent human. He did not move and his appendage was limp. My throat contracted at the thought of having to take another into my mouth.

"Give me pleasure and then give me a child," I told the human, in a voice little above a whisper.

For a moment, I thought the human had not heard. Then, he turned and moved on top of me.

I panicked, but once again my voice died in my throat. His mouth pressed against mine and his tongue slid between my lips. This was not entirely unpleasant, but it was unexpected. Did not the human need to put his face between my legs?

Something was between my legs, pushing inside me. I realised it was the fingers of the human, sliding in and then out, before stroking me between my legs. The whisper of heat at each stroke was a faint echo of the heat I had felt twice tonight, but the whisper began a slow burn that grew hotter as the human continued. This time I felt the rush building. When it came, it was surprisingly stronger than before and I found I cried out in pleasure and not pain. The sound was muffled by his mouth on mine.

Before the heat could fade, the human had pushed his appendage inside me. It was no longer limp and felt quite hard. He pumped it with considerable vigour for a few minutes, before he withdrew and moved off me.

When I left this room for the corridor, I ignored the sticky trickle down my leg and had a thought that would have been unthinkable yesterday. *If I do not conceive a child from this breeding event, I would willingly do my duty again among humans,* I reflected, as I walked slowly on aching legs. *Just as long as I don't have to do it all night.*

JOE

It felt like forever 'til the woman on the jetski returned with Vanessa and Marina riding on the back. Every minute had been its own eternity. I ran all the way back down the sandbar to the beach to meet them. Vanessa had Marina in her arms, wrapped up in the filmy skirt. She passed Marina to me as soon as she was close enough. I hugged them both tightly, not wanting to let them go. I was so scared I'd almost lost them.

"Shall we take Mummy's skirt off you now?" I asked, starting to unwind the cloth from my daughter.

"Only if we get her clean clothes out of the bag," Vanessa replied, with a pointed look at Marina. "Marina ripped her bathers on a rock while she was swimming." She started rifling through the backpack, throwing a little dress over my shoulder. "I'm going into the shop to get ferry tickets because Marina is NOT walking on the sandbar again." She disappeared.

I let Marina down onto her own feet and she dropped the skirt on the sand, holding her arms up for the dress. I noticed her bathers had been ripped across the bottom, as if a tail had gone right through them. *No wonder Vanessa's angry at her.*

"What did you see while you were swimming?" I asked Marina carefully.

She giggled. "I saw seagrass and blue octopussies and red lobsters and a sea lion and some penguins! And lots of fish, where there's a wooden boat."

"What were the penguins doing?" I asked her, curious.

Marina moved her hands like dolphins

swimming. "They were flying through the water, catching fish in the seagrass. They were so fast! But I was faster." She beamed.

"Of course you were, sweetheart," I replied absently. I bundled Vanessa's skirt up and stuck it in my backpack.

Vanessa appeared at the shop door, but she was waylaid by an excited-looking staff member. "You have no idea how amazing a find it is. We've been looking for that boat since the 1830s, when it first sank. There was illegal salvage and the blokes were sent to Van Diemen's Land when they were caught, but no one else ever found it. The Museum is going to be thrilled…"

Vanessa smiled politely and came over to us.

"What was that about?" I asked, puzzled.

Nessa sighed. "There was a wooden vessel in the water, which had broken up and was hidden inside one of the reefs. It had the word "Cumberland" on it, so I asked the shop assistant when it sank. It turns out the wreck had never been found before, though it went down in 1834 with all hands." She held out some small pieces of paper that I realised were the ferry tickets. "Right, shall we get on the boat?"

We trooped down the jetty to the flat ferry. With the shallow draft on it, it looked like it would wallow like a pig offshore or in a decent swell, but for this sheltered, shallow water it was probably okay.

We were the first people on board and there weren't many others. Maybe this was a quiet day.

When we got to the island, we were greeted with a sign. "*No penguin show today, closed for DEC Christmas function,*" I read. I looked down at Marina. "Sorry sweetheart, you can't see the penguins at the Discovery Centre today. Maybe if we look around the island, we'll see some more."

Marina giggled. "The penguins have all gone fishing, Daddy."

Vanessa smiled at me and nodded, so I shrugged and didn't say anything else.

"Daddy, I'm hungry," Marina announced.

"Okay, so let's have a snack," I replied, leading the way over to the picnic tables and sitting down. I took Vanessa's skirt out of the bag and dropped it on the table, before digging deeper for the bakery bag. The skirt smelled faintly of fish. I pulled out the savoury rolls and handed them out.

Marina bit into hers greedily, scattering crumbs all over the grass. There was a rustle and a large, dark lizard, as long as her arm, came out from under the table, tonguing up a piece of bacon. Marina took another bite and a big piece of bacon broke off, tumbling to the grass. She reached down to pick it up and shrieked when she saw it had already been eaten. The lizard was eyed her hand for more.

"A cheeky lizard!" Marina screamed, scrambling up onto her feet on the seat. Unlike the Abrolhos king skinks, this one was bigger, fatter and more sure of itself. It didn't back down. She jumped up and down and dropped the remainder of the roll. The lizard took it in its mouth and slid under the table with it. "He ate my roll!" Marina wailed.

I pulled another one out of the bag and handed it to her. "Then don't give him this one."

She nodded fiercely, her teeth closing over

the new roll. She managed to eat the second one without incident, though she did watch the lizard under the boardwalk with narrowed eyes as it finished off her first.

She washed the roll down with some of the bottled water before she cautiously climbed down from the picnic table. She reached up for Vanessa's skirt and pulled it into her arms. I heard a strange quacking sound, like an angry duck.

"What did you say?" I asked Marina, worried.

Vanessa shook her head at Marina, not pleased.

"I didn't say anything, Daddy," she replied sweetly.

"Where is it, Marina?" Vanessa asked, her voice suddenly serious.

Marina pulled the skirt closer. "I'm going to call him Quackie!" she shouted.

Vanessa held out her hands. "Give him to me."

Marina backed away. "No! He's for Daddy!"

"Then will you give him to Daddy?" Vanessa asked slowly, nodding to me.

Marina's face spread into a beaming smile as she held out Vanessa's skirt to me. "Here you go, Daddy, just for you. Merry Christmas."

I took the skirt from her and it emitted a pretty pissed-off quack. I quickly set it down on the ground and opened it up. The angry penguin inside fastened its beak on my finger and hung on 'til it drew blood. Then it ambled off under the boardwalk with another grumpy quack. The lizard fled.

"Did you like your penguin, Daddy?" Marina asked, looking proud of herself.

I looked at Vanessa as I stuck my bleeding finger in my mouth. It tasted of rotten fish. I pulled it out again, but it was too late. The rotten fish taste didn't go away.

Vanessa nodded with a tight smile on her face.

"Sure, sweetheart," I told Marina. "Next time, can you ask him not to bite me?"

LAILA

In the corridor, I was greeted by three Atlantic sisters.

"The humans are spent and so are we. It is time for disposal, to protect our people." Salina smiled and beckoned. *"Come, we will watch from the water."*

Together, all four of us dived from the deck of the vessel into the cool waters. It felt refreshing to wear my tail again, to breathe cool water and not pant warm, stale air. The ache deep inside me remained, dulled and cooled by the water.

A deep booming came from beneath the

ship, with the screech of metal parting under water.

I felt the wave building, shaped by several Atlantic sisters. The wave washed over the top of the vessel, followed by another. Successive waves topped the deck, until the vessel sat lower in the water, closer to the surface. The waves became smaller, pushing the vessel onto its side, so that it filled with more water. I watched in horror as it sank.

Some of the large, metal boxes that I had seen on the deck of the vessel floated free, bobbing just beneath the surface. I watched for more debris, but the large boxes were all that surfaced. I ventured to ask about them. *"Do we need to hide the evidence of those large boxes, too?"*

I looked around at the Atlantic sisters on either side of me. After a moment, one of them replied in a casual dismissal. *"Shipping containers like these are lost in the oceans every day. These will travel with the currents and pose no threat to us, though they may inconvenience the humans."*

I felt the most inconvenienced humans were those on the vessel sinking to the sea floor beneath me. I had not seen any lifeboats surface and I dreaded to ask. *"What about the humans who were on the vessel?"*

This time, I did not turn to face the Atlantic sister who replied.

"They will not live to spread stories of our kind. Even now, our sisters who were not breeders are ensuring that the humans drown in deep water. It is a fitting price for a blissful night with the ocean's gift. They will carry our secret to a watery grave. We give them a chance to live on, in the children they created tonight with us. For this, as it always has been among our people, the humans must die."

I could still feel the ghost of heat from our joining inside me. I realised that my faint feeling was now the ghosts of those humans whose bodies were already cooling beneath the ocean's surface. I felt sad and fought the rising panic.

I joined with five humans in one night. One of them heard my cries, felt compassion and helped to ease my pain. Three of them gave me pleasure I had not believed possible. Any of them might have given me a child through our joining. And now they were all dead, because they touched the ocean's gift. Me.

Mother came to me on the swim home, her satisfaction clear on her face, a strong contrast to my complete desolation.

"Mother, please permit me to go home," I begged her. *"I wish to birth my child among my own people, in familiar waters."* I had no hope that she would agree, but in my desperation I said the words. I tried to keep my expression controlled. I need not have bothered.

Mother's expression held a faraway, distracted smile. *"Then you may, provided you send the child to me when she is old enough to travel the distance. You will take my place on the Elder Council as I fill the empty Black place here. Send me word of anything that happens in the Indian Ocean and I will do the same here."* She eyed my midsection. *"The first news I expect is that of the birth of your child. Once I hear of that, I will send word of my resignation from the Council so that you may take your place."*

I breathed a sigh of relief that sent bubbles all the way to the surface.

"Farewell, Mother," I said with finality and respect. I turned tail and headed home, hoping that my mother's mania did not harm her

people or mine.

JOE

"Is there anything interesting in the news?" Vanessa asked as she passed. She glanced at the TV screen, but continued on to the kitchen without stopping.

"Politicians arguing, the Eagles' best player is facing suspension because of how some bastard tackled him and it looks like someone's lost an entire freighter off Brazil." I responded, ignoring the news about some politician calling the other a drunken womaniser, because everyone including his now ex-wife knew she'd slept with him, so it was hardly news.

Vanessa stuck her head around the doorframe. "Seriously?"

I shrugged. "Yep."

She stepped back into the lounge room. "Then it's as bad as I thought," she said sadly with a sigh.

"Hey, it's okay," I told her. "He might get off. You can see in the videos of the match that he was tackled by the other bastard. He only accidentally elbowed him in the face and broke his nose because he was off balance..."

"What?" Vanessa looked confused. "Oh, I don't mean the news about the football player. I meant the freighter."

I snorted. "Yeah, well, if a shipping company can lose a boat that big, they probably deserve it."

Vanessa looked more worried than before. "Brazil...that borders on the Atlantic Ocean, right?"

I shrugged again. "I don't know. Probably."

"How often do big freighters vanish without a trace?" Vanessa asked quietly, her voice deadly serious.

"I never heard of it happening before. Oh,

maybe once when I was a kid…" I waved it away.

Vanessa's voice was still quiet. "You mean the *Alexandre*, which left Dampier and disappeared back in the early 1990s? Where there were no survivors?"

"I don't remember the name, but that could have been it," I admitted.

"Do you remember any of the details of the recent freighter that's been lost in the Atlantic?" Vanessa's voice was urgent now.

I didn't understand why it was so important to her. "It was due in port yesterday, but they lost contact with it a couple of days ago. Search planes haven't found any sign of it yet and there's been no other communication with the boat."

Vanessa was shaking her head. "I told them this would happen. I only hope it will turn out okay."

I wasn't worried. "Yeah, they'll probably find the ship and discover that some idiot shorted out the power systems so the ship's communications are down. It wouldn't happen if they had a decent sparky on board."

Vanessa's smile was tight. "Joe, even if you'd been on board, you couldn't have saved that ship." She looked sad.

"You think it's sunk?" I asked her.

Her eyes met mine, full of some dark knowledge I suddenly didn't want to know. "I think that freighter's gone down with all hands. My sisters in the Atlantic are nothing if not thorough. Especially after the mess they made of the *Alexandre*."

My jaw dropped and I couldn't seem to pick it up again. "You seriously think mermaids sank a whole freighter? Those things are huge!"

Her eyes held pity now. "They killed everyone on board and then sank the ship in deep water off the continental shelf. They've done it before and they'll do it again. Don't underestimate my sisters, Joe. My people are stronger than you know."

Horrified, I tried to reply, but it took a couple of tries before any words came out. "What do you mean?"

Vanessa's expression became businesslike and less worried. "I must inform the others. I think we're going to have some visitors from my people. I'd best prepare the guest room, before I go for a swim." She headed down the passage toward one of the unused bedrooms.

I stared wordlessly after her. *She's expecting hitfish who kill people and sink ships to come and visit us? Shit, I'm going to go buy me a shark shield and wear it in the house.*

I got up and switched on the computer, to search for a shop that sold them, before the next thought hit. Would a shark shield even work on mermaids? If they could sink ships, a shark shield wasn't going to hold them up for long.

I paused for a second. *All it has to do is give me a few seconds to shout for Vanessa.*

I decided to get the biggest heavy-duty shark shield I could find, and hope for the best.

DARMA

"What the fuck?"

It was the voice of a human male that jarred with our more careful, measured tones. He wore as little as we. I thought this unusual behaviour for a human, but I had not seen a human in many years. Perhaps they did not wear clothing here.

"Nessa, what the fuck are these girls doing here and why," he swallowed uncomfortably, a lump in his throat bobbing as he did so, "are they all naked in our dining room?"

I wondered who he addressed, until I

remembered that Elder Sirena went by the name of Vanessa on land. She also evidently answered to the diminutive, Nessa.

Elder Sirena stood, smoothing the short blue garment she wore, majesty in every move. "These are the Elder Council, Joe, the government of my people." Her hand swept around the table, encompassing all of us. "They have come to speak to me."

At her summons, I thought. I wondered if she had shared this information with him.

The human male looked distinctly uncomfortable, staring at us as though he could not remove his gaze.

As he continued to stand in the doorway, all of our eyes turned to him with similar intensity. He was a well-built man, with more muscle than those humans I remembered seeing the last time I ventured on land. His procreation equipment matched his physique, too, I noticed, standing ready to attention as if he anticipated joining with one of us. Quite impressive, I admit. My taste ran to smaller, darker men than he, but I felt a warming curiosity to know what Sirena's human was capable of doing with such equipment. She was not one to choose an inferior specimen, even for a casual joining.

I looked around the table. Sunitha's eyes were wide with wonder, as she remarked on the man's size to Indah, pointing with a shaking hand. Only Nafula seemed unimpressed.

The human noticed Sunitha's gesture and reached for a piece of fabric that was draped over a nearby chair. He used this fabric to cover his sizeable equipment, to Indah's audible disappointment.

Elder Sirena smiled at the human. "Go back to bed, Joe. I won't be long."

I reached for one of the salt sticks in a bowl on the table, curious to find out how they tasted. It made a crunching sound as I bit into it, but the taste was pleasant — salt and powdered grain.

He looked as if he wanted to obey her order, but still he hesitated. After a few moments, he planted his feet firmly on the floor and raised his voice. "Look, don't any of you even think about taking Vanessa away from me. She's my wife and you're not taking her back to the bottom of the ocean. She has a life and a family and people who love and need her here. I'll go up against any one of you, if you think you can take her without going through me first."

Not all of the Council members understood English as Sirena and I did, so there were confused looks around the table, all of which settled on me. My confusion was no less. Did this human not know who Sirena was? Even if she did not give him her true name, he clearly knew she was not human. Of all of us in the room, the woman he called Vanessa posed a greater danger to him than the rest of the Council combined. At a word from her, he would cease to live. None of us would dare defy her.

I swallowed the mouthful of salt stick and spoke slowly, trying to remember the correct words in the human's language. "You should listen to her wise words, human. She holds your life in her hands. It is well known that she does not forget, nor forgive." I smiled gently at him, hoping to soften the warning in my words.

He opened his mouth, but no reply seemed forthcoming.

Elder Sirena pushed her chair back from the table and approached the human. She curled her arm around his and turned him around. All the eyes at the table followed his well-rounded behind with admiration.

Sirena guided him out of the room and into an adjacent one. She kept her voice low, but I heard her reassure him, repeating the same things she had already told him, but in different words. When this did not have the desired effect, she surprised me by asking him a question.

"Why did you want me, Joe?"

"I woke up and I…wanted…you…and you weren't there, Nessa," the human said in a tone that sounded like he was distracted. We all clearly heard the man gasp.

"If you still want me, I'm here now," Elder Sirena replied. I heard the squeak of wood under tension, as if something heavy had been placed on an item of furniture. I tried to remember what the furniture in the adjacent room was. I could only remember a bed.

The wood began to squeak in a slow rhythm, like a chained buoy in the waves.

"Nessa…What about the…others…in the dining room?" the human hissed, as if trying not be heard. He sounded a little short of breath.

The squeaking ceased. "Would you like one of them instead? Or in addition? Which one? I can ask…"

Indah half rose from her seat and I felt a considerable pull to do the same.

"No…" gasped the human. "Just you, Nessa. Just you. I meant…won't they be angry when you don't come straight back?"

"They will wait," was Elder Sirena's response, followed by a quiet moan, "Ohh…yes."

We were the Elder Council, the government of her people, as she said, but we were her people, too. I'd never seen such a blatant display of her power as I did that night. She permitted a human to interrupt a very important meeting, took her pleasure with him in the next room, all the while knowing that we would wait, not daring to proceed with our meeting or move from our seats until she returned. And wait we did. With all mouths open, as if to moan with her, and many eyes closed, I noticed, far from immune myself. Sunitha had a salt stick part-way to her mouth, but the stick sat in mid-air, forgotten. Nafula had her finger in her mouth.

Sirena's moaning continued, almost a song, the beat kept by the increasing tempo of creaking wood under stress. I lost track of all time, the moments seeming to stretch endlessly, yet I was not impatient for them to end.

Sunitha's hands were over her mouth, whilst Indah's were under the table, when we heard Elder Sirena's scream of pleasure from the next room. The human followed soon after with a deeper groan, in which I could clearly hear the word "Nessa," no less heartfelt than her, before the squeaking ceased.

I heard Sirena's voice murmur something softly, too low for me to hear. The wood gave an extended creak and I heard footsteps on the floor.

I looked around the table. Not a single one of us was unaffected, some more than others.

Elder Nafula cleared her throat, her blush barely showing beneath her dark skin, and asked softly, *"Elder Darma, could you explain what the human said?"*

The footsteps approached and I watched Sirena kiss the human softly, smiling as she pulled away. "I love you, Joe. I'll be upstairs again with you soon," she said.

"I love you, too, Nessa," he replied. He caressed her bare breast, just once, staring into her eyes like a human who had been sung into submission, though she had not. His skin gleamed with sweat and the lingering salt on my tongue left me with a desire to taste some more salt that was not from the sea.

I kept my eyes on the human as I spoke. *"He said that he would not let us take Elder Sirena to the depths against her will or his. He offered violence in response to any attempt we made to force her from land."*

I heard Nafula's musical laughter first, before the others joined in. Even I had to laugh at such a ridiculous notion. Elder Sirena, coerced to do something against her will? When she had summoned us to land with a command so strong we all felt forced to obey? This human knew nothing of the woman who captivated him so completely without even a song.

He stiffened at our laughter, the muscles in his behind growing taut in a very attractive way. I watched those tight muscles move as he started down the corridor and up the stairs, out of sight.

Elder Sirena had seated herself at the table whilst I was distracted. She patted the perspiration from her breasts with the blue garment she had been wearing earlier, before reaching for one of the salt sticks and popping it in her mouth. Her cheeks were flushed pink. I'd never envied her as much as I did now. I wanted her human.

Sirena sipped from her teacup and swallowed. *"Now, where were we?"* she asked, her voice a little breathless.

"About to discuss the fate of Laila, the child who will soon return from the Atlantic," I began, before I blurted out with bluntness I had not known I

possessed, *"Will you share your human?"*

Now all eyes were on me, before sliding to Sirena. Her smile was almost coy. *"He prefers me alone, so I must say I will not. He is my consort and under my protection still."* Her last words held a potent warning.

The others visibly shared my disappointment at her answer. *"Then we will not touch him,"* I forced myself to say.

Sirena stood up. *"As for Laila, when she returns you must send her to me to do her duty, accompanied by my granddaughter, Estella. The two are still close friends, are they not? I will see to any further discipline for her actions in the Atlantic. You may be sure she will do her duty before she returns home."* She finished with a dismissal, already headed toward the stairs and the delectable human.

She turned as she started up the stairs. *"It is still early. There is a human drinking establishment not far from here, called the Left Bank. I suggest you wait in the car park. Though not as skilled as Joe, you might find a partner to join with before you take to the water."* She winked. *"Until we meet again, sisters."*

All of us rose to our feet, making our way out of her house and down the street to the drinking establishment by the water. It seemed I was not the only one craving human warmth tonight.

JOE

Nessa slid into bed beside me and I eased my arms around her, pulling her close.

"That was incredible," I told her, though she hardly needed me to.

She pressed her body against mine, still naked, and I inhaled sharply in anticipation.

"Have they gone back out to sea?" I asked hesitantly.

Vanessa laughed softly, so that her breasts bounced against my chest. "They've all gone down the hill to the pub."

I tried to imagine the four women who had

been downstairs walking into the Left Bank. "They wanted a drink?" I suggested.

Vanessa shifted to distract me even more. "No, they wanted you. I think they went to find consolation in other humans in the pub car park, when I wouldn't share you."

Somehow, the thought of those four naked women getting with random guys up the road didn't do anything for me, but it didn't matter. Nessa knew I was ready for her and she didn't waste time. "Four mermaids wanted me? What for?" I groaned as she moved her hips slowly.

I thought she hadn't heard me, but I was too focussed on her to care for a while. I felt her body stiffen as she let out a quiet gasp. Breathlessly, she replied, "This, Joe," as she blew my mind for the second time that night.

Afterwards, when she was lying in my arms, as sated and happy as me, Vanessa laughed. "You made quite an impression."

I brightened. "You mean I made four mermaids hot?"

Vanessa shifted slightly under my hands. "Five, Joe," she murmured, pressing harder against me. She felt softer than before, almost like…

I felt her tail flukes caress my calf. *Oh God, if we hadn't just had sex twice in one night I'd be ready to go again. Shit, no, wait...*

"How am I supposed to do this?" I mumbled, remembering the last time I got turned on by her tail. I'd gotten nowhere.

"Like this…" she breathed.

I learned that you can make love to a mermaid, but only if she really wants you to. Not many men get to see heaven while they're still alive, but that night, I did. *Oh, Nessa…*

LAILA

Elder Sunitha approached me first. *"What tidings have you of our sisters in the Atlantic?"* Her words were brisk and businesslike.

My eyes could not cry in the depths as they could on the surface. If they could, I would have cried a new ocean for the slaughtered humans. This was immaterial to the Elder, so I did my best to suppress my feelings as I spoke of more practical matters.

"Their ocean changes more than ours does. From the shifting of the sea floor to changing currents, warming waters and overfishing by the humans. They perceive the

changes with pleasure, for it means more trouble for the humans than for our sisters. They feel that fewer humans are no loss, for humans present increasing danger for our people and theirs." I closed my lips firmly, not wishing to venture another word, knowing all I could say would reveal my own feelings and thoughts, which were not pertinent.

Elder Sunitha looked grave. *"Have you recovered from your long journey? Long enough to attempt another?"*

My confusion was complete. I had expected her to comment on my report, not send me back. I looked to her in wordless panic. I could not fathom the thought of returning to the Atlantic. Not now. My words came out hesitantly. *"I have recovered somewhat. What journey would the Council have me take?"* My voice shook, but I could not yet bring myself to beg to stay home. I dared to hope.

Elder Sunitha looked sympathetic, but her words were not. *"The Council would have you do your duty. You and Estella. Elder Sirena has summoned you, that immediately on your return you must present yourself to her. You will travel to Perth, where Elder Sirena awaits you."*

Elder Sirena knew me better than most and she knew humans better than any sister alive. I shaped my thoughts into hesitant words. *"Does Elder Sirena know that I was in the Atlantic?"*

Elder Sunitha looked as if she felt sorry for me. *"Elder Sirena sent word of events in the Atlantic before your return. The humans communicate faster than we do and with more detail."*

My heart sank. Elder Sirena does not forget and she does not forgive. She would require atonement for slaughtering the humans. My heart buoyed up a little at the thought that Estella would accompany me. I would not be alone. I could stand anything required of me, if Estella were beside me.

"I will do my duty as the Council commands. Estella and I shall leave with the dawn." I swallowed my dread, where it lay like a sunken ship on the sea floor.

JOE

"Daddy, do mermaids go to heaven?" Marina chirped, an eager smile on her face.

"Ah…what?" I asked, stunned.

"Do mermaids go to heaven?" Marina repeated dutifully. "Mrs K said that all good girls and boys go to heaven, so all we have to do is be good and God will know and take us to heaven when we die. But when Charlie asked if his pet fish could go to heaven too, she said heaven was only for humans. Mummy won't let me ask Mrs K, because I can't talk about mermaids at school. So, do mermaids go to heaven?" She looked expectant, as if she had every confidence in my ability to answer.

I floundered. This wasn't something I could search on Vanessa's computer, like what the Great Wall of China was built for, if it didn't keep out rabbits. "Um, Vanessa?" I heard footsteps on the wooden floors and I'd never been so relieved to know my wife was in the house. "Sweetheart, your mother knows more about your people than I do. This is one she'll have to answer."

"What do I have to answer?" Vanessa appeared on cue. I wanted to kiss her more than usual and that's saying a lot.

Marina's shining eyes were on me, so I spoke for her. "Marina was telling me that she learned at school today how all good humans go to heaven and she was wondering about mermaids."

"I didn't ask Mrs K, Mummy, just like you said," Marina announced proudly.

Vanessa held her arms out to the little girl and leaned over to lift her up so they were nose to nose. "Of course, sweetheart. If you're a good girl, you'll go to heaven, the same as all the other children in your class." She hugged Marina closer, so Marina couldn't see her mouth the word, "NO" to me over our daughter's shoulder.

My mouth was open, ready to contradict her with all I'd learned at Sunday school as a kid, but I closed it before Marina saw.

Marina slid down Vanessa and skipped away to her room. "Can I play with my Lego before dinner?"

"Sure, sweetheart," I replied as I sank onto the couch.

Vanessa sat close beside me. "You can't tell a little girl she won't go to heaven, no matter what you think," she warned me in a low voice.

I struggled to find the words. We hadn't really discussed religion before, as she'd made it clear that the subject was not a welcome one. Now I had to say it. "But…in the stories…mermaids aren't supposed to have souls. They're not like humans…" I trailed off, not sure what else to say.

"You mean in the stories written by humans about creatures they'd never seen? Do you believe everything you read?" Vanessa looked at me with angry eyes and I shook my head quickly. "How can you be sure that heaven, or hell, or gods, or human souls, or any of these religious things exist? I've been into human churches and I've taken Communion. I've been mistaken for the Virgin Mary on at least one occasion." She closed her eyes, cleared her throat and continued before I could say anything in response. "Her soul will go to heaven with all the certainty that yours will. Like all my kind, we are closely related to humans and at least as intelligent. I can pass for human so well that you are the only one of your kind to have suspected otherwise and that is because you saw my tail."

She stood up. "Do you honestly believe that if I die, my body becomes foam on the water and I'll have to spend hundreds of years bringing cool breezes to hot climates? After everything I have done for your people and mine?" She was furious now.

My mouth was dry. "I don't know what you've done for your people or mine, Nessa. I just know that you make me happier than I've ever been. I have heaven here with you." The last line slipped out before I realised I meant it.

Her expression softened. "If this is all we get and there is nothing after, then I am content with you, too, Joe." Her smiled turned wicked. "But if there is a heaven and the gatekeepers try to keep me apart from you, I will move heaven and hell until they reconsider."

I laughed. I believed her. I thought back about everything she'd said and realised I wanted to know more. *The Virgin Mary? How'd she manage that?* I turned to ask her, but she'd already gone.

LAILA

"Together, we shall do our duty. There is safety in numbers," I tried to reassure Estella, for her fear ran as deep as mine had. Now all I found in the depths of my heart was despair and dread.

"I admit I am afraid. Is it as difficult as Cantrella and Mother have described?"

I drew a breath, before telling her what I had learned in the Atlantic. "No. *If the human is cooperative, then there is very little pain and even some pleasure in joining."*

Estella still had doubts. *"But what if the human is not cooperative? Mother could not join with a human and Cantrella, your own mother, encountered humans who were not cooperative. Cantrella experienced significant pain…"*

I told her my plan, inspired by my Atlantic sisters. *"All humans are cooperative with the right song. If we sing together, the song will be all the more powerful."*

Estella's smile was nervous. *"I am still afraid. What if my song is not strong enough? I was never good at singing."*

I thought of my first human and how a song had not been necessary. *"For your first time, we will find a human who is already cooperative. And I will be there, to add my song to your own."*

Estella was timid, but her face set with resolve. *"If you can do your duty among strange people in a different ocean, then how can I do less?"*

I felt my failure.

"But I have not yet done my duty. I still have not borne a child for our people," I confessed. *"Come, we are in shallow water, near humans. We must be careful."*

Estella changed the subject. *"Why did you choose this place to come ashore?"*

I explained with some apprehension, *"This is*

where Elder Sirena lives on land. She keeps a human house and she will assist and advise us." My shame was deep at being summoned here, so I did not state it.

Estella's expression cleared. *"Grandmother Sirena will help us? She has borne three children for our people, more than any other. With her guidance, I may no longer be afraid."*

Together, Estella and I crept from the water on unfamiliar legs. It was very dark and there were no humans nearby. We approached the dark house. I knew we had the right one, because there was a square tile on the wall beside the back door, with a picture of a mermaid painted on it. She looked a little like our people, but she was a human creation. There were shells over her breasts, a discomfort none of our people would bear.

I retrieved the key from behind the tile and opened the door with it. I returned the key to its hiding place before we ventured inside the dark house. There were voices and movement on the upper level above our heads, but this room was dark and empty of people.

Estella raised her quavering voice, fear

colouring it. I could see her shaking. I took her hand.

"Grandmother Sirena? We are Estella and Laila. We were sent to land to do our duty for our people and we seek your guidance."

I heard footsteps outside the room. Elder Sirena stood before us, wearing a short dress of some shiny fabric.

Estella dropped to her knees on the square-tiled floor, dragging me down with her. She bowed her head. *"Grandmother Sirena, we are Estella and Laila, the daughters of Maria and Cantrella. We have come to land to do our duty among the humans. As an elder with great knowledge of humans, we beg your guidance."*

Elder Sirena stood thoughtfully for a moment, before she smiled down at us and said, "I advise you to speak in the humans' tongue when on land."

"Please, Elder Sirena, tales of your exploits among humans have become legend. Please help us." I spoke up for the first time, awed by the powerful Elder who was not my kin, as she was to Estella. What did she want with me?

A click sounded and the room flooded with

light. A human wearing very short pants and nothing else walked clumsily into the room to stand next to the Elder. He slid a proprietary arm around her shoulders. She did not move away or reprimand him in any way.

The human looked angry as he demanded, "Who the hell are these two, Nessa, and why are they dripping and naked on the kitchen floor? And why do they call you Elder Sirena?"

His disrespect made me angry, but this was the Elder's province. She had not asked for my assistance or advice.

Elder Sirena's voice was gentle. "Joe, these girls are from my people." She signalled for us to rise. "This is Maria's daughter, Estella, and Maria's partner's daughter, Laila." We both inclined our heads as she spoke our names.

The human turned so that he did not face us. "Can you introduce me again when they have clothes on?" The human spoke the words with difficulty.

Elder Sirena's laughter was friendly and infectious. I felt my lips draw up into a smile. I wished my heart would lift with it.

"Come, Laila, Estella. I will give you some

guidance. First, I think you should wear some human clothes and get some sleep. I think I have some of Belinda and Maria's clothes that will suit you. Tomorrow, I will take you to purchase your own clothing." Sirena gestured for us to follow her down a corridor to a small, dark room with beds and cupboards.

JOE

I grabbed an old towel and roughly mopped the floor with it, before sticking the wet towel in the laundry basket. Then I went back upstairs to lie down in bed. I stared up at the ceiling, trying to work out what I'd just heard downstairs.

Elder Sirena? Legend? Vanessa, what do these crazy girls know about you that I don't?

Eventually, Vanessa returned to our room. She closed the door carefully behind her. She shook her head, as if to shake out the memory of the two crazy girls in the kitchen. "Where

271

were we?" she murmured.

I held out my arms, eager to have her back in bed beside me. *Or on top of me. Or underneath me. Or any position she cared to have sex in.*

She chose to sit on top of me, rubbing against me so it felt like no time at all before I was ready for her. As soon as I slid inside her, she moved her hips slowly. She pulled her nightdress off so my hands were on the bare skin of her hips, her boobs, her arse…*Oh God, please don't stop.*

A slight sound made me open my eyes. At the end of the bed, staring at us, were the two crazy girls. They were dressed now, but we weren't. My voice died in my throat.

"Grandmother Sirena, what further guidance have you for us?" one of the girls said. Her companion's eyes on us were hungry.

Vanessa's voice was cold and firm. "I strongly suggest you retire to your assigned room and sleep until the sun rises. I will have no further guidance for you before then." Vanessa didn't break her rhythm, her hips still moving against mine. *Oh God, I'm so close to coming and so is she. I can't do that with those two crazy girls watching.*

"Get out," I gasped out. I reached for the quilt, to cover us so they wouldn't see.

The girls didn't move.

Vanessa moved more slowly, deliberately. Her voice was angry. "You will remove yourselves from this room and close the door behind you. You will not enter this room without my permission at any time. Now, get out."

I squeezed my eyes shut, trying desperately not to come when I wanted nothing else.

I heard the door click shut. Vanessa's lips touched mine, softly.

"Ready, Joe?" she murmured.

"Oh God yes," I breathed.

I felt her come, just before I did. It was such an incredible high I barely recognised my own voice, shouting, "Oh God I love you, Nessa."

Her lips were on mine again. "I love you, too, Joe. And I like the sex."

We both laughed. *I'll never get over the amazing feeling of her laughing while I'm inside her. Unless maybe those crazy girls were watching.* Despite myself, I shivered.

She moved off me. "What's wrong?"

I shook my head. "Those crazy girls. Calling you Elder, grandmother, Sirena. Legends."

She blew out a breath. "I don't know anything about legends. I never heard any. I've only been on land for three years, it's surely too soon for legends to evolve. I am an elder among my people, one of our leaders. That's why you're still alive, despite your knowledge of my people. "

"They aren't going to kill me?" I brightened at the thought.

"No," she said with a smile. "As long as you are not a danger to us, you're under my protection."

"Under any part of you sounds good to me," I returned, without thinking. I moved closer to her, to hold her and kiss her. I tried to pull her on top of me again. For a moment, she resisted. Then she changed her mind and shifted with me, so she lay on top of me, her breasts squashed against my chest.

She lifted her head a little, pulling away from my kisses. "Once, you would have bitten your tongue instead of saying something that direct to me."

"I figure you probably won't bite my head off for it now. And you've made it pretty clear you like sex with me." *Now, please don't bite my head off for asking questions about things you haven't told me.* I took a deep breath. "Please, tell me why they call you different names."

Vanessa hesitated. "Are you sure you want to know, Joe?"

You're my wife and I adore you. There isn't anything about you I don't want to know. "Yes," I said slowly.

Vanessa's eyes closed, then opened wide above me. "Sirena is my real name, not Vanessa."

*Sirena, Serena…*memory itched. "Skipper said your mother's name was Serena. It's weird for you to have the same name."

Vanessa sighed. "My mother died before Skipper was born. Her name was Sephira. The Serena he knew thirty years ago was me. I came on land then and had to take a different name now."

There were a million questions in my head now and I didn't know which one to ask first.

"How old are you?"

"Older than you, Joe, you know that," Vanessa was smiling, but her voice was sad.

"One of those crazy girls called you grandmother. Are you...can you really be…you don't look older than me!" I blurted out.

Her voice sounded pained. "Estella is Maria's daughter."

My memory had some sort of rash, it was so itchy. "You said Maria was older than you. How can she be your daughter?"

Vanessa hesitated, again. "No, I said Maria was older than I was when I had my first child. Maria was my first child."

"How old were you?" My voice came out in a whisper.

Her voice was small. "I was sixteen. I didn't want to have a child and I was careless..." Her voice faded and a tear dripped onto my chest.

She had a baby when she was only sixteen? Just a child. No wonder she's so upset and didn't want to tell me.

Vanessa started to sob and I held her tight. "I'm sorry," she sniffled.

I kissed her again and her lips were salty

with tears. "There's nothing to be sorry about, Nessa," I told her. "I love you." I paused and thought for a moment. "Or should I call you Sirena?"

She sniffled again and managed a laugh through her tears. "Call me whatever you like, Joe. Legally, Serena died before I met you and I'm Vanessa, but I'll always be your Nessa."

I felt a warm glow. *My Nessa.* I realised the glow was hotter in some areas than others. Close contact with Vanessa's naked body definitely turned up the heat. "How much do you want to go to sleep, my beautiful Nessa?" I asked her gently. I pressed closer against her, so she couldn't help but notice what she was doing to me.

She slid her legs around me, so her feet were under my arse. Holding tight to me with her arms and her legs, she rolled to the side, pulling me with her. Now I was on top and between her legs. I was hard and she was wet...

"You still want sex with an old woman like me?" she murmured.

I took a deep breath. "I always want sex

with you." I thrust inside her. I lost all interest in anything else but amazing sex with the most beautiful woman in the world. *My wife. My Nessa.*

LAILA

The unfamiliar human beds were soft and comfortable. Both Estella and I slept easily, for we were tired from the long swim to shore. We were woken by conversation in another room of the house.

I spoke quietly to Estella. "*She has a human child and a human male in her house?*"

Estella's voice was a murmur. "*My mother told me that she keeps a human in thrall, who knows of us but cannot speak of us to other humans. I heard rumours of a child she bore him, out of love…*"

I tried not to snort in disbelief. "*These are*

stories. That is all. Come, we must put on the clothing she has given us."

On rising, we donned the unfamiliar human clothing. Mine were a fiery red and Estella's were the dark of ocean depths. We left the room for a corridor and were greeted by a small human, whose piping voice had been audible from our room. Her head was as high as Estella's round breasts, all but the curve now hidden by dark fabric.

"Oooh, who are these girls, Mummy?" the human girl asked.

Elder Sirena appeared behind her, dressed in the colour of the ocean's surface in the sun when the currents run deep beneath it. "The taller one with the darker skin and curled hair is Laila and the shorter one with the paler skin and straight hair is Estella." The Elder's eyes went from Estella to me. "This is my daughter, Marina."

"Not a human child. One of our people. The stories are true!" The words stole from Estella's lips before she realised and clapped a hand over her mouth.

The child replied before the Elder spoke.

"Do you have tails too, Laila and Estella? What colour are yours? Mine is silver."

I answered the child. *"Our tails are the colour of bronze, little Marina. Estella's is darker than mine."*

"Perhaps one day we can all swim together and you can see, Marina. Now, run to your room and get dressed. The girls are hungry and would like some breakfast," Elder Sirena told the little girl, who moved quickly down the corridor. She turned to us. "We have some fish that I have just defrosted, or we have human food, if you would like to try it. You must eat human food outside of this house."

Estella still had her hands over her mouth.

I bowed my head. "I would prefer fish, if I could, Elder Sirena. Human food can wait until I must eat it."

Estella nodded emphatically.

The Elder dropped two small fish on each plate in front of us, then gave each of us a steaming cup of brown liquid. "This is coffee," the Elder told us. "Maria is fond of it, as are many humans. You must drink it in small volumes at a time, however, as it is very hot."

She lifted a cup from the table that

contained a steaming green liquid and took small sips to demonstrate.

"What do you drink, Grandmother Sirena?" Estella ventured to ask.

"Green tea," the Elder said slowly, before she smiled. "It reminds me of a kind of kelp I am partial to. A touch of salt and it is the taste of home."

Estella and I bit into our fish. They were cold and tasted stale. I could understand why I might consider human food instead of stale fish. Perhaps tomorrow.

The Elder took a breath and let it out. "I take it you are here to do your duty for our people, to come to shore and carry home a child?"

Estella nodded, her mouth full of fish.

"Then we will purchase clothing that is simple and also revealing. Do you have preferred colours?"

I pointed at my bright dress.

Estella swallowed and said shyly, "I like the colour of your shirt, Grandmother."

The Elder nodded. "Red for Laila and royal blue for Estella. If we purchase clothing carefully, you may not need underwear, if you are only on land for a few weeks. It complicates matters, at times."

JOE

Vanessa had gone up to bed, but I stayed downstairs to watch the football. It'd been a long day after a night without much sleep, but it was a live Dockers match and I'd missed a few lately.

I must have fallen asleep on the couch without realising it. I woke up suddenly in the dark. The only sound was the voices of some after-game footy commentary show. The TV screen was dark, but the surround sound was still on.

I thought I heard dolphins. Disoriented, I

felt around desperately in the dark, trying to make sure I really was in my own lounge room and not in the water somewhere with murderous dolphins. I'd never been so glad to get my hands on couch cushions.

I groped for the remote and turned the TV back on. The light glinted on bare skin. One, no, two naked women stood in the shadows beside the TV. One of them opened her mouth and began to sing, like a Smurf trying to imitate a dolphin. My thoughts started to go hazy, like I was going back to sleep.

The other naked woman reached for the remote control and took it from my suddenly nerveless fingers. She pressed a button and switched the TV off again.

I tried to sit up, to protest, but I couldn't move. One of them squeaked something at me. She repeated it, twice, but I didn't understand and couldn't speak to tell her so. The other approached me and started tugging at my pants.

"Vanessa?" I asked quietly, my heart lifting at the thought. The woman tugging at my pants held still for a second, then started pulling harder. I managed to lift my hand to push the woman away from me, swatting at her limply.

The singer started again, louder this time. My hand felt boneless and dropped to my side, no longer under my control. The other woman found my belt and started to unbuckle it.

I was helpless to stop them. I couldn't move. My pants slid down my legs. A naked woman crouched over me. She was too little to be my wife. *Vanessa will kill me. She'll never believe I just lay here paralysed and let two girls smaller than she is take advantage of me...*

"Vanessa!" I shouted as loud as I could. "Vanessa!"

I heard her feet running down the stairs. "Joe? What is it?"

I couldn't speak or move any more.

The steps skidded to a stop. "Silence! Leave him!" Vanessa's voice roared, in an eruption of volcanic temper. "How dare you touch a human under my protection?"

It was her hands that pulled my pants back up. "Joe, are you okay?" she murmured in my ear.

I tried to reply, but I couldn't open my mouth or shake my head. Her lips touched mine, briefly, before she stood up again.

"What did you do to him?" she barked at the two naked women.

A voice I recognised as the taller crazy girl, Laila, ventured a reply. "We did not intend to harm him. We thought that, as he had given you one healthy child and you enjoyed his attentions, he might be amenable to do the same for us."

Vanessa didn't let up. "And when he was not amenable you tried to force him?"

"I tried a song of control, so that he would be more cooperative," Laila protested.

"You think that forcing a human, even under a song, will not harm him? Do you not remember your mother's story of her first journey to shore?" Vanessa thundered. "You would force yourself on an unwilling human when you know the pain such forcing cost her?"

"The Atlantic sisters sing the humans under their control. The humans don't object to this and they are not harmed by it. They did not resist like this one," Laila insisted, pointing at me.

Vanessa's voice was deceptively soft. "And after the Atlantic sisters are done with the humans, they kill them. No human under their control may live to tell the tale. Are you suggesting this is not harmful to the humans?"

Laila squirmed uncomfortably. "No. I returned to our people because I did not want to kill the humans. Our people live in harmony with humans, but in secret." This last sounded memorised.

Vanessa nodded, slowly. "Touching a human without their permission is harmful. If you ever touch or sing to this human again without his or my permission, I will send you both home in disgrace. You will be sent to do your duty on some less hospitable shore. Do you understand me?"

The two girls murmured, "Yes, Elder Sirena."

Vanessa smiled a little. "Besides, neither of you is a strong singer, yet. Believe me, you will get better results with two beers, a pair of visible breasts and a willing human than you did with a song. In addition, the humans will not suspect you are anything but human. I suggest you try beer first." She took a breath and let it out slowly. "At night, you may swim or sleep, as you please. But now, you will leave us." This last was a firm command.

Both girls disappeared from sight.

"Oh Joe, I'm so sorry," Vanessa murmured, kneeling on the floor beside the couch. She slid her arms under my back and started to sing.

This was no dolphin Smurf. It wasn't her faint humming on our wedding day, either. Her voice was high, rich and powerful. This was the sound of a dolphin singing of the dawning of a perfect morning, or it would be if dolphins could sing like this. Her song burned away the mist in my head and gave me back control of my fingers, then my arms. I managed to sit up and the first thing I did was throw my arms around Vanessa.

Her last note faded into the air. I fully expected the sun to be rising, but it was still dark.

"Are you all right?" Vanessa asked softly.

"I am now," I said slowly. "But I think your granddaughter tried to take my pants off. And I thought you said you couldn't sing."

She laughed quietly and replied, "You mean karaoke in the club? Oh, when I said if I sang, you all would have gone home. And you would have. I would have sung a powerful song of control and told everyone to go home to bed, because that was what I wanted to do."

I tried to wrap my head around what she was saying and I couldn't. "You can control a room full of people with a song?"

"I can. There are many songs among my people. Songs for summoning fish, calming sharks and controlling humans, to mention just a few." Vanessa sounded sad.

Oh God, please don't let my love for her be just a trick, some sort of mind control. Don't let me be just some fish she summoned. This is the happiest I've ever been, my whole life. Don't take that away from me.

"Have you…" I cleared my throat. "Have you ever used a song to control me?"

She hesitated. "Once," she admitted.

I took a deep breath. "When?" I asked, trying hard not to let my voice shake.

"The night my daughter flooded your boat with a misplaced wave. You grounded your dinghy on a rock, but a wave upset the boat and tipped you out. The girls were…not human when they found you, and you were sufficiently conscious to notice and ask questions. I sat beside you in the boat and sang you to sleep so I could take you back to your shack safely without betraying the secrets of my people." She smiled at the memory. "You took some waking, once you were safely home. It took even longer to get you warm."

My head was spinning. I managed to get the words out, almost as fast as I thought them. "You saved me from the water that night and tied the dinghy up at my jetty. You got me back to my shack. You got me out of my wet clothes and washed them. And you…" I swallowed. *You inspired the most amazing, sexy dreams I'd ever had.* "I dreamed about you that night."

She laughed. "I'm surprised you had time to. I must have left you perhaps half an hour before Skipper woke you to pull the pots." Her voice turned soft. "We made Marina together that night."

Oh my God. In that one night, she saved my life, took me home, gave me the best blow job a man can have, had incredible sex with me all night and gave me a child. She's God's gift to man and she'd chosen to be mine.

My mouth went dry. "You're amazing," I told her thickly. "I love you."

She stood up and held out her hand. "And I love you. But if you'd like to sleep with me and not on the couch, we should head upstairs because now I'm really tired."

My fingers closed over hers. Hand in hand, we headed upstairs together.

LAILA

For our first foray alone among humans, the Elder took us to a drinking establishment called Little Creatures.

There were large numbers of humans inside, particularly male ones. The Elder spoke of a ship in port from another land and cautioned us to choose only single humans, or those with only one companion. She stressed that we should stay together as much as possible for our own safety.

Her warnings ringing in my ears, I looked fearfully at all the humans pressing close around us in the place she called a pub. Both Estella and I drank some form of fermented fruit juice that left me feeling as bubbly as the beverage with a disturbing desire to belch.

There appeared to be two kinds of humans. There were the fairly relaxed ones who spoke as the Elder and her consort did, sipping their drinks, consuming food and engaging in conversation with the small groups that surrounded them, which were both male and female. The other kind was louder, with a different manner of speaking. The majority of these were male and their eyes roamed frequently over us and the other girls in the pub. The female humans who joined them were quickly pulled into close physical contact with the loud humans, though they did not appear to know the men very well. Several times I saw pairs leave the pub – most pairs consisted of one female and one loud human – and head for the hotel nearby.

I stayed close by Estella at a small table, my fear growing each time one of the humans approached us. I kept my eyes firmly down on the floor or the table, drinking deeply from my glass. Estella sat smiling and looking around, sipping her drink until it was gone. She took my hand and squeezed it, surprising me into looking up to meet her smile.

"Shall I get you another drink?" she asked softly. Her eyes were sympathetic – she knew how little I liked being among humans.

I pressed my lips together, feeling an overwhelming desire to cry. I nodded quickly, hoping the tears forming in my eyes would not spill.

I closed my eyes for a few moments, before opening them to study the surface of the table in front of me. There were sticky circles on its otherwise smooth surface from the bases of countless glasses that had rested on it over the course of the evening. I sat rigid in my seat, hoping no one would approach me until Estella's return.

Of course I was not so fortunate. Three male humans came up, jostling each other for the seats around my table. "Why are you sitting here alone, sweetness?" one asked, a lazy smile on his face.

The second one winked. "You should come

over and join us." He nodded his head toward a larger table where their fellow loud humans were seated.

The third one attempted to put his arm around me. "I think you're just beautiful. What's your name?"

I jumped to my feet, pushing the stranger's arm away. I'd never been so afraid in my life, not even on the ship. Then there had only been one human at a time – now there were three. I backed away from them, looking around in panic for Estella.

I backed away too far and bumped heavily into the table behind me. I whirled around, sure I was being attacked, but I realised that I was mistaken. Those seated around the table asked me if I was okay as they steadied their drinks on the surface. I nodded quickly and headed for the bar in search of Estella.

She had turned around at the sound of me crashing into the table, so she was smiling when I saw her. Estella stood at the bar, holding her drink and mine, with a strange man's arm around her waist. She set the drinks down and beckoned me over.

I weaved between the sea of humans standing around the pub with their drinks in hand, my eyes not leaving Estella, my safe harbour. When I was close enough, she reached out to pull me to her side, trapping the human's hand between us, her eyes glowing. I reached for my drink and downed half of the pint of cider, almost choking.

"Laila," she shouted in my ear as she leaned in closer. "This is my friend Dan. He's studying engineering at the University nearby. He's invited us back to his house to have some quieter drinks." As she spoke, the human's fingers caressed both her side and mine. She smiled and winked.

I looked at the dark-haired man uncertainly and he smiled. "As I was saying to Estella here, my car is parked outside and I live not far from here. I'd be happy to have you both over at my house."

I felt a weight of dread lift from me as I heard his voice, which spoke in the same way as Elder Sirena's consort. He sounded far more pleasant than the brash, loud men who had frightened me from my table. Still I hesitated, unsure. I took another large gulp of my drink, wiping my mouth with the back of my hand.

Estella looked from me to Dan. "We'd love to," she told him, lifting her face to kiss him.

All three of us finished up our drinks and clunked the empty glasses down on the bar. Estella fitted herself under Dan's arm and seized my arm in hers. "Together," she murmured to me as she towed me out of the pub in their wake.

The cider swirled in my head, but I didn't stumble as I followed them outside to the cool, salty breeze in the car park. Dan approached a dark, shiny, metallic vehicle with an open box on the back and opened the door for us. Unlike Elder Sirena's car, this had only one row of seating, including the driver's seat. "This is my Ford ute," he told us proudly, as he noticed me staring at the strange vehicle.

I heard loud laughter behind us and moved closer to Dan and Estella. Almost without thinking, he curled his other arm around my shoulders and I did not throw it off.

"Nice pickup, bud," shouted a voice from across the car park.

I turned to see the three men who had frightened me earlier staggering across the pavement with some difficulty.

Dan looked from Estella to me and grinned, his arms tightening around us both. "They sure are, mate," he called in response.

The three men laughed loudly. "I meant the car!"

Dan shouted back, "Thanks mate. Can't beat a Ford ute!"

Estella and I quickly climbed into the front of the much-admired Ford, eager to leave. The man's house sounded so much safer than a pub.

JOE

"Come watch a movie with me," I coaxed. "The crazy girls are out, Marina's asleep and you've read every book you own. This one's a classic and you said you'd never seen it…"

Vanessa gave in and cuddled up to me on the couch. I started the DVD and left the remote control in easy reach. I wasn't moving far when I had her so close and it was just us awake in the house.

I think I was about as close to content as I could be with my clothes on. I had my arms around Vanessa's boobs, my breath fluttering the neckline of her nightie so I got a good view of them any time I cared to take my eyes off the TV screen, and we were watching *Fight Club*. I even had a cold beer within reach.

When the sex scenes appeared, I watched Vanessa's face carefully, wondering if I should broach the subject of unusual positions.

"You might like that one, but it does nothing for me," Vanessa said suddenly, as if she was reading my mind. "The other one, though...I recall we both enjoyed it immensely the first time we tried. If you'd like, later..." she trailed off, a faint flush on her cheeks as she looked at me.

I stared at the screen, trying to work out how to phrase my response. "I'll have sex with you in any position you like, Vanessa, you know that. I don't remember that one, though, and it's not one I'd forget..." I had vague memories of a dream once where...*shit.* "Unless it was the night we made Marina."

She cuddled closer to me, so there was no way she couldn't tell I was ready for her. "After the movie, I'll remind you," she murmured. *Damn. At least she's promised later...*

I shifted so I wasn't poking her quite so aggressively. I tried to distract myself with the movie again.

At a point which I didn't think was funny at all, Vanessa suddenly lost it laughing. "Oh, that's Cantrella!" she gasped out.

"Cantrella?" I asked, more confused than ever.

Vanessa tried to catch her breath. "Cantrella. Laila's mother. She's a Watcher. Just…like that!" She burst out laughing again.

She cuts guys' balls off? Great. I'd better start wearing that shark shield…

I wasn't as turned on as before and Vanessa noticed the difference. She moved closer to me again as she started to explain. "Watchers are our security. Laila will choose to be one, too, I think. That bit where he says, 'We guard you while you sleep. Do not fuck with us,' is exactly the description of what a Watcher is and does."

I turned cold and even Vanessa on top of me wasn't enough to warm me. "You mean that crazy girl who paralysed me last week does shit like that? I'm going to wear my shark shield in the house, Vanessa. She's not safe around people!"

Vanessa's voice was soothing, though her hands on me were far from it. "She wouldn't dare try that with you, not after her misguided attempt last week. She won't even speak to you now without permission."

"Where did they go and when will they be back?" I asked, hoping they'd be gone a long time. I had a real strong desire to christen the couch with Vanessa tonight and I didn't want us interrupted.

"To the pub, to seduce a human man or two," she replied, demonstrating how effective she was at seducing her own human man. "They should be back by morning."

"You set those two on the human population of a pub? What the hell will they do to the bloke who pulls them?" I felt almost sorry for their prey.

Vanessa laughed. "I don't know what they'll choose to do to him, but I suspect he'll be in for an interesting night. Hopefully he'll survive it." She pulled her hand away from me, kissing my lips. "Now, let's watch the end of this movie you like so much and then we can do something else, if you'd like."

God help the bloke those girls picked tonight, I thought, then shifted my thoughts to pleasanter subjects as Vanessa cuddled up to me again.

LAILA

I pressed my back to one side of the door frame and my toes to the other, watching them. More correctly, watching Estella, as I'd promised I would. When I returned to the deeps, I would be a Watcher, like my mother, so she could not ask for a better companion.

She gave a loud squeal and I looked more intently at what her male companion had done to provoke such a response. He had one hand between her legs and possibly inside her, too, judging from the squelching sounds. His mouth was fastened over one of her round breasts, evidently sucking. Her hands were kneading his back and her head was thrown back, her eyes closed but her mouth lifted in a smile, so I assumed she still derived enjoyment from his attentions.

I breathed a sigh of relief and relaxed a little.

"You know, you can join them, if you're bored," a voice said. "He won't mind."

I tore my eyes from the bed to see a human who looked identical to the one pleasuring Estella, standing behind me. I looked from one to the other, wondering if all humans looked so alike.

He looked like he understood my confusion. "My brother Dan, you've met. I'm Dave. We're twins."

"I don't remember seeing you earlier in the pub, or in the house when we arrived," I replied, warily.

He shrugged. "I'm studying for end of semester exams. I was in my room." He jerked his chin toward his brother's room. "He should be studying for exams, too, but he said he wanted to go to the pub for a break." He looked at me. "I'm taking an hour's break, too." He settled against the passage wall beside me.

"Yes!" squealed Estella, louder than ever. Dan appeared to have moved his mouth from one breast to the other, his spare hand squeezing her right breast. Her nipple glistened wetly between his fingers.

I squinted at his hand between Estella's legs, trying to work out precisely what he was doing to excite her so much. Some of his fingers appeared to be sliding slowly in and out of her, whilst others rubbed against the lips between her legs. Which motion made her writhe in such pleasure, or was it a combination of the two?

"Did you want a beer or something?" Dave offered.

I shook my head, not shifting my gaze from the bed. "I promised her I wouldn't leave her alone. She was a little nervous." I could see Dan press down on Estella with his thumb, moving it only slightly, eliciting a long squeal from her.

"Oh." Dave paused. "It's not like he's going to hurt her or anything. I don't think she'd notice if we left."

I did not reply. Estella lifted her back off the bed a little, pushing her breasts higher. The movement was mesmerising, particularly as she was now breathing hard.

The man beside me was silent, whilst the couple on the bed were not.

Dan took his mouth from her breast and began murmuring, "Come on baby, come on baby…" in a litany that punctuated Estella's frantic panting. After some minutes, she let out another loud squeal, longer than before. Dan had removed his underwear and was easing his way between her legs before she was done squealing, her breasts and her face hidden from my sight by his hairy back.

Her hands closed on his equally hairy behind, pushing on it as though she wanted him deeper inside her. I did not find such copious dark hair attractive. I shuddered delicately.

"Your sister's pretty noisy," Dave said, poking his head through the doorway. His eyes were fixed on the bed as much as mine.

"She's not my sister. She's my best friend," I

responded. My best friend was now making little yelps at each thrust of the hairy bottom. One yelp ended with a gasp, a few more thrusts, before yet another loud squeal. Estella was definitely enjoying her hairy human.

"Friend, then." He paused, shifting back into the passage so the couple were out of his sight. "You know, I'm better in bed than he is." He sounded offhand.

"Can you make me squeal like that?" I blurted out wistfully, as I caught sight of Estella's blissful expression.

He pushed off the wall and shifted to stand close beside me. He looked at me for a moment, before he replied, "You don't look like you'd squeal at all. But I could make you want to."

I looked up at him, expectantly. "All right, then."

He looked flustered. "Well, we'll need to get you out of your knickers, at least." He reached slowly under my skirt and I made no move to stop or otherwise hinder him.

I felt his hand on my skin. "Fuck!" he said, dropping to his knees. "You're not wearing any!"

I edged the hem of my dress up, the stretchy fabric keeping it in place around my waist. "No."

He looked up at me. "Are you sure you don't want to lie down for this?"

I shrugged. He pressed my hips against the wall and put his face between my legs.

Oh, fuck!

My knees went weak and became difficult to control. I couldn't focus on anything else, other than what he was doing with his tongue. I heard him laugh.

Dave was correct. When the time came, I did not squeal – I made a sound more like a low moan. I heard Estella giggle at me, but the happy sound only made me smile more.

"My turn?" At the sound of his voice, I opened my eyes. He had his pants off, his stiff appendage ready for action. "A blow job, or would you like me to stick it somewhere else?"

Now it was my turn to be flustered. I didn't understand and I didn't much care. "I want to be able to watch my friend still. What would you like?"

"Me?" Dave sounded gleeful. "I'd like to do you from behind, doggy-style, with you down on your hands and knees."

I assumed the position he described, facing Estella. Whilst I had been distracted, she and Dan had changed position. Now she sat astride him, leaning forward, facing me. Her sweet, round breasts glistened with perspiration, bouncing with each thrust of his hips. The joyful smile on her face said it all as her eyes met mine. She lifted her head, squeezing her eyes shut, as she squealed, "Oh yes!"

I felt the man slide in from behind me and thrust his way to his own groaning release, but it did little for me, aside from leave a sticky, wet mess behind. I envied Estella, as she bounced her way to another squealing climax. Presumably the human she rode enjoyed the experience, too, for he kissed her with considerable passion afterwards, requesting a repeat performance, which is more than his brother had of me. Dave disappeared after his hour break was over and did not emerge from hiding to farewell us when Estella and I had arranged our clothing to cover us once more.

It was Estella's squeals that rang in my mind from that night, as she endlessly reached yet another climax with Dan on the bed, her breasts bouncing in a happy rhythm in my head.

JOE

"Come on, sweetheart, I have your bag packed. Just get your socks and shoes on and we can go," Vanessa called from the kitchen.

"I can't find the pink ones, Mummy, and I have to have the PINK ones!" Marina shouted back from her bedroom.

Vanessa looked at me. "Can you get some socks for her? She has blue and pink sneakers — you can tell her blue or white will still work with that." She returned to putting lipstick on in the mirror on the wall.

I managed to persuade Marina to wear white

socks with pink hearts on them, after considerable effort, before she'd agree to put the things on.

"Okay, we're all ready then?" Vanessa asked, standing with her keys in hand.

Marina struggled into her school backpack. "Yes, Mummy."

I dropped my voice low so they wouldn't hear me. "What about the crazy girls? Are you going to leave them here on their own? Will the house still be standing?"

Nessa laughed. "I'm sure they'll be fine. They'll both sleep for a while, I suspect, and they can fend for themselves well enough. They had a very tiring night." Her smile spoke volumes that she wasn't going to say.

I wanted to ask, but decided I didn't need to know. If the bloke had ended up dead, it'd be in the news by now, unless they'd dumped the body really well. "Okay," I replied.

We all headed out to the garage, me to the ute and the ladies to the Mazda. I kissed both my beautiful girls goodbye.

"Have fun at school, sweetheart. And don't let the screaming sea cucumbers get to you,

Nessa," I called, getting into my ute.

"I will!" chirped Marina.

Nessa smiled. "They don't scream any more, Joe. I hum a little song when the children first come in and it's amazing how well-behaved they are. I haven't lost a single one to the children since." She laughed. "And the researchers are surprisingly cooperative if I show up to a meeting singing under my breath."

She pulled out of the driveway before me, both of them waving, as I tried to decipher what she'd just said. Oh shit, yeah, she'd said she could control a roomful of people just by singing. It looked like she'd infiltrated the Australian government with a vengeance and a song. I wondered what would happen if the mermaids wanted to take over the world.

If Vanessa wanted it, then she would, and I couldn't stop her. Good thing she was happy with me.

I started the engine and headed to my first electrical job of the day.

LAILA

Estella came in, looking thrilled. "I'm going to see Dan again tonight, we'll have dinner and go back to his place afterwards."

I looked hard at her. She didn't move as I had after my first joining – she didn't look as if she was in pain at all. Perhaps she simply hid it well.

"You should wait until the pain from the first time subsides before you permit him inside you again," I told her. "Even if it delays our time here, I can't bear the thought of him hurting you again."

Estella giggled. "He didn't hurt me. He did plenty of other things to me and I'm hoping to try some of those again tonight, after dinner." She looked at me in concern. "Did you…your first time…oh no! You missed that lesson, you were already in the Atlantic…" She stumbled over to hug me tightly. "Oh Laila, that would have been terrible for you!"

I hugged her back, her sympathy a balm that meant more to me than anything anyone else had said. I felt tears form and flow. "It was at first, but it wasn't all bad. Some of the men gave me pleasure, like the one last night." I wiped the tears away with my hand.

She looked aghast. "More than one man hurt my dearest friend? Oh that's barbaric! I missed you so much that lesson. If I'd known…"

I sniffled and tried to smile. "What lesson did I miss? Another with Teacher Darma telling us how we must behave on land?"

Estella took my hands. "No, it wasn't that at all. She was telling us how to avoid pain and she gave us homework…"

My smile was watery, but it was there. "I would have liked to have learned that lesson before I climbed aboard a freighter in the

Atlantic."

"It wasn't the lesson so much as the homework. She gave us all these dolphin-shaped things she called 'dildos' and suggested we experiment with them, either alone or with a partner, over the course of the week." Estella squeezed my hands. "Oh, I missed you so much that week!"

I felt sad that she'd had to choose a partner for a lesson activity and I had not been there to help. "Did you…" I began, not sure I wanted to know who she had chosen to partner with in my absence. I would resent the time she'd spent with the other girl, when she had wanted me.

"Did I?" Estella smiled. "Of course, dearest. You know I always do what I'm told. And it worked — no pain on land!"

I was wistful. "I could have done with one of your dildos, then, when I was far from home. What are they and what do you do with them?"

Estella looked thoughtful. "Elder Sirena mentioned that she had procured some for us, if we needed them. Would you like to see?"

She led me back to our shared room.

Once there, she started opening drawers until she found what she was looking for. She pulled a long package out and held it up. "That's exactly what we were given!"

I took the box from her and examined the object inside. There was a picture of a smiling dolphin on the outside and it was shaped like an elongated dolphin, but neither was a very good representation of a marine mammal. It was too long.

I removed the object from the packaging and held it up. "It looks like a sea cucumber with pseudopods extended, or a nudibranch." The whole thing wobbled. "Or maybe a little like a misshapen man's appendage..." Realisation dawned. "Is that what it's supposed to be for?"

Estella laughed. "I have to go meet Dan now, but maybe later I'll show you what you can do with it. Have a play with it whilst I'm gone." She kissed my cheek and left.

I flicked the dildo again and it wobbled. Why in water would I need a floppy, misshapen man's appendage?

JOE

"There's something wrong with the lobsters in the US," I called to Nessa, my eyes on the newspaper.

Nessa stopped wiping the bench and came closer. "What's happened?"

"Apparently they're dying in huge numbers in the Gulf, wherever that is, and up just past Florida," I said, trying to read more so I could tell her. "The prawns, too. Some disease, but no one knows where it came from. They're saying it's bioterrorism." I looked at it again. "Kind of like anthrax for lobsters and prawns, or something."

Vanessa held her hands out for the newspaper. "Milky haemolymph, I'll bet," she murmured, scanning the page.

"Milky what?" I asked, wondering how in hell she knew this stuff.

"Milky haemolymph syndrome. It's a bacterial disease that kills crustaceans – lobsters, prawns, crabs, crayfish. We don't have it here and I hope we don't get it..." Vanessa looked worried. "I wonder where it came from?"

I shrugged. "Apparently, terrorists."

Vanessa shook her head, still looking worried. "Something tells me the Atlantic sisters have something to do with this. Oh, I hope they didn't..." She shook her head and changed topic completely. "The lobster prices will go through the roof. The fishing industry here will clean up."

"What?" I asked.

"If there aren't any lobsters, prawns or crabs being fished out of US waters, then ours will be worth more. I'll keep an eye on it – but I think a few years of fishing at a time like this would be a lucrative investment. I'd be able to fund any research I want, if we take advantage of this." Vanessa looked determined, but to do what, I didn't know.

LAILA

I threw the plastic pregnancy test into the round bin and lay on the small bed, wondering why I felt so empty when I had accomplished all I was sent to do. I had done my duty. I had conceived a child with a human and I could carry my doom home with me to take up the destiny my mother had decided for me. The destiny I didn't want.

I heard the click as Estella's negative test landed on top of mine. She looked down at me in sympathy with her sweet smile. "I would take your burden from you, if I could, dearest."

I shook my head. "You don't want that. A lifetime of Council meetings, the responsibility for our whole people on your shoulders? I would not wish it on you."

Estella darted quickly out of the room and returned within a few moments, a bowl in her hand.

"I know how to cheer you up," she said with a smile.

I stared at the white ceiling, moulded into shapes of leaves and flowers at the joins. "What would cheer me up is if the Elder's consort had succumbed to my song to join with you on our first night and given you a child so that we could now return home."

Estella laughed and set the bowl down. "I do not. Grandmother explained to me that sung humans are somnolent, reducing their skill and the pleasure they can provide. She sang her consort to sleep once out of necessity and it took her half a night to rouse him before he was any use to her." She selected something from the bowl and transferred it to her mouth. It was so small that I couldn't see what she held. "I'm quite enjoying the delay, even if it means I must join with a human who is less skilled than the Elder's consort. Dan is skilled enough with sufficient simple instruction to give me some pleasure, every night. I think I may even miss him when the tests are positive."

I sat up and looked at her, unsure whether she was serious or in jest. Estella smiled at me.

She shifted the small bowl of raspberries from the bedside table to her lap, so that I could see the frosted red fruit. She popped them into her mouth, one at a time, savouring them before swallowing. "As for the Elder's consort, she told me she has never met his like in all her life, nor known one of the gift who has. A true consort must come willingly, for there is no honour in controlling such a rare, skilled man. He must be both eager and inspired, awake to the possibilities, able to support and excite – an irresistible man in every respect. She put it very succinctly in human – 'I like a man with spirit who also knows what to do with it.' She told me he even had the strength to resist her for a time, though I find it hard to believe."

"Perhaps she was joking. I do not believe he could." I looked longingly as Estella, who had certainly inherited her grandmother's attraction for humans. The human she'd chosen in the pub was her willing partner, any night she cared to name. Last night she had not returned 'til morning and I'd slept in our room alone. The human I had joined with had made no attempt to contact me, to my relief. I was fortunate that our joining had already resulted in the child I now carried and no further sticky encounters were necessary.

She giggled. "And we thought we could tempt him when even Elder Sirena found him a challenge." She came over and sat close beside me. "You are not too unhappy, waiting for me to conceive a child, too? You could return home without me."

I felt bereft at the thought of leaving without her. "I am content to wait and watch. Elder Sirena has not yet given me permission to return home." I had not yet asked her, either.

Estella folded me into a hug. My breasts ached at the touch of hers, even through the layers of fabric between us – a sure sign of my early pregnancy. "It is not so bad. You could join Dan and I one evening. I know he won't mind…"

I thought of the hairy human she enjoyed so much, but he attracted me as little as his brother. I didn't want a human. I craved the pleasurable sensations they could deliver, it is true, but I did not want it from either man. I shook my head. "Thank you, but no. When will you return to him today?"

Estella smiled. "Not until the weekend. He has study matters to occupy his time and has no time for me. And I have nothing to do for the rest of this week. What would you like to do?"

I felt listless. I shrugged.

Estella's smile brightened. She pulled her dress over her head and dropped it on her bed, bouncing a little where she sat in eagerness.

"I've been speaking to Elder Sirena and paying particular attention to Dan…" she began.

I reflected bitterly that she had paid so much attention to the human that I barely saw her. I tried to concentrate on her words, reminding myself that at least I had her attention now.

She eased my dress up until she'd removed it from my body. She threw it onto the bed beside hers. "Would you like to try?" she asked with an excited smile.

"Try what?" I replied, suddenly confused.

She leaned over and kissed my tummy, over where my embryonic child was growing. She looked up at me with wicked eyes. "You weren't listening, were you, dearest?"

"No. I'm sorry," I whispered. My eyes filled with tears. I felt like I was losing my only friend to a human, yet I was the one lost in the dark.

She lifted her head and cupped my aching breasts. She planted a light kiss on each of my nipples before she smiled at me again. My skin tingled where she'd touched me, to the point where my tears stopped. I wondered why she would show any interest in my breasts when they were so insignificant compared to hers.

"Now I have your attention," she said gently. "We have the house to ourselves for the whole day and I think I've worked out what these skilled human males do to provoke pleasure in joining. It doesn't look difficult – after all, humans do it – and I'd like to try it with you." Her eyes held mine as she sucked gently on my nipple.

I gasped, feeling the pull of her mouth far deeper than my breast, even after she let go.

"Let me show you, dearest," she whispered. Her lips opened on mine, kissing me so that I could taste the raspberry juice on her tongue. I yielded to her downward pressure until my head rested on the pillow once more.

I combed my fingers through her hair, kissing her back as hard as I could. She broke away with a smile, her eyes full of sincerity, as she took my hand.

"Here," she said as she pressed my fingers to a place between my legs that made my skin jump when we touched it. She touched my fingers to the same place on her body and I felt the jolt as she moved in response. I moved my hand, dragging my skin against her, and felt her gasp as much as I heard it.

"You first," I murmured. I knew I was

clumsy, but within a few minutes I heard her breathing quicken until she let out a squeal that left me almost breathless with desire.

"My turn," she responded before I knew what was happening. She reached for the bowl of raspberries and pulled out two that were still covered in ice crystals. Carefully, she placed them over my nipples. The cold was stunning, an icy stab to my insides, as I gasped.

"Leave them, dearest," she murmured as she kissed me. "I'll take care of you."

She was far more skilful than I, her delicate touch precise and tantalising. Now I could hear my own voice moaning in pleasure, but I couldn't focus on anything but her hands, on me, in me, never ceasing…I could feel the heat build deep inside me, like a subsea vent about to blow a blockage. So could Estella, because she started giggling. Then she was quiet. I felt the orgasm bubble up as she sucked the first raspberry off me and I screamed. Before I could catch my breath, she took the other one in her teeth and sucked hard on my breast. I sobbed out her name and clung to her, lost in the sensation of my sweet, sexy Estella.

No man could compare to her.

JOE

"I can read, Daddy! Listen!" Marina announced, climbing into my lap on the couch. I shut off the TV with the remote and turned my attention to my daughter.

She opened up a purple book with a penguin on the front and began sounding out the words, her finger beneath the letters. "Where's my Mummy?"

She recited her way through the whole book, stumbling occasionally, 'til she reached the end and slammed the book shut. She looked up at me, her eyes shining with pride.

"I can read!"

I clapped for her with a smile. "Well done, sweetheart."

"Give Daddy a kiss. After you've read him his story, it's time for bed, Marina," Vanessa said softly from behind me.

I turned and said, "Did you know Marina can read? She's amazing!"

Vanessa's smile grew wider and Marina's looked like her face was going to split. Little lips touched my cheek before Marina's hands crept around my neck for a hug. She skipped off to bed, Nessa following her out.

Nessa was back in a few minutes, still smiling. "She is amazing."

I put the penguin book down on the coffee table. "It's better than the picture books I learned to read with. They were full of, 'Hello Jack. Hello Jill. This is Dick. Play with his ball.'"

Vanessa laughed. "My students learn from waterproof copies of *The Rainbow Fish*. I need to get some more soon, to give to the girls when they leave for the depths again. They do deteriorate in the salt…"

"Doesn't Marina have that one? I thought it only came out recently," I replied, puzzled. "You can't have learned from that, unless you haven't been reading long."

"It did," Vanessa responded. "I learned to read long ago, from a book with words that were not so simple as yours or Marina's, though it sounds like it was closer to your reading primer than any penguin or fish book."

"What was the first book you read called?" I asked. "Darwin's *Origin of Species*?"

She laughed. "No, though my mother was there when he did the research for his treatise on coral reefs."

What? That was a joke…

"I learned to read from a leather book with no pictures," she continued. She gave a grin. "I still have it."

It was my turn to laugh, though it was a pretty nervous laugh. "Show me."

Nessa took my hand and led me to the library. From one of the higher jarrah shelves, she pulled down a small, brown book that looked pretty worn and boring.

"What is it?" I asked, turning it over. There

was nothing written on the cover or the spine.

"It's an Indian book of etiquette," she replied, trying hard not to laugh.

"A what?" I stared at her. "You learned to read from an Indian book on manners? Is it even in English?"

Vanessa laughed. "Yes, it was translated into English. Here, you should read it." She pushed me into one of the armchairs, opening the book in my hands. "I'm just going to do some washing, I'll be back in a minute."

I started to read the old book. The date on the inside cover was 1926 and the publisher was listed as one in Paris. The title was something Indian that didn't mean much to me, so I just kept going 'til I got to some more words. Then it started to get interesting. I still didn't get how it was a good book for a young girl to learn to read from, but if Vanessa said she had...

I heard her come into the room, but I was trying to get my head around what it was saying. I wish it had pictures, but Vanessa's reading primer didn't have any. Maybe they were too expensive to print then. Or maybe...

Nessa slid into my lap, beneath the book. I reached out to steady her, as her perch seemed a little precarious, and my fingers touched skin. I looked up, to see that the stupid book blocked my view of her perfect bare breasts. I closed it and tried to put it down on the table. I wanted both hands free for Vanessa.

She took the book from my hands and opened it against her stomach so I could still see the pages and almost everything else as well. She started flipping through them, looking for something.

"Nessa, the last thing I want to do is read when you're on my lap with no clothes on," I protested.

She found the page she was looking for and held it out to me. When I took it from her, I saw that it had a muddy outline of her fingers beneath them, but her fingers were clean. I looked at her for a moment, before turning my eyes to the page, at precisely the point indicated by the brown fingers stained into the page.

Nessa shifted in my lap as I looked at the words, then tried to make sense of them.

She started to undo my pants. I stood up to help her, still looking at the page. She managed to undress me as I read, pushing me down on the chair when she was done, so the velvet was soft under my bum.

I looked up at her face as she slid back onto my lap. "You seriously learned to read from this book? How old were you?"

Vanessa took it from my hands and closed it on the table. "I was twenty-two, and that's not all I learned." She lifted her legs so that they were on the back of the chair behind me, taking my hands and placing them on her body, very precisely. "Even today, the Kama Sutra is considered a manual for love." She shifted and I slid in effortlessly.

Arching her body back as she held onto the arms of the chair, her head was almost resting on my ankles, yet she was definitely in control as she started to move. "Make it good, Joe," she murmured. "Maybe we'll have time to try a couple more tonight."

I wanted to wonder who'd taught Nessa to read from a sex manual, but it was bloody hard to concentrate on anything but her. *Ah, fuck it.*

My curiosity got the better of me. I held tight to her and did my damnedest to find out what it was like when she came upside down.

Vanessa seemed pretty pleased at the result and I was bloody proud of myself, too.

"Are you all right, Elder Sirena? Why are you permitting him to hurt you like that?"

Both of the crazy girls came into the room at the sound of Vanessa's loud cry of joy.

Oh, fuck.

Any hope I had of further sex with Vanessa fizzled at the sight of them. I got a big, floppy one at the memory of being paralysed and terrified she was going to kill me as those two did that freaky, squeaky shit they did.

Nessa felt the change in me and pulled herself up so she was just sitting in my lap.

"Get out," was all she said to them and they obeyed.

Her eyes went to my face. "I'm sorry, Joe," she said.

"Not as sorry as I am," I replied, looking down. I was about as useful to her as a wet sock on the washing line.

I went to find my clothes again

LAILA

I shared the shower with Estella, watching the water cascade over her body, her skin now as familiar to me as my own. Perhaps more so, as I'd tasted every bit of hers over the last few days.

The feeling of water flowing over us as we made love in the shower was so smooth, I longed for the open ocean and the feel of being surrounded by cool water with her warm body.

Estella gave me a lingering kiss and stepped from the shower, reaching for a towel to dry her captivating curves. I turned the water off and let my skin drip, just drinking her in.

She flicked the towel at me with a giggle before hanging it up. "You'd think I was leaving for a week instead of just a few hours of the evening. If you'll miss me so much, come join us. Dan won't mind."

I shook my head. I didn't want the hairy human and I didn't want him to have her. "I don't want to see you with him. I know you're only using him to give you a child, but I still don't like it."

Estella's smile held sympathy. "Good. I don't want to share you with him, either. You're mine." She kissed me again, her fingers lightly stroking my side.

"Do you have to go?" I murmured.

"Yes!" she returned with a smile. She pulled a dress over her head, adjusting her breasts so that they sat close together with a tempting chasm between them. "Cheer up, I'll be home before you know it. I'm going to let him try without a condom tonight. He'll be lucky to last fifteen minutes."

I did not understand her words, but covered

my confusion with a smile as I realised that she would spend the night in my bed tonight and not his.

She gave me one last kiss. "Then I'll be all yours again, dearest." She winked at me before she turned and left.

JOE

I was already sitting at the table, sipping my coffee, making sure Marina ate every bite of the Vegemite toast she'd insisted upon for her breakfast, when the two crazy girls walked in.

They walked straight past me, without a word or look of acknowledgement, but I was getting used to that.

"Good morning, Laila and Estella!" Marina sang out with a big, black-lipped smile. *One day she'll learn to eat Vegemite without getting it everywhere,* I thought, grabbing a tissue to wipe the worst of it off her face.

"Good morning, Marina," Estella, the shorter one, replied with a smile. Her eyes glanced across me as she spoke and I know she saw me, but her gaze slid away before I could say anything.

"Mummy says you should try the raspberry yoghurt for breakfast!" Marina announced.

I wondered why Vanessa would offer them her favourite breakfast food, when she guarded her yoghurt from me most days, but I was roused from my thoughts by the unfamiliar sound of laughter. I looked up.

Both of the girls were giggling, exchanging glances as if neither of us were here.

"Okay, what's so funny about raspberry yoghurt?" I asked, not expecting an answer.

Cool lips on the back of my neck. "I believe it's a private joke, Joe. They'd tell us if it weren't." Vanessa's voice sounded like she understood the joke better than I did, though.

They might tell you but for them I don't exist, I thought with annoyance, but didn't say.

Vanessa opened the fridge and then the freezer, scanning the shelves. "We need milk and bread, so I may as well do the food shopping later today. It looks like we're low on raspberries, too." She glanced at me.

"Don't look at me," I said defensively. "I haven't eaten raspberries in a long time." I hadn't been able to touch Mum's Christmas pavlova because the raspberries on top reminded me of Vanessa and the last time I had raspberries and her on the *Siren*…

The giggling resumed, louder than before. The smaller one clutched at the bench as she attempted to control herself. "I'm sorry, I've developed quite a taste for them," she gasped out, with a look at the taller girl. "So has Laila." Both dissolved into giggles, the smaller one doubled over, she found it so funny.

Vanessa regarded them with a slight smile on her face, but the smile vanished quickly. "In that case, I'll make sure I get plenty more."

"Please do, Grandmother," Estella said, smiling at Laila.

"Yeah," I muttered. If those crazy girls were snacking on our raspberries, there'd be none left for me when Vanessa and I found the time to fool around.

For a moment, I wondered if they knew

what the raspberries were for, then dismissed the thought as quickly as it had come. Coming from a purely female underwater population, there was no way they'd know what to do with fruit. They'd probably never slept with anyone in their young lives and I sure wasn't about to volunteer to educate Vanessa's young relatives on the joys of sex. Or even the theory.

LAILA

I could not find Estella, so I called her name softly.

"I am here, in the library," came her reply.

I entered the library, to find her seated in an armchair with her legs curled beneath her. She held an old book, full of equally curled writing. She looked up with an excited smile. "Look, all of our history is held here – written down!"

She offered the open book to me, but I shook my head and settled on the floor beside her. I could read human letters, but I did not enjoy it.

"This one holds some of the older stories, ones I have not heard from our teachers. Listen:

"*When Aurelia and Manyara were children, dragons had long since died out. We have only stories of their existence, males of our kind who lived once but no more. When our people arrived in the Indian Ocean from the Atlantic, there were no more males and we were required to venture on land for the services of humans.*

"*The two girls were grown, summoned to attend a Council meeting so they could be sent to do their duty on land, but they obtained permission to investigate a cave island where stories said a dragon had once lived.*

"*The two entered caves and swam through dark mazes, finding fish that never saw light and dwelt only in darkness, caves full of sweet water with no salt and many other things. In one deep cave, they heard the noise of a large creature roaring. Aurelia was a skilled singer, so she sang as few can, to send the creature away. It approached closer and the girls tried to flee. The creature pursued them through dark caves it knew better than they and Aurelia caught her tail between rough rocks. Stuck, she commanded Manyara to leave without her, to tell the Council that she would die bravely and do honour to her line in fighting to the end.*

"Manyara hesitated, for she could not in conscience leave her friend so that she could escape in safety. She did not lack courage, but did not have the reckless pride that was Aurelia's undoing. She returned to bear her sad tale as a lesson to us all.

"So the Council lost a promising young woman who might have made a strong leader. Recklessness in the ocean is not rewarded. Children must learn to..."

Estella looked up from her book. "Did you know there were dragons?"

I shook my head.

She lifted another book from the table beside her and flipped feverishly through its pages. "There is another story of Aurelia, but it is different. This one..." She pointed and I stretched up to read it with her.

"GO!" I shouted.

Manyara hesitated, but she went.

"I am Aurelia of the Gold line and I will not go lightly into the deeps! You will pay dearly for the damage you do today!" I roared, drawing myself up with all the majesty of my mother. No monster would find me lacking in courage.

"I have paid dearly for much in my lifetime, child,

but what new damage do you speak of today?" The voice which spoke was deeper than any of my sisters' and hinted at laughter.

I struggled to free my tail, but it was firmly caught in the rock. I could feel the grate of broken bone on stone and knew I would require the help of a healer before I could swim home. That is why I sent Manyara away — not false courage or a desire to die. I knew I could not swim as fast as she but I could provide a distraction that might save her life.

"Now, you've hurt your tail. Let me assist you, child." Dark claws clutched at my tail. I struggled more, but to no avail. With a painful wrench, the claws pulled my tail from the rock cleft that held it.

The pain was shocking, but I was my mother's daughter and I knew how to behave. "Thank you," I managed to say with the proper degree of respect.

"You will need more assistance than that, child. The bones in your left fluke are broken. You cannot swim far."

I drew myself up. "I am not a child and I have a name."

The voice laughed. "Oh, I heard you shout your name, child, and I know from the way you hold yourself that you are a child still. You are no mother, not yet."

I could not see him in the darkness, but as he approached I began to discern his shape more clearly. I backed away.

He shook his head, as dark as his clawed hands, so that it was hard to see him in the inky depths of the cave. "I have trained as a healer. I can help you, and it will be easier if you do not try to swim." His claws closed over my hand and I found they were more like my own hands than true claws, with nails that were longer and sharper than mine.

He pulled me through the water, deeper into his cave, at a greater speed than I could swim.

"Who are you?" I asked bluntly as we headed into the dark.

He laughed. "You ask for a proper introduction, Aurelia of the Gold line? I played with a girl of the Gold line in the shallows as a child, but she was too high-born to join with me, the youngest and the lowest of the Black. She chose the oldest and most powerful of the Silver, to give her a strong child. She damn near killed him, too, though perhaps that was her intention. She would have done better to choose someone younger and stronger, but her choice was made and did not include me."

I was mystified more than ever. "Who are you?"

"You are a true child of the Gold line, Aurelia — you do not give up. I am Dubhan, the last of the dragons and after me there will be no more."

I almost choked on my laughter. "There are no dragons. They all died out, hunted to extinction by humans, whilst the women retreated to the deeps and hid from them. Only we remain."

"My father and many others were hunted to their deaths by humans, though some said it was the desires of our women that were our end. I would choose death by desire, had I a choice. I found there is no honour in killing a human or even a hundred humans. They are weak without the ocean's gift. Whereas death by the hands or the tail of a woman of the ocean's gift…ah, there is honour and more besides in being conquered by one of our own. Use your eyes, child, and see that what your Elders have told you is wrong. I am the last dragon and I have not died yet." He pulled me into a cavern where daylight shone through, turning black water to glowing blue.

The only darkness remaining was — him. His dark, iridescent skin covered him from top to tail, colouring his face almost black. Yet, as I watched, he changed his colour, from black to dark blue to an almost icy silver.

"How do you do that?" I blurted out, staring at

him in fascination. I stretched out my hand, unable to resist my desire to touch his smooth skin. I touched his chest, running my hand down his stomach. Beneath my fingers, his colour began to change again, to the dark colour I had first seen. He gave a shiver and showed me his legs — and more besides.

He removed my hand from his body and laughed. "You are indeed a child, Aurelia of the Gold. How old are you?"

"I am one and twenty," I returned, my eyes still on his body though my hands were not.

"And you have never seen a human, or a man, so you stare at the last man of your kind, who is more than ten times your age." His smile was broad, as he closed his eyes and shifted his skin to show me his tail once more.

"I will be ordered to do my duty at the Council meeting on the morrow," I replied defensively, then realised the truth. "I will not be able to attend the meeting…"

"Until you are healed, you will not be travelling far," Dubhan said gently. "You may share my island and its reefs, if you wish. I have enough fish for two, for a little while, at least."

I thanked the kind dragon-man, but he dismissed

this as unnecessary.

He bound my tail with kelp and cautioned me against shifting my skin until I had healed. I agreed to his condition, for shifting my tail flukes caused me great pain. I would not wish to put pressure on those broken bones by attempting to walk on land.

My tail took weeks to heal, but I did not go hungry. I raised my voice to sing my meals to me, and the fish came, as I knew they would. Dubhan was impressed by my voice, but he did no more than smile as I sang.

One evening, as he unwrapped the kelp from my tail and together we tested my flukes, I found the pain had lessened. With Dubhan's help, I swam to one of the island's tiny beaches, where we lay on the sand beneath the stars.

I let out a big sigh as I relaxed, which made Dubhan sit up. "Do you miss your sisters so much?" he asked.

I reflected before I replied. "No, but if I had gone home as I was supposed to, then perhaps I would be closer to being an adult than I am now. Who knows how long it will be before they see fit to send me to land?"

His hand stroked my tail. "You are in a hurry to bed a human?"

I shrugged. "I am in a hurry to take control of my life, which I cannot do until I have borne a child. Until then, I am a slave to the Council, like every other child." I took a deep breath. "When I am my own, I can choose my calling, where I live and whether I take a partner. I can refuse a task they give me, or request one. One day, I will take my grandmother's place on the Council."

His hand felt warm and pleasant, as the warm water lapped at my tail flukes. "You are no one's slave here. The Council think you are dead."

I felt sadness for my family and my friends who would mourn me, but there was little I could do. I could not return home until I had healed. "But when I am healed I must return home to do my duty, or I will never be an Elder."

"If you returned carrying a child, or already a mother, they could not send you anywhere against your will." His words came softly, his hand settling on my hip as he ceased stroking. "I could give you a strong child, stronger than the spawn of any human."

I brightened. "You could?"

His hand felt hotter as he resumed stroking my tail, harder this time. "It would be my pleasure."

"As soon as my tail is healed, then?" I asked

hopefully.

Dubhan laughed. "Why wait?"

I hesitated. "I shouldn't change my skin until I am healed and I thought…"

"Did your Elders tell you that you could only join with a human in human form? But we are not human, Aurelia, and you have such a beautiful tail…"

I gasped as I felt his hand inside my tail — I know not how — in an intimate caress that tantalised as he touched me.

"Join with me, Aurelia of the Gold," Dubhan whispered as he pressed his body close to mine.

I was close to losing control in a way the Elders had not warned me about. "Yes," I whispered, so softly he did not hear.

The sensations he provoked all but took my breath away, yet I was panting.

"Will you join with me now, Aurelia?" he asked.

"Yes!" I gasped out. "How?"

"Turn your body so your eyes are on the sand and not the stars," he directed. "Lift your hips — like this." With one hand still inside me and the other beneath me, he lifted, leaving me breathless. I could feel the heat of him close behind me as he hesitated. "You know that your first time may cause some pain?"

I did and I felt a frisson of fear, but I did not permit it to show. I was Aurelia of the Gold and I was to join with the last of the dragons, to produce a more powerful child than any I had known. I would do my duty and do it well. "I do," I breathed, as calmly as I could.

I heard him sigh in relief. "I will be quick for your first time, for I would not prolong your pain. The next time will be better."

I concentrated on my breathing, trying not to tense up as he withdrew his hand. I would not shed tears like a weak human. There was pain, yes, sharp at first and then just an ache, as Dubhan ebbed and flowed like waves pounding a cliff inside me. And my duty was done.

We lay on the sand, the waves lapping at our tails, and I thanked a dragon for allowing me to do my duty among my own kind.

A week later, Dubhan kept his promise. The next time was better, longer and far more satisfying, with no pain. As was every night following.

A year later, I delivered our child into his waiting arms. We called her Sephira, for the way her tail caught the sun like the brightness of a blue surgeonfish. I had never seen him so happy — he lightened his skin to match hers every time he saw her.

One night, as Sephira slept in her seagrass cradle, swaying softly in the light current, we made love slowly for what may have been the thousandth time. I had not kept count, though perhaps I should have, for this time was to be our last.

I felt him reach his peak, but he stiffened with a groan that did not sound like enjoyment. Frightened, I asked him what was wrong.

He had difficulty speaking, or even drawing breath. "Thank you…Aurelia… Sephira…"

They were the last words of the last dragon, Dubhan of the Black. My Dubhan died and I took his body into the dark depths of the cave where we had met. I carried our dragon-child home to my people, ready to take my place in the Elder Council that one day Sephira would rule.

Recklessness is not rewarded in the ocean. Since my childhood, I have taken calculated risks for the honour of my line and the good of my people. Sephira and Sirena, when you succeed me, remember this. You are of the Gold line, but you carry the blood of the last and most powerful dragon of the Black line. Make my Dubhan proud. He deserves no less.

"That makes me his descendant, too. Do you think Sirena knows she is descended from dragons?" Estella almost bubbled in her excitement.

I shrugged. It made little difference to me, for it was common knowledge that dragons did not exist, if they ever had. The Atlantic sisters believed in myths, legends and misinformation that I did not subscribe to. This sounded like more of the same, for it even used the same name. "Elder Sirena said that many of these books are stories written by humans which have little basis in fact. This could be one of those."

Estella shook her head slowly. "I have read the human stories. The letters are printed, not written like these, and the writing in both of the stories about Aurelia is the same. No human would know enough about our people to write this…" She stopped abruptly and her eyes grew wide. "Grandmother Sirena!"

Elder Sirena entered the room. How long she had waited in the doorway I did not know.

"Did you know we are descended from dragons, Grandmother?" Estella asked breathlessly.

The Elder smiled. "They were not really

dragons. That was what the humans called the rare males among our kind, as they called us mermaids. My grandfather Dubhan was the last of them, but now he is gone." When she spoke the dragon's name, she made it rhyme with *gone*.

"Why did Du…Du-vawn…why did he die so suddenly?" Estella looked sad as she said it.

"Aurelia was not a healer, so she did not know, but my mother believed his heart simply failed, for it was the end of his life. Aurelia was a powerful woman and the energy she possessed in her youth was formidable. It is likely that his happiness with Aurelia shortened his life, though he did not appear to regret it." Elder Sirena crossed the room and took the books from Estella's hands.

"My line has less human blood than most and perhaps that is why I lead as I do. Aurelia did not wish it widely known that she had joined with a dragon. She returned to her people with a child and the truth that the child's father no longer lived. As an adult, she was not asked for more detail." She raised the books. "But she wrote an account of her time with Dubhan, for those who would come after her. She infused our blood with his strength, but I believe she did love him." Sirena's smile was soft.

"Why do you say that, Elder?" I asked.

"She knew that we would need to be strong in the times to come, yet she bade my mother and I to honour his memory and not her own. She was the most powerful leader in living memory and a legend in her own right, but she attributes our strength to him. He was a man I would have liked to meet." The Elder's eyes appeared wistful, but still she smiled.

I did not speak the words aloud, but I wondered. The most powerful leader now was unarguably Sirena, who eclipsed Aurelia even in the stories told to children. This could have come from her grandmother or her grandfather. I wondered what else her dragon blood meant for her and our people. I did not know, so I did not ask, for there are questions best left unsaid and, perhaps, unanswered.

JOE

Vanessa was in the garage, lovingly running a chamois over her Harley. She barely noticed me come in, she was so intent on the machine.

"You prefer him to me?" I asked, after a while. I admit I was happy enough watching, because her stroking the metal was a hell of a turn-on, but there's a point where a man wants his parts stroked, too.

Nessa looked up from her motorcycle. "No, though I haven't been riding for a while."

Now I felt uncomfortable and not just because my jeans were feeling a little tight in places. "I'm up for a ride with you any time you want."

She smiled. "Have you ever ridden a Harley, or any other motorcycle?"

I shook my head. "No. I had a go on my sister's scooter once, but that was like a bike that buzzed a bit. Then she kind of took a wall with it and it got damaged, so she got a car instead."

Nessa unlocked the lockboxes on the back and pulled out a couple of helmets. "Go get a heavy jacket and some boots on. I'll take you for a ride."

I headed back into the house and returned with the coat and boots. While I'd been gone, she'd changed into a clinging leather suit that looked so sexy, I was ready to beg her to take it off. Well, maybe after a minute or ten of watching her move around in it.

I turned my attention to the motorcycle and sat on it, my hands on the handlebars. "So, how do I drive one of these?"

Nessa laughed and handed me a helmet. "You don't drive one of these." She squeezed between me and the bike, using her arse to push me further toward the back. "You stick real close behind me and hang on tight while I drive this baby."

The leather clung to her like her own skin and I made a point of keeping close to her so she couldn't miss mine. She rubbed her arse against me with a wicked laugh before she started walking the Harley out of the garage.

"Ready, Joe?" she asked, without looking at me.

"Shit yeah," I replied. I was ready for anything she wanted.

"Helmets on and we'll go. I'll take it slow for you, Joe, as it's your first time. Hold on!"

I jammed my helmet on as she did and held on as ordered. Then she opened up the throttle and took off.

Fuck, it was like flying. Only better.

LAILA

I sat in the sun on the grass outside, as Marina played on the metal structures she called a playground. I had agreed to care for her whilst Elder Sirena and her consort were out of the house and Estella was spending time with the hairy human.

I angrily hoped that the hairy human would finally give her a child today. If he was not fertile, she should choose a better human who could give her a stronger child. Or perhaps artificial insemination, as her mother had, so no further joining with a human would be necessary. Then she would be mine alone. I thought on this with considerable satisfaction.

An animal approached me across the grass, perhaps as large as the biggest lobsters, though that is where its similarity to a crustacean ended. It had pointed ears atop its head and a pointed nose, too. The creature stood on four legs, with a long tail like that of a bosunbird. It had fur like a sea lion, though its colour was that of the underside of a storm cloud. It made a sound not dissimilar to the vehicle the Elder drove.

It had no fear of me, butting its face against my hand. I lifted my hand away, only for it to rub its face against my foot instead.

I looked askance at it, before asking Marina, "What is this creature and what do I do with it?"

Marina giggled, a tinkly version of my Estella's laughter. "That's Fluffy the cat from next door. She's really stupid but she's really friendly, too. Look, you can pat her." Marina raced over to me and proceeded to stroke the animal's fur, from her head to her tail. The animal closed her eyes and increased the noise volume.

"You try it," Marina coaxed, pulling my hand toward the animal's fur.

I knew it was soft, so I lightly ran my fingers down its spine, feeling the animal shiver a little, still making the sound. I smiled at it.

"You can pick her up, round the middle, go on," Marina said in excitement.

I placed my hands around the midsection of the cat and lifted her up. She was surprisingly light – her fur must have been very fine, not thick like that of a sea lion. She brought her face up to mine and touched my nose with hers. She licked my face, too. Her breath smelt of fish, just like a sea lion.

"I like this creature," I told Marina, smiling, as I put the cat down on the grass once more.

Marina smiled back, then ran back to the playground to continue with her activities. The animal curled up beside me and went to sleep.

JOE

By the time we were back in the garage and climbing off Vanessa's Harley, I felt like I was going to break the zip on my jeans and split the leather on her pants. I couldn't take my helmet off quickly enough to get my lips on hers.

I dropped my coat on the ground and started on her zip. Hers was a much more snug fit than mine, but as the zip came down I realised there was nothing between me and her boobs — she had nothing on beneath the leather.

My jeans were so tight it hurt, but I was torn between getting her pants off first or mine.

"Upstairs," I managed to say between passionate kisses, as Vanessa pulled me with her toward the house.

I had my hands between the jacket and her boobs and I wasn't letting go for anyone, stumbling with her toward bed and getting my damn jeans off.

Once up the stairs and in the bedroom, Vanessa shrugged out of the open jacket, her boobs bouncing a little as she moved.

I gave a moan of relief as I unzipped my jeans and let them slide to the floor. I sure as hell wasn't floppy tonight.

Her body slammed against mine without hesitation. I clutched her leather-clad arse, wanting to tease her just a little before I helped her out of her pants.

"Mummy, Mummy, Laila's trying to make me eat yucky fish! I want cucumber!"

Marina's high-pitched wail preceded the sound of her feet off the stairs. Vanessa and I broke apart, panting. I grabbed my jeans to at least shield what was too hard to hide.

Vanessa was putting on a singlet top when Marina came into the bedroom, pouting. "I don't want yucky fish! I WANT CUCUMBER!" She screwed her face up as she demanded the vegetable.

"Sure, sweetheart," Vanessa said, sounding as out of breath as I was. She held out her hand to Marina. "I'll come down and cut you up a cucumber. Then maybe we can go eat it together while we watch a movie..." She and Marina headed down the stairs.

Shit. I collapsed on the bed to catch my breath. Well, most of me collapsed. Aching with how much I wanted my wife, I headed to the ensuite for a cold shower. Sex would have to wait.

LAILA

"Goodbye. And thank you," I heard Estella say. I heard her kiss the human.

"You'll call me when you're back in Australia, right?" he asked, sounding uncertain.

"Of course," Estella cooed softly. I heard another wet kiss.

I vowed to keep her in the water at all costs, never to set foot on land again if it meant I would have to share her with a human. She had spent her last night with him.

The door shut and Estella entered our shared room, sunshine streaming through the window and setting red highlights in her hair. She smiled and sat astride my thighs, her hands gentle on the rounded mound that now rose between my hips. "It is done, dearest. I carry a child now, though not as clearly as you do." She pressed her lips to my tummy.

"You just got home. Did you test for the child with *him*?" I struggled to sit up, shocked.

Estella placed her hands on my shoulders. "No, dearest. I did the test just before he arrived and left before I could tell you."

I was horrified. "And you let him use your body when it was not necessary? How dare he!" I tried to get up from my bed.

Estella shook her head, her weight still firmly on my legs. "I wanted to say farewell. And I have enjoyed his company. He gave me considerable joy and a child. I wanted one more memory to take with me to the deeps and he gave me that, too." She laughed. "I gave him a parting gift, too. I sang to him to make sure he will never sleep with another, not after me. I left the man with a limp…" She shook her head, still laughing. "I spent too much time teaching him what to do to waste him on a human girl. Only a singer of our own kind can arouse him now and she will need to be a stronger singer than I."

She sighed as she lay down on the bed beside me, stretching. I ached with want for her, but she might have been sated by the human, in their sweaty coupling in the darkness of night. I would deny my own needs to ensure my Estella was well-rested, for her wellbeing surely meant more to me than it did to the hairy human. A human who would never join with another again, for who among our kind but Estella could find such a hideously hairy human attractive?

"I was saving something special for our last day – something we haven't tried before. Are you too angry with me, or would you like to try something new? I promise you'll like it." Estella smiled, her eyes closed as she lightly ran her fingers up my sides.

I was angry at the human for taking her time from me, for daring to touch her, to venture inside her. I was furious at him, but never at her. "What is it?" I asked grudgingly.

"I'll be right back," Estella said in

excitement, leaping up and running to the kitchen. I heard the clink of something in a bowl, growing louder as she returned to me. She dropped the large bowl on the table, where I couldn't see its contents. She slid a hand beneath her skirt, then withdrew it. She pulled off her dress, looking at me expectantly as I did the same.

She knew me so well by now that she could bring me to the cusp of a climax within a few minutes. "Are you ready, dearest?" she asked sweetly.

I gasped out an incoherent reply that she nevertheless understood. I heard her reach for the bowl, unable to focus on anything except her mouth on me. My orgasm came with a new sensation – of something long and hard pushed deep inside me by her hands. It wasn't until I came down off my high that I realised what it was. "Ice!"

Estella gave me one last lick before shifting up my body to kiss me with her cold tongue. Her hands were already busy, caressing me and shifting the ice so I could only moan in response. Once…and again…and a third time...I didn't know I could peak so many times in such quick succession. My skin felt so sensitive after her onslaught a single breath from her lips could push me over the brink again.

She kissed my lips, then bent down and sucked the much-reduced ice from between my legs. She crunched it in her teeth with a wicked smile. "Did you like it, dearest?" She lifted her head to look in the bowl. "We have two more – one each?"

I felt spent, but I wanted to make Estella forget the human today. "You first," I murmured, sitting up and reaching for the ice.

Her breasts bounced as she laughed. "I was first, dearest, but you made me so hot it melted clear away." She lay on her side beside me on the bed, her hair in dark ribbons on the pillow. I stared at her for a moment and she smiled back. "How about both at the same time?" she whispered.

I eagerly complied, shifting my body for better access to hers. Her first breathy squeal sent a waft of hot air that melted the ice inside me, blowing away all thoughts of humans.

Estella was mine and I was hers.

JOE

I could hear voices in the kitchen, so I came closer to find out if Vanessa was there. The voice I heard was Estella's, sounding very serious.

"If I do this, then I can offer to be your ally in all matters of policy, to support you as long as you lead. But she will be mine."

Vanessa laughed. "You are still a child. I can order either of you and you must obey. Defy me and I will ensure there are consequences that see you never dare to consider disobeying again."

"But you will not have a willing ally and she will oppose you, even as her mother did, until she is ruined beneath the strain. You will have a far more capable ally for much longer if you support my candidacy. I am your best choice, grandmother, for I have your blood and his."

"I would like to have known your father." Vanessa still sounded amused.

Estella's voice contained far less emotion. "What does he matter? He was a man who sold his seed for a profit, hoping to people more of the world with his progeny in the process. He was ambitious and took calculated risks to forward his ambition. As did your grandmother and mine…as do I.

"I will do all that you ask and willingly, but she is my price. Mine and mine alone. You will ask nothing more of her. I will take care of her, whatever may come." She paused for a moment, before continuing, "Thank you for your guidance and assistance, Grandmother. With your permission, when the time comes, I will do what is necessary and reveal what you have told me of the Black line. I will take her place when she falters. I will do you and

Dubhan proud."

I entered the room, just in time to see Estella place her hands by her sides as she stood straight and tall, though she barely came to Vanessa's shoulder. She bowed her head deeply, so her chin almost touched her collarbone. She lifted her head again, throwing a quick glance at me before her eyes turned to Vanessa. "With your permission, Grandmother?"

Vanessa smiled. "Go ahead."

Estella spun on the spot to face me, before she did the same head-bow in my direction. "I thought Elder Sirena would make you forget my lapse of judgement when I first arrived on land, rendering an apology unnecessary. Now I understand that you are her consort and as such you are permitted to know more than any other human." Another head-bow.

She'd spent weeks ignoring me, but now she wasn't just acknowledging me, she was offering me some sort of respect that was full of big words. I looked askance at Vanessa, but she only smiled.

Estella continued, "I wish to apologise for

my behaviour when I first came to land. I took poor advice and gave in to bad guidance. If my actions caused you harm or discomfort, I express my deep sorrow and remorse for having caused such. I understand now that as the Elder's consort, had you granted my desire it would be an honour I do not deserve. I offer apologies for the behaviour of my Laila, too, but I can promise you that she will have better guidance in the future." She regarded me gravely as she spoke, then finished with yet another head-bow.

"Ah, no worries," I began uncertainly. "Your Laila?" I asked, feeling stupid.

"My Laila," Estella said with some satisfaction. "I will take care of her, for we will be life partners. All but the brightest star needs darkness to shine." Her smile said a lot more than I could understand, possibly because I couldn't get past the thought of lesbian mermaids.

I stumbled to Vanessa's side, wanting to remind myself that I had someone better than any pair of lesbian mermaids. *Two of them...who'd consider it an honour if I...Shit. If I didn't have Vanessa, I'd...*

"As long as the brightest star does not crush the darkness," Estella finished cryptically. She repeated her head-bow, for longer than before. "Farewell, Grandmother. Farewell, consort."

I waved automatically as she left the room. I heard the front door open and close.

I looked at Vanessa. "What was that all about?"

Vanessa laughed softly. "I think my granddaughter has more strength and ambition than her mother. She would be formidable if she were to lead the Council. I'm lucky that she will not. I pity the other Elders who are not strong enough to withstand her, though. It's a good thing for Laila that Estella wanted to bed her instead of eliminating her. Poor Laila doesn't have the strength to fight Estella, but she'll thrive as her subordinate. Now both girls have gone home to take their places among my people."

When I was game to go into the hallway, I saw the clothes Estella had been wearing lying neatly folded on the door mat. She and her crazy friend were really gone and they'd left their clothes behind. *Naked lesbian mermaids…shit, think of something else!*

LAILA

"Where would you like to sleep, dearest?" Estella asked, swirling the waters around me in her joy to be beneath the surface once more.

The visibility was low in the muddy water. I longed for the open ocean. *"I don't care, provided we are at sea."*

"An island or the surface?" she mused. Before I could answer, she had decided. *"Come, dearest. We shall swim for a couple of hours and we will sleep in safety together. No need for Watchers where we're going."*

She flicked her tail and headed off, as I

accelerated in her wake. I matched her speed, as muddy waters gave way to the pylons and shadows of ships in the port, before we were out of the shipping channel and into the open ocean.

There were dolphins and some large sharks, but I made sure that the fish were told to keep well away.

Estella led me to an island off the coast, surrounded by rocky reefs and low cliffs, with some sandy beaches. She chose a cave near the waterline, shifting to her legs to trudge up the rocks to the sandy beach inside.

The sand was big enough for the two of us, but no one else.

"Just us, dearest," Estella whispered. She licked the salt water from my cheek before she kissed me. Her kiss was salty, too.

"Are you too tired from the swim, or would you like me to pleasure you?" she asked, her hands already on me.

I laughed, more freely than I had on land. *"You first."* I rolled in the sand so that I ended on top of her.

I had her squealing and clawing at the sand

before she could do the same to me. We slept, sated, secure in one another's arms.

Of course, that was until the usual inhabitants of the cave came home to sleep.

A snuffle and the sound of sand being compacted woke me. The strong smell of fish was unmistakeable. A damp nose touched my hair. *"This is our cave. Go sleep somewhere else,"* I murmured. This had no effect on the fur seal.

I heard a slap. Estella had an amorous fur seal, too.

"Fuck off, fur seals!" Her angry shout echoed through the cave. "No boys allowed!"

The male New Zealand fur seals slunk reluctantly back into the water.

"You tell them, Estella," I murmured, cuddling up to her breasts.

Her laughter set my soft pillow moving. *"Oh I will, dearest."*

JOE

"I hope we have a boy next," I murmured sleepily, much later.

"A boy?" Vanessa asked.

"If you have another baby, I hope it's a boy." I explained. "I always wanted to name my son John Giuseppe, after my father and my mother's father."

I heard Vanessa take a deep breath and let it out. "Joe, my kind don't have boys."

"What, you only have girls? I thought that was up to the man…" I drifted off, uncertain. I didn't know much about genetics.

"No, all of my kind only have girls. There are no males." Vanessa's voice was gentle.

"But our child will only be half mermaid. It'll be half human, too," I tried to explain.

Vanessa laughed. "It's a genetic predisposition among my kind. We only give birth to girls."

I thought for a moment. "So, if mermaids are all girls, where do the little ones come from?"

"From sex, the same as humans," Vanessa replied shortly.

"But if there's no male mermaids, does that mean..." I began. My voice died before I could get the words *lesbian sex* out of my mouth.

Vanessa came to my rescue. "It means that when one of my kind wishes to conceive a child, she has to come on land and find a willing human male."

My mouth hung open. "You mean...you seduced me so you could have Marina? I was just...a sperm donor?" I sat up in bed, horrified. *No wonder she hesitated about marrying me.* "Is that what you're here for now?"

Vanessa sat up, too, and slid her arms around me. "No. I wasn't on land to conceive a child. In fact, we weren't supposed to get too friendly with humans at all. Then, as now, I'm among humans to collect information on changes to tectonic plates, subsea volcanic activity and the marine environment, and how it will affect both of our peoples." She laughed softly, her breasts bouncing against my back. "My time with you, and Marina, were…not planned."

I started to relax, then thought of something else to worry about. "And how many other men have you slept with who weren't planned? How many other children have you had, who were not planned?"

"None," Vanessa answered softly. "Joe, unplanned doesn't mean unwanted." She pressed her body against my back and kissed my neck. "I've wanted you since the day I first met you."

I wanted you the first time I saw you, too, but then I didn't know that all you wanted was my stud services. She just wanted a guy with a functional dick, one who didn't shoot blanks. Anyone would do.

She shifted so that she was up on her knees, then swung around so she was kneeling astride me. My head was a mess, but my dick had a mind of its own. It was already hard and ready to go. She could feel it and she was angling her hips so I'd slide right in.

I could feel all my willpower draining away as my sex drive took over. "No, I don't like being used for my stud services. I don't want to have sex with you," I lied through my teeth. *Dead kittens, dead, smelly lobsters, getting electrocuted…shit, please let my dick go down…a pair of naked, lesbian mermaids taking my pants off…fuck, no, that won't help…big, gay, hairy bikies with prison tattoos…*

She laughed gently. "Just a few minutes ago you were saying how much you wanted to have children with me. Now you don't. You can always wear a condom, Joe." She rocked her hips against mine.

"I don't have any left," I managed to say. *Once I'm inside her, I won't care why she's decided to sleep with me. All I'll care about is how incredible it feels to come inside her.*

"Oh, well," she said indifferently, moving

off me.

I wanted to tell her I'd changed my mind and I'd take sex with her at any price, but the words died in my throat. *I've married a woman I barely know.*

She kissed my cheek. "Good night," she said softly, before lying back down and turning away from me.

I stumbled into the ensuite bathroom and closed the door. I waited a few minutes, then realised there was only one way I was going to get rid of my hard on. Weeks of impotence because I was terrified of those two crazy girls, the first night I had Vanessa all to myself and no worries…then this. *Fuck. Oh, and the shower's fucking cold, too! Big, gay, hairy bikies with prison tattoos…* I froze my arse off in the shower 'til I wasn't in the mood any more, then dried myself and went back to the bedroom.

I lay back in bed, beside the beautiful woman who was my wife. *I'd give anything to be able to take it all back, the whole stupid argument. I'd tell you I'm sorry, Vanessa, and how much I want to have sex with you, in any position you want. I'd tell you that I'll be happy to sleep with you as many times as you want, because I'd give anything to see you carrying my child.*

But she was fast asleep. I lay awake beside her, wishing I could sleep, too.

LAILA

When dawn approached, there was a large vessel near the island, slowing as it approached the port to unload. It was a container ship, like the one the Atlantic sisters had sunk in their own ocean. They unloaded and loaded in a day or two and moved very quickly. I looked at Estella. *"What do you think? Would you like to ride on it and be lazy?"*

She laughed. *"You mean climb aboard a human vessel and travel with it north to as near to home as it gets? What if they see us?"*

"We can hide beneath," I replied, showing her

the underside of the vessel beneath the water. *"There are sea chests with soft algae in them. We would have a bed and a secure place to conserve our energies."*

She smiled. *"Or to expend them in exercise other than swimming."*

We chased after the vessel and prised our way into the largest sea chest with the most luxuriant algal growth. Whilst the ship was in port, switching one set of sea containers for another, we made our compartment as comfortable as we could. Together, we detached anything hard – molluscs, barnacles and anything else – evicting some small purple swimming crabs that waved their claws at us in impotent aggression. When the compartment beneath the ship was soft once more, we pulled the grate shut, checking to make sure we could open it from the inside. Satisfied that we could, we both lay in the green growth on the walls of the sea chest, luxuriating in our lazy journey home.

"What shall we do now, dearest?" Estella asked, stretching so that her back arched out of the green cushion beneath her. There was a piece

of algae caught on her nipple.

I reached over and picked the algae off, placing it carefully in my mouth. Chewing slowly, I looked at her.

"I would like to do you," I replied after I'd swallowed.

She giggled. *"You are reading my mind."*

I didn't reply, for my tongue was already busy.

JOE

"Daddy, Daddy, I'm hungry!" Marina shouted, bouncing on the bed.

I managed to open my eyes. It was 10 am and Vanessa wasn't in bed beside me.

Oh God, what did I do? Is she gone?

I wandered into the kitchen, Marina tugging on my hand to make me walk faster. In a daze, I made her some toast and poured her a cup of juice. I emptied the juice carton and went back to the fridge to check for more. *Nope, we need to buy more juice.* I found a pen and turned to write it on the bottom of the shopping list. I paused when I realised the sheet was blank. *I thought we had a pretty long list, but now it's gone. Maybe Vanessa's just gone to do the food shopping?*

Slightly reassured, but still worried, I made and swallowed my own breakfast without tasting it. I coaxed Marina into eating her toast, then helped her to brush her teeth and get dressed. We played together with some of her stuffed toys, until she got bored and wandered back into the kitchen.

By then, it was lunchtime, so I made us both sandwiches and spent the next hour persuading her to eat every bite. When she finally finished, she was tired, so we sat down to watch her favourite movie, *The Little Mermaid.* She fell asleep less than halfway into the movie, so I carried her little body to her bedroom. She seemed heavier than ever, so it took more effort than I remembered. She was growing fast. I tucked her into bed and closed the curtains. Just before I closed the bedroom door, I heard a glass door shut.

Vanessa's home. Oh thank God, she came back.

I almost flew down the passage to the side door. Vanessa dropped her shopping bags on the kitchen table and looked at me, her eyes sad.

"Oh, Joe, I'm so sorry," she burst out before I could even think of what to say. "I've never felt so lonely as I did last night. I went and bought some condoms, so even if you didn't want me to be able to conceive children, we could still have sex. I didn't know which ones you wanted, so....oh!" As she reached for the bag, it tipped over, spilling its contents all over the floor. Boxes of condoms went everywhere. Vanessa dropped to her knees and started crawling across the floor after them.

Oh my God. Underneath her short blue dress, Vanessa was wearing a blue lace g-string.

My shorts felt way too tight. "Vanessa, stop," I managed to say, before I dropped to my knees behind her. I touched my shaking hands to her almost bare behind.

She was still and I was as tongue-tied as the first time I saw her naked. After a moment, she said gently, "What is it, Joe?"

I swallowed and prayed that I wouldn't say the wrong thing again. "I...wasn't telling the truth last night. I did...and I do want to have sex with you. Even here and now on the kitchen floor." I let out a breath I hadn't known I was holding. *At least it was better than telling her I want to bend her over the kitchen bench and fuck her from behind.* I still hadn't worked out why she let me do it instead of feeding me to the sharks.

She looked back over her shoulder at me. "Pick whatever condom you want, Joe. I've been ready for you since last night."

Breathing hard, I slid my fingers under the blue lace. She was already wet, but I was going to do this properly. *This isn't something I can afford to fuck up. I have to make sure she enjoys this even more than I do.* I dipped my finger inside her and rubbed her with my wet finger. She gave a little gasp and I rubbed harder, trying to keep my hand steady. I struggled to get out of my shorts one-handed, as her breathing quickened.

Her breathing came in short gasps by the time I had my shorts out of the way and I wanted to be inside her when she came. I yanked down the blue lace and plunged in, faster and faster, so that I could come with her. She screamed out my name and squeezed me so hard it felt like I'd burst. I guess in a way I did.

I was suddenly aware of how hard the tiles were under my knees and sat back, pulling Vanessa with me onto my lap.

She surveyed the mess of boxes all over the floor. "You didn't use any of them," she said in wonder.

Oh shit. Did she want me to use one? "All I wanted wrapped around me was you," I told her honestly, praying I hadn't just stuffed up worse than last night. "You're my wife. If you want me to sleep with you so we'll have children, I agreed to that when we got married. My stud services are all yours, along with my dubious parenting skills afterwards."

She smiled, squirming around in my lap until she faced me. "I told you, I already have all the children I can handle." She suddenly looked around. "Where's Marina?"

"She just went down for a sleep," I said proudly.

She looked thoughtful. "So, we probably have at least an hour before she wakes up?"

"I guess," I answered.

Her hands slid up my sides, pulling my shirt up over my head. Now I was naked, but she was still wearing her dress. I helped her take that off, too, followed by her bra. She moved closer to me in my lap, so her knees were on either side of my hips. *She's astride me, just like last night, before I fucked up royally. Please, don't let me fuck up again now.*

She rocked her hips against me and I rose up to meet her, sliding in easily because she was so wet. I felt like I was going to slide right out again. Then she squeezed me deep inside of her and I just let her take control. By the time she let me blow for the second time, she'd already come twice.

Oh God, that was so good it's going to be days before I can get it up again. I kissed Vanessa, long and lingering. My tongue was still tangled with hers when she moved off me, leaving me as limp as a garden hose. I grabbed hold of the table and pulled myself to my feet. I rested my backside on the table for a minute, because my legs felt shaky. Vanessa was still on her knees on the floor, looking up at me thoughtfully.

"Hey, Joe," she said, her impish smile

already in place. "How about we go for third time lucky?"

I laughed. "After two rounds of sex that good, even the most beautiful woman in the world wouldn't be able to make me get it up again today. And as I've just gone two rounds with the most beautiful woman in the world, I hope she'll forgive me." I closed my eyes. I could still feel her, hot around me, even in the cool air-conditioned air of the kitchen. *I just want to hold onto that feeling for a minute longer…*

She laughed, and then sucked me so hard it almost hurt. I could feel my dick hardening and lengthening inside her mouth. I was glad I was sitting on the table, because my legs couldn't have held me up under her onslaught. I had my hands in her hair as I gasped out her name. This was better than the incredible blow job she'd given me in the air strip shed all those years ago. Fuck, this was like something out of a dream.

She had the full length of me inside her when I came for the third time and I don't know how she managed to swallow that without choking. Hell, like the first time,

Vanessa sucked me dry before she let me out of her mouth.

Vanessa meticulously put her clothes back on, from the g-string to the dress. I sat on the table, so much adrenaline coursing through my blood that I felt like a rag doll. I felt her lips on my dick again, a cool kiss on the shaft, but it hung as lifeless as a dead elephant's trunk.

I wanted to apologise, but she helped me pull my boxer shorts and then my shorts up my legs. I slid carefully off the table as I put my shirt back on.

I put my arms around her and kissed her.

"Now we're even," she murmured, before I kissed her again.

I moved one hand down so that it rested on her perfect bottom. I pressed my lips to the top of her equally perfect breast, just visible at the front of her dress. *How can we ever be even, when you're the most beautiful woman in the world and also the most gifted at sex?*

I answered dreamily, "Whatever makes you happy."

She smiled and started picking the boxes off the floor again, flashing what was now a damp lace g-string. This time, I settled down to admire the view, happy just to watch. For once.

LAILA

I was called to the first Council meeting after Estella had given birth to her twins. I had wanted to remain by her side, keeping watch over her, but the summons was urgent and Estella insisted that I go.

The meeting commenced with my arrival.

Elder Sunitha spoke first. *"The whales have brought a message from Cantrella. She intends to remain with our sisters in the Atlantic. She has resigned her position on the Council and we must appoint her successor. She has named Laila as her heir."*

Darma nodded. *"What has Laila to say to this?"*

I had known this day would come, but I was still not prepared for it. I took a breath, then another, willing my heart to slow. It felt like a fish flapping on land, desperate to escape to water where it could breathe freely. I reminded myself that I was in water, no longer on land.

"Laila?" Elder Sunitha prompted.

This was why I had ventured far from home, why I had offered my body to join with humans in the Atlantic and on land. Why I had borne my twin children, Blythe and Joy, with all the pain that entailed. To live my life as an adult, to make choices of my own, to take Mother's place as the Elder of the Black line on the Council as I was destined to.

"I wish to be a Watcher, as my mother was, to watch over our people and the children, to guard my people while you sleep. But I do not wish to be on the Elder Council. This honour is too much for me. Let the place pass to another who is worthy and wishes for it. I have no desire to lead." I let out all of my breath, feeling my shoulders slump, though the weight had lifted.

Darma looked shocked. *"You mean you decline? You have the strongest claim of any in the Black line, for there are few left. It will take time to find a replacement, to work out who has the next strongest claim..."*

She continued and the other Elders murmured in discussion, but I sank into dejection and did not listen to more. I felt guilt for placing such a burden on the Council. I wondered if I should offer to take my mother's place temporarily until someone more suitable could be found. I opened my mouth to make my offer.

A hand closed over my open mouth, as lips kissed my neck. *"Don't, dearest. You don't owe them this."*

I relaxed as my sweet Estella's arms slid around me. *"What about the children? Are you rested enough to be here? You gave birth only yesterday..."*

Estella's breasts bounced as she giggled. *"I would not miss this day for the world. Aunt Apalala and Healer Pearl have the children. They are safe, dearest. Today I must take care of you."* She pressed her lips to my neck one more time.

I did not understand her meaning, but such was my relief that I didn't question her.

"I, Estella of the Black and the Gold lines, offer to take the place of Elder Cantrella on the Council," Estella announced, her voice as majestic as her grandmother's.

Darma shook her head. *"You are not summoned by the Council, child, and you cannot claim to be of the Black line until we check the records."*

Estella's voice was clear and commanding. *"I am no child. I am a mother of two children — Diana and Danielle. My claim to Cantrella's place is greater than Laila's. My great-grandmother was Sephira and she was the daughter of Elder Aurelia and Dubhan of the Black, the last and greatest of the Black line."*

Indah gently ventured, *"But Elder Sirena is not here to approve such an unusual claim. We must send word to her…"*

"I voice my claim at her command. She holds the records of her and my ancestry. Send word if you must, but she will support me," Estella's voice thundered through the water.

I shrank in terror for her, dreading the response of the Elders at being commanded by one so young. I reached for Estella's hand, thinking to offer comfort but needing hers more than she did mine.

"You don't need to take this burden for me, Estella..." I began, aching for her sacrifice.

As my fingers touched hers, she turned to give me a triumphant smile. *"This is no burden. I have wanted this for longer than I have wanted you, though perhaps not as much."* She pressed her lips to my breast, swollen with the milk that I must feed my daughters with soon.

Darma broke into our intimate exchange. *"The Council will accept Estella's candidacy, pending confirmation from Elder Sirena. Welcome to the Council, Elder Estella."*

All four of the Elders bowed their heads to Estella, as did I.

She bowed in response, not letting go of my hand. *"Thank you. Is there more business to this meeting, or may I return to my children? Both I and my partner have newborns to feed."* I felt a thrill at the sound of it. My partner! She had formally acknowledged me to the Council. We were officially partners!

Darma nodded slowly. *"The meeting is concluded."*

Estella pulled me through the water in her excitement, as I could barely keep up. *"It is done!"* she squealed.

"It is," I replied in relief. I would not have to be an Elder. I could care for my family and not my whole people. And Estella was mine.

She swam around me, until she stopped beneath me, her hands on my breasts. *"They're enormous,"* she said in wonder. She touched her lips to mine, opening her mouth to deepen her kiss as I pulled her closer.

The pressure sent a thin stream of milk to cloud the water. Estella giggled, putting her lips to my nipple instead. A soft touch inside my tail had me looking down. The end of her tail was inside mine, a delicate tickle that I found hard to resist. *"Celebrate with me,"* she said softly, stroking.

I could never refuse my sweet Estella, but I worried for her. *"Are you recovered enough from your ordeal yesterday?"*

She giggled again. *"For an hour with you? I think so."*

JOE

"The lobster disease has spread, all the way up the US coast. It was detected in Maine this morning," Vanessa told me as she came in from work, looking excited. "They've found a shipping container washed up not far from there, which tested positive for the disease. It was identified as part of the cargo of the container ship the Atlantic sisters sank."

"Mmm?" I asked, my eyes on the TV.

"Call Skipper. Ask him who has quota left and doesn't want to fish it this year. I'll buy anything that's going. I'll buy anything going

for the next ten years — licences included."
Vanessa's voice was businesslike and brisk.

"What? You want to quit your job and go
fishing for ten years?" I struggled both to sit
up and grasp the idea. "What do you want me
to do with my business?"

"Sell it, too, Joe. We're going fishing."
Vanessa smiled.

I wondered if she was joking. "You know, if
I told anyone that my wife had just told me to
quit my job and she'd quit hers so we could
just go fishing for the next ten years, they
wouldn't believe me. Are you serious?"

She laughed. "Yes, Joe, I'm serious. My
sisters in the Atlantic have caused an ecological
disaster on a mass scale through their stupidity
and we're going to cash in on it when lobster
prices go through the roof. In ten years, we'll
be able to retire and you'll never have to work
again."

I shook my head, still not really believing
her. It sounded too good to be true. "Retire
before I'm fifty? Seriously?"

Vanessa smiled. "Whatever you want, Joe.
But I need the best deckhand I've ever had on

the *Siren* at my beck and call until then."

"What about Marina?" I asked.

"She can fish with us as much as possible in the school holidays and we'll make arrangements for her schooling up there." Vanessa smiled. "I am a teacher, Joe. I'll ensure my daughter receives a full education."

Idly, I wondered what a mermaid education involved, but I didn't think about it for long.

I had phone calls to make and then we were going fishing. For ten years.

Fuck, I hate lobsters.

Maybe in ten years' time I wouldn't mind them so much.

LAILA

"Mother has sent word that I must send one of my children to her in the Atlantic, to be trained properly!" I wailed to Estella, the moment I found her.

Six years had come and gone, a brief respite from the doom I knew floated over my head. My baby girls were growing up fast. Even as I watched them with delight, I still felt the dread of what their future held.

Estella watched our four girls and the daughters of Nafula and Indah, as they practised walking on land. Their balance was not good and more than once a girl would fall in the shallow water, landing with a splash. Diana was the youngest of them all, but she seemed to have the most poise. Blythe as the bravest was the first to run, but very clumsily. When she fell, she landed in front of Joy and Danielle, tripping both so they all landed in a heap on the sand.

I watched my two beautiful girls, my heart aching at the thought of giving either of them up to my mother and the Atlantic Elders. I loved them dearly and I did not want them to be subject to the cruelty of our sisters to the west.

Estella's arms around me were a welcome distraction. *"Did you promise to send her your child?"*

"No. It is far worse — she ordered me to do my duty for the Atlantic sisters when I was still a child in their ocean." I regretted having my head above water, because my eyes were filling with tears.

Estella's voice was calm. *"Your duty was to provide the Atlantic sisters with an heir of your line, as it was here, yes?"*

I nodded, sniffling. I hugged Estella tighter. If I was to lose one of my girls, I would need her comfort more than ever.

"Then we will ask the girls once they are adults, which of them would choose to go to the Atlantic, to replace your mother as Elder on their Council," Estella announced, unperturbed.

"But I was ordered..." I began, sure she did not understand.

Her lips were soft on mine, cutting off the words I didn't want to say. Her kiss continued for some minutes, cool and calming and caressing.

"I order our people, dearest, not her. She has no authority over me or mine and you are mine," she said softly with her sweet lips. *"And as the Elder of the Black line I will not permit any of our children to be hurt by her madness as you have been. As adults, the girls may choose to become elders in another ocean, but not before. Your mother has no power to overrule me and nor do you."*

Her eyes were intent on mine and I could not look away. All my worry flowed away beneath her gaze.

I heard a shout that broke the moment and we both turned to look. The girls ended up in the water once more, with a larger splash than before. Diana looked particularly put out.

Estella clapped her hands. *"Class is complete for today, girls. You are dismissed and you may return to your mothers, or fish until dusk."*

All six of them headed off as one for Blythe's favourite fishing spot, leaving us alone.

"You would do that?" I stared at Estella in awe. *"You have never ordered me as my matriarch before."*

Her smile was loving. *"Of course I would do that. In fact, I'd like to order you to do something else, too."*

"Anything," I answered immediately.

She rose and revealed the shapely legs she had hidden beneath the surface. Sauntering up to where the waves met the sand, she stretched out on the empty beach with a sigh of contentment.

"Make love to me, dearest," she commanded.

I laughed, shifting to my legs so that I might walk to the sand beside her. I looked down at her beautiful body, barely changed in six years, as she lay spread on the sand beneath me.

I dropped to my knees beside her. *"How*

many times?" I asked timidly. This was the first time I felt a thrill at obeying the command of my matriarch and I fully intended to enjoy it.

Her smile turned wicked. *"Until I tell you to stop, dearest. And then, I shall have my way with you."* She caressed my breast lightly, then pulled her hand away.

"Only until dark, though," I answered with regret. *"I must watch tonight."*

Estella laughed. *"I will have you 'til the stars fade in the morning sunlight. Someone else shall watch tonight. You answer to ME."*

She pushed me onto my back on the sand, rolling until she straddled my chest. Sand grated between her bottom and my breasts as she slid forward slowly. She looked down at me, still smiling.

"Start, dearest. The sooner I am sated, the sooner I start on you."

My mouth was dry with desire for her, but she was wet enough for us both. Tonight I was hers to command.

JOE

After six years of hard fishing, the *Siren* was much the worse for wear and I didn't feel any younger, either. If anything, I hated lobsters more than ever. The lobster prices had been so high, year after year, that our profits from the last season alone were enough to buy a new boat.

Vanessa sold the *Siren* to someone who wanted to retire and start a charter business in the far remote north of Western Australia. We wished them luck. I hoped they didn't learn how hard fishing could be right away and that they enjoyed it. They even renamed the boat, something to do with rebirth.

Vanessa bought us a new boat, bigger than the first, and she also named this the *Siren*. The dark blue paint of her name had barely dried on the side before the boat was in the water and we were aboard.

This would be our first fishing season without Marina. She was in high school now and she had chosen to stay with Nonna so she didn't miss school and her friends.

I loaded boxes from the wharf to the deck and Vanessa took them to where she felt they belonged.

My job was finished first, so I stood on deck and watched her. Thirteen years had passed since we'd first met at the Abrolhos and at the end of this year, we'd have been married for ten of them.

Vanessa was amazing. Wearing a tiny pair of shorts and a fitted t-shirt, at first glance she looked exactly like the girl I lost my heart to on the cliffs on Rat Island. All she was missing was the groper and the shark.

"Almost time for a break," she announced

as she stacked up the esky boxes around the ice box.

She dusted off her hands, then twined her arms around my neck. As we kissed, the fire was still there, but it was more like a smouldering glow than lighting a flare. Under the shade of the canopy, I could see fine lines around her eyes, because of how much she smiled and went out in the sun. Her fair hair was a little lighter now, with threads of white through the gold.

"You haven't changed a bit," I told her, my hands in her hair.

She laughed. "Wrinkles and white hair? Hardly. Still, I have less than you." Her hands touched my hair, where I was starting to go grey at the temples. "I'll still love you, Joe, even when your hair is more silver than gold."

She let go of me and darted excitedly into the cabin. "Come and see. This *Siren* is better than her little sister."

I followed her into the main cabin, which was laid out pretty much the same as the first. *But there are no memories of mindblowing sex on this kitchen bench*, I thought sadly.

Vanessa already stood at the bottom of the stairs, in the lower cabin. "Come on, Joe!"

I ducked my head as I went down the stairs, though there was no chance of hitting my head. This lower cabin was bigger than the previous one. This *Siren* had partitioned bedrooms, two on either side, where the bunks had been before. On either side of the stairs were a shower and a toilet.

She opened the door of the shower, an impish smile on her face. "This one's big enough for two!"

Hey, that's the one thing we've never done: have sex on a boat in the shower. The little *Siren* shower had been cramped for one and nearly impossible for two. I shrugged. *Well, it's something to try. I want to christen that kitchen bench first…*

Vanessa entered one of the little bedrooms and bounced on the bed. Instead of the tiered bunks, there was a double bed below and an upper single bunk folded flat against the wall. She stretched out. "What do you think?" she asked, her eyes shining.

I sat on the edge of the bed beside her. "I

think it's going to take us at least a week just to christen this cabin." *Thirteen years ago, we'd have had sex everywhere on the boat in a weekend, but my stamina isn't what it was.*

She laughed. "It's going to be a busy week, then. Shall we head out?"

I shook my head. "No. We should wait 'til tomorrow morning."

She looked stunned. "Why?"

The Abrolhos had grown on me. I was turning into a superstitious skipper and I was still only a deckie. "It's bad luck to head out in a boat that hasn't been christened."

Vanessa laughed again. "You mean we need to smash a bottle of wine over the side, where her name is painted? I think we have one here for that..." She went up to the main cabin and produced a bottle of bubbly wine. "So we smash it and head out. Shouldn't take long..."

I followed her out to the deck and together we broke the bottle over the blue letters at the stern.

Vanessa cheered and clapped. "Now we can go!" She skipped back into the cabin.

I caught up with her and laid my hand on

her arm. "I want to make sure this boat is christened properly before we take her out to sea."

She looked puzzled. "But that's what humans normally do for a boat, they smash a bottle, right?"

I laughed. "You're not human and not normal, either. This boat won't be christened properly until we've both come at least once on that kitchen bench."

She shook her head. "What is it with you and galley benches? Your first season out here, I spent three weeks tempting you in every way I could think of so you'd agree to sleep with me again. Then we were in the galley of my boat, waiting for dinner to be ready, I offered you a drink and…"

I told her I wanted to fuck her from behind. I will never, ever live that down. "I meant to say I wanted a beer," I admitted, in way of apology.

Her body was already pressed against mine, so she knew how much I wanted her, yet she massaged the front of my shorts with one hand and made it worse. "Do you still want that beer?" she asked softly. "Or would you prefer me?"

Yes. My mouth was dry. "You weren't wearing any underwear," I tried to explain.

Something soft landed on my foot. I looked down and met Vanessa's t-shirt as she pulled it over her head. *Blue lace. Boobs. Oh God, naked Vanessa. Thirteen years and I'm as hard for her as the first time I saw her naked.*

Salt, sea air and Vanessa, a potent cocktail that was better than Viagra.

We headed out to sea in the morning. We'd christened all four beds, the shower and the bench. I ached all over – I felt like I'd be sore for a week. God it felt good.

APALALA

She was fire in the water. My fiery daughter, Zerafina. All grown at eighteen years of age. No longer a goldfish, now she might rival her father for height, for her tail was longer than mine. She would be a gifted healer one day, when she made her choice of calling, but she was not an adult until she ventured on land. Once the fishing season was complete, she intended to ask Mother if she would permit her to do her duty soon.

She was nervous and excited about going on land, as I had been my first time, but I had told her all I knew. She would not go unprepared. Whiskey would not take her by surprise, nor fiery, hairy men.

I thought of the man who had sired her, but briefly. Aidan was part of my past that I wished I could prolong, but how many men could be trusted to be consort to an ageless beauty?

Apart from Mother's stupid consort, of course.

"Mother! The dolphins are asking for you — they wish to show you the new calves. Come here!" Zerafina called with a smile.

I laughed and rippled through the water, feeling a little stiff for being stationary so long as I watched her play.

Together with their mothers, Zerafina recited the names of all of the new children to the pod. Each calf bowed his or her head to me in acknowledgement. I waited until they were all done before I responded with a single nod to the whole group. *"I hope you will all be ready to assist if a whale needs help birthing in your islands."*

A clamour of squeaky voices responded

with eagerness. *"Of course, Healer Apalala. We will!"* They took their leave and swam away in search of a finned meal.

Zerafina hugged me as she said, *"Thank you, Mother, for bringing me here. The Abrolhos are beautiful and I love the dolphins."*

My fingers tangled in her red curls as I hugged her back, snarled like a shipwreck in seaweed. *"I have wanted to for a long time, but I waited until you were old enough to enjoy it. If Mother consents, we will part ways here, and you will carry a child of your own when you return to me in the depths."* I let go of her reluctantly.

"They will be here soon, will they not, Mother?" Zerafina asked, suddenly excited. *"Will she permit me to meet her consort?"*

I remembered the stupid human and how carefully she protected him from contact with us. *"I doubt it, sweetheart. She is very protective of him."* Privately, I hoped I would not have to see him again, either. He could remain on her vessel or on land and I would remain in the water. I knew my place and I hoped he knew his.

JOE

Abrolhos life fell into a pattern, as always. Before dawn, we pulled the pots and dropped them again. We crated up the catch and sent it back to the mainland on the carrier boat.

When we ran low on supplies, we took the *Siren* back to Geraldton and went shopping.

For the rest of every day and every night, it was just me and Vanessa. It was like the honeymoon we'd never had.

We took some days off and went snorkelling, both up in the Wallabis and down in the Pelsaert Group.

Sometimes, late at night, she'd slip over side of the *Siren* and go for a swim on her own beneath the surface. She always came back with fish. One night, when we were moored off the end of Pelsaert Island, I woke up alone. I stepped out on the main deck to find her sitting on the ladder on the side of the boat. She wafted her tail flukes aimlessly through the water.

I watched her for a minute. She didn't show her tail often and almost never out of the water. It stunned me as much as the first time to be reminded that she wasn't human. *But still my beautiful wife, Nessa.*

I came up behind her and slid my arms around her before she noticed I was there. "Can't sleep?" I asked her gently.

She shook her head slowly. "I miss my people and sometimes I want to go home, but at the same time I want to go back inside and sleep with you. Am I a traitor, for not returning to my people and staying on shore for so long? Yet if I swim home to take my place among the Elder Council again, it is a betrayal of a different kind. I will be leaving you and my responsibilities here."

"Marina would be really upset if you left, too," I reminded her.

She turned so I could see her face. "I would take Marina with me, Joe. She is one of my people and she still has so much to learn. Only you couldn't follow us."

My heart sank, like it'd dropped right out of my chest and onto the sea floor below. I tried to keep my voice light. "So don't go. It's not like you to be so dark."

She took a deep breath. "But Joe, I'm carrying another child. I'll have to stay with her in the water from late pregnancy until she's weaned. She will be born in the water, at our Nursery Grounds, with the assistance of one of the healers among my people. I won't be able to bring her on land until I know she can control her tail." Her hands went to her tummy, where blue skin blended with cream.

Now I looked, she did seem a little rounder than usual, but I'd put that down to more beer and frozen pizza than was good for us. I was a bit rounder than usual, too, but I sure as hell wasn't pregnant.

I reached out to touch her tummy, caressing her soft skin with my fingers. *Our baby's in there. A baby we made.*

From the depths, my heart suddenly soared, like an osprey's fish breakfast. I was in bliss. "You mean we're going to have another baby?"

"Yes," Vanessa said softly, smiling at my obvious happiness.

I'm going to see her increase, swollen with my child. My perfect wife is carrying my child.

I lifted her off the ladder, tail and all, staggering under her weight. I laid her down gently on the main deck, stroking every bit of her I could reach. "Thank you, Vanessa, thank you," I told her. There were tears in my eyes.

I lay down beside her on the deck, hugging and kissing her. I felt her tail slowly split as I pressed against her. Somehow hugging and kissing gave way to more intimate caresses. In the pre-dawn darkness, we made love on the main deck of the *Siren*. *Me and my beautiful, pregnant wife.*

APALALA

I watched Sirena swim off in her human swimwear, but I waited 'til she was some distance away before I hauled myself aboard her boat.

Her human consort had aged considerably, but his habits had not changed. He stumbled around the galley of the new *Siren,* too somnolent to notice my entrance as he made coffee for himself. I selected one of the damp towels strung up over the line on the back deck and wrapped it around myself. I knew what happened when I showed my naked body to a human male.

I was angry at him for placing my mother in such danger, danger he surely did not understand. I would make him understand.

"There is considerable risk to her in carrying this child," I told him with disapproval.

His sudden start told me that I was correct in my surmise that he had been oblivious to my approach.

"Belinda, right?" he asked.

I looked at him with little patience. Sirena had named him her consort, privy to any knowledge of us that he pleased, but I did not wish to tell him my true name. Grudgingly, I acknowledged the land name he used, permitting him to call me by it.

"What do you mean by considerable risk?" he asked next.

I attempted to state the words slowly, so this stupid human might understand. "She is older than any other new mother I have known, and her time on land has aged her further. Age increases the chance of danger in the birth, both to mother and child. It also means there is greater likelihood that the child will not survive."

"Why do you care?" he burst out with considerable anger.

"I am a healer, the most senior among our people. I was trained by my grandmother, Sephira. I will assist Vanessa in the delivery of this child, if she carries it to term." I let my eyes beg him to understand, as I gave him more information than I thought wise. "It was I who delivered Sister Marina, a birth also fraught with risk for her mother."

"Marina is your sister?" he demanded.

I had indeed told him more information than Sirena had. I lowered my voice to explain, hoping Mother would not mind.

"Yes, Marina is my sister and if this child lives, she will be my sister also. Vanessa is my mother and our people will not thank you if your careless relationship with her results in her loss. She is too important." I met his eyes. "I will gladly take your life in payment for hers."

The human was brave, I will grant him that, though still no less stupid.

"Bring it on," he replied icily. "If you kill my

wife by not letting her deliver our child in hospital, I'm not going to let you survive, either. I don't care whose daughter you are."

I bowed my head in acknowledgement. I didn't want to tell him that he did not stand a chance against me in any form of combat. Reluctantly, I realised I did have more to say. "I have never lost a mother during a delivery, but the child is another matter. If she loses this child, it will devastate her."

He looked surprised at my change of topic. "Why tell me?" he burst out. "Why talk to me at all, if all you want is to kill me?"

I swallowed bile at the thought of having to deliver compliments to this human. "Because my mother loves you. You can bring a smile to her face when her heart contains nothing but salt tears. No one else makes her as happy as you can. As long as she lives, you are under her protection. None of us may touch you or even speak to you without her permission."

"Are you here with her permission?" he asked abruptly.

I struggled to control my anger at his impertinent question, when I wanted his assurance that he would assist her. "I had to speak to you, to beg for your help. Please help her, support her through this difficult birth. Do anything she asks of you and do not desert her. If we lose her, both your and my people will be lost." I bit back the names I wanted to use for him, as they were far from complimentary. "She knows the risks, but she chose to carry another child for you. Please help us."

I waited a moment, hoping for an answer, but he still looked angry and uncooperative. As Sirena would not permit me to damage or kill him, I left the vessel and dived into the water before I took my frustration out on him.

Stupid human. Because of his anger and stubbornness, my mother could die carrying his child. And if she did, I would see to it that he died in the slowest, most agonising way possible.

JOE

Back at Rat, I woke up alone in our bed. I dressed quickly and wandered through the house, but Vanessa wasn't home. I went up the jetty and checked out the *Siren*, but Vanessa wasn't aboard, either. Her dinghy and the Naiad were tied up, too.

So she's either gone for a walk or a swim, I decided. Back on the veranda, I checked and her shoes were gone. I ducked inside to grab an iced coffee from the fridge, before heading down the path.

I looked around as I wandered between the

shacks, but no one was around. Most of the boats were still off checking pots. I scuffed my feet through the coral shingle until I reached the airstrip. I stopped by the shelter shed and looked around again. *There's something blue across the southern end of the airstrip,* I thought. I crossed the airstrip and followed the sand track south.

She knelt on the ground near the grave on the southern cliffs, her shirt almost the same colour as the ocean. She didn't hear me approach, so she must have been lost in thought.

"Nessa?" I said softly. "Nessa, are you okay?"

"Joe?" She turned and then stood up. Her eyes were red as if she'd been crying, but her smile was as clear and happy as ever.

"Why were you crying?" I asked her.

She wiped her eyes and sniffled. Her smile turned rueful. "You don't want to know."

Probably, but I'm going to find out anyway. "Yeah, I do. I don't want you to be sad."

Now her eyes were sorrowful. "Sometimes life is sad, Joe. Sometimes you lose people and there's nothing you can do about it."

Shit. Not you. Not our baby. Please don't tell me the ice queen was right. Don't let me lose my Nessa!

"Are you okay? Is the baby okay?" I blurted out, worried.

She smiled again. "No, the baby and I are just fine, Joe. It's not as if she's my first child."

Now's the time to ask her. Now or never.

I took a deep breath. "How many children have you had?"

The way she looked at me, I swear she was scanning my brain, every thought and memory laid bare. After a few moments that felt like longer, she said, "I have borne three children. She will be my fourth child." Vanessa patted her tummy.

"Maria, Belinda and Marina, right?" I ventured.

"Yes," she replied softly. It was like she was waiting for me to say something else.

I'm either going to be really jealous or really scared, but I have to know. "What happened to their fathers?"

She regarded me warily, but her voice stayed soft. "Both Maria and Belinda's fathers died. Marina's father proved irresistible in bed, so he's still alive." She looked like she was trying not to laugh.

Part of my head glowed at being called irresistible in bed, but the rest of my mind froze with fear. *Nessa's killed two men and one day she might lose interest and kill me, too.*

"How did they die?" I stammered.

"Belinda's father died in a motorcycle accident with his wife," Vanessa replied immediately, then hesitated. "Maria's father drowned."

An accident could happen to anyone. But drowning? I don't want to, but I have to know. "Were you there?" I asked. *Say no, please say no.*

"I was in the water," she began haltingly, then looked at my face. She turned defensive. "It was an accident! His boat capsized and he couldn't swim, so I saved him and took him to a little sand island. I tore strips off his clothing to bandage his wounds and...I warmed him up in the only way I could. I was fertile and he was very gentle." She looked down at the ground, not meeting my eyes. "When the storm died down, I tried to take him back to his people, but he was bleeding and some sharks attacked us. I sent them away, but I lost him in the water. When I found him, he was dead." She looked up at me, her eyes filled with tears. "He called me an angel, Joe, because he thought I'd save him. But I didn't, because I forgot he couldn't swim." She rested one hand on the gravestone and wiped her eyes with the other.

"If the last thing he did was have sex with you, then he died a very happy man," I said after a moment. "What was the lucky bastard's name?"

Her eyes were on my face as she pointed to the gravestone, not saying a word.

Giuseppe, who died in 1921? You have to be joking. "You can't be serious. He's been dead a hundred years!" I burst out.

He eyes held mine. "He was the first man to touch me as a woman. That's not something a girl forgets, even after a hundred years."

Shit. I know she's not lying, but it's just not possible. "How old are you?" I asked her.

She looked thoughtful. "I was sixteen then, and so I am around a hundred and twenty now. I do not know the date of my birth, for my people didn't record that."

More than a hundred. Older than my grandmother was when she died. How the hell is that possible? She doesn't look any older than me! "How?" I managed to say.

"My people live longer than yours," Vanessa explained. "In the ocean deeps, we age slower and live perhaps twice a human's lifespan. On land, we age faster, more like humans."

My wife is a hundred and twenty and pregnant. No wonder the midwife's worried about the birth. "How much longer will you live?"

"Perhaps another thirty years, depending on how much time I spend on land," Vanessa said slowly. She looked at me. "Probably about as long as you, as human life expectancy is around seventy to eighty years."

I only get another thirty years with her? Right. "Let's go back to camp," I told her suddenly, taking her hand.

"Why?" she asked, surprised. She followed me back along the track.

"I need to find a way to stay with you every minute I can, right up until the baby's born," I replied, striding as quickly as I could. "We're going to get a boat so I can follow you even in the water, to your mysterious Nursery Grounds. Where are they?"

"For most of the year, we use Rowley Shoals. It is easy to avoid humans there and the water is warm and shallow."

Rowley Shoals is somewhere up north. "Where in Rowley Shoals?" I asked.

She laughed. "Mermaid Reef, of course."

Shit. Don't make it obvious or anything. "Then I'm going to get a boat that can take us out to Rowley Shoals and that's where we're going."

Vanessa stopped and looked at me in wonder. "You'd do that for me?"

I snorted. "Yeah I would. I'm going to be there when you have our baby."

She laughed. "Then don't go to Rowley Shoals. She'll be born in summer, the cyclone season, which is when the Nursery Grounds are not at Mermaid Reef."

"Where then?" I demanded.

She hesitated a second. "North Keeling Island," she said finally. "It's where I was born."

DARMA

"I do not want to learn about fish and humans. It is stupid. I have lived among them for ten years and I do not need to learn how to walk!" the angry girl shouted at me.

I was taken aback. Not even Elder Sirena had shown this little respect as a child and this child was hers. Any other child and I would have been well within my rights to discipline the little she-shark as I saw fit, but Sirena's child was special. So special she deserved a slap.

"Your mother has said you will attend school with

the others and you shall. Even if I have to tie your tail to a rock in order to arrange this," I replied calmly. With a gesture, I summoned Zerafina forward. A flash of fire and the older girl floated beside me. "I trust you to ensure she remains in school as Elder Sirena directed. You may use any force you deem necessary."

Zerafina smiled. "With respect, Elder, no force will be necessary."

Marina's eyes blazed. "Want to bet?" she spat. "Fuck you." The human words made little sound as the bubbles floated up to the surface, but I understood the words her lips shaped.

Zerafina settled herself gracefully in the water, the image of patience. "I was there the day you were born, you know. It was my first birth. I was permitted to assist — I helped Mother hand you to Grandmother." She smiled at the memory. "I kissed you first when she told our people your name."

Marina said nothing, her expression still angry.

"I will have to visit land soon — it will be my first time. I am very excited, but very nervous, too. There is so much I do not know and yet I want to. My mother speaks of the warmth of fire, wood that burns in air, *and the need to cover our skin because humans are driven mad when we uncover it. She also speaks of a liquid fire that humans drink, but I do not believe that is possible."* Zerafina laughed, rippling her tail so that it looked like fire. *"Tell me — is there such a thing?"*

"There's alcohol," Marina replied grudgingly.

Zerafina slapped her tail with her hands. *"There is a fire drink? Ha! What does it taste like?"*

"I don't know," Marina admitted. *"I never have."*

"I'll make you a deal," Zerafina purred. *"You keep an eye out for me on land and persuade Grandmother to let me try some of Mother's fire drink. I'll keep an eye on you here and not tie your tail to a rock, if,"* she looked askance at me, *"Teacher Darma agrees to let you add to the information she can give us on human life on land."*

Marina looked tempted. I held my breath as I waited.

Zerafina was of her grandmother's line, of that there was no doubt, but she had qualities all her own that she could only have inherited from her human father. I wondered what kind of man could have tempted Healer Apalala to try for another child, after the heartbreaking death of her first. A persuasive one, like his daughter, I presumed.

One of the younger twins – Danielle or Diana, I could not tell which, for I could not tell one girl from the other – swam up, her expression worried. Her bow was deep as she caught her breath from the speed she had needed for her journey.

Zerafina took Marina's hand and the younger girl did not resist. Her face had gone pale.

Estella's daughter managed to state her message. *"Elder Darma, Zerafina, Marina. Please come quickly. It is time."*

JOE

"Joe, it's time," Vanessa's voice called from the water. I was down in the cabin, but I took the steps two at a time to reach the deck.

"Time for what?" I asked, confused. We'd been out on the boat at North Keeling for a couple of weeks now, and we hadn't seen anyone else. What possible appointment could we have? Did she invite some dolphins for dinner? Or some fairy terns?

"Oh!" She sounded like she was in pain. Panting, she managed to say, "It's time for me to have the baby, Joe."

Oh God. Oh God. I took off my shirt and jumped into the water, swimming to her side. She wasn't alone. Belinda and another girl I didn't recognise flanked her, one on either side. They swam with her to shallow water, gold and cream tails with Vanessa's legs between them. They were followed by a pair of dolphins.

For a minute, I stared after them. *Why doesn't Vanessa have a tail?* I thought about it a minute. *She said she loses control of her tail when she gets turned on. Maybe it happens when she goes into labour, too.* I realised that they were rapidly outdistancing me, and I swam as fast as I could to catch up.

They took her to a pool of shallow water, perhaps knee deep if she'd stood up, but she couldn't. The pool was surrounded by reefs and slight waves broke over the surface, but they were little more than ripples. When the two mermaids sat her down on the sand beneath the water, it came to her breasts. Her swollen belly stayed submerged, looking enormous. She doubled over in pain again.

Belinda was talking to the dolphins and it

sounded like it was more than a one-way conversation, the dolphins taking it in turns to duck beneath the surface and squeak in Vanessa's direction. Belinda nodded gravely at whatever the creatures told her.

"What can I do?" I asked, anguished. I wanted to take Vanessa to the best hospital back in Perth and make them give her pain drugs so she didn't have to hurt like this, but it was too late now. She had mermaids, dolphins, a shallow pool and me.

She stretched out a hand to me. "Hold me, Joe. She's coming."

I splashed through the pool to take her hand. She gripped it hard as another pain came. I dropped into the water to sit behind her. I put my arms around her and moved closer, supporting her back. She didn't let go of my hand.

Belinda and Cream Tail were talking in low voices and didn't notice me at first. When Vanessa cried out at the next contraction, they both turned to her and saw me. Belinda's mouth closed firmly and she looked like she was gritting her teeth, but she didn't say a word. Cream Tail said something in the mermaid language and she sounded angry.

Vanessa gasped out something in response, glaring at Cream Tail.

With a malevolent look at me, Cream Tail spat out, "No human has ever watched a birth of one of our kind. Never has a human seen us in such numbers and lived to tell the tale."

Vanessa and her volcanic temper. "Then, Pearl, my consort will be the first. He will be my support in this difficult birth and I…will vouch for…his spreading…no tales amongst humans." Her voice started out majestic, but the last few words came out strained as she doubled over in pain again.

Pearl muttered something I didn't catch. Even through her pain, Vanessa heard her and understood.

"This human has helped our kind more times than I can count." Vanessa broke off suddenly for the next contraction. No one dared to speak while they waited for her to continue. "Our people owe him a large debt. As my consort you will give him equal respect to what is due me. Anyone who thinks to harm him will answer to me."

Heads rose from the water across the reef. There must have been at least ten mermaids in the water, between us and the outer reef, with another five patrolling the outer reefs. All the heads dipped in acknowledgement, before sinking beneath the waves.

I married the queen of the mermaids, I realised. *Please don't let me lose her now.*

Vanessa started to say something else, but all that came out was a wordless, horrible shout. Belinda and Pearl pushed her knees up and apart while Vanessa reached for my other hand with her free one. Holding tight to my hands, Vanessa let out another shout as she started to push.

"She's coming," Belinda said encouragingly.

This was Hell. Vanessa held so tight to my hands I lost all feeling in them. She bellowed so loud with each push that I was certain she was in agony and there was nothing I could do about it but hold her and wish her pain would end. I would have done anything to save her from this, but there was nothing I could do. *Oh God, please let her be okay. Please let her deliver this baby safely so the pain will stop hurting her...*

"I can see her head, Vanessa. One more big push..." Belinda began.

Vanessa pushed so hard every muscle in her body went taut. Then she took a deep breath and did it again.

Between her legs, I could see blood in the water. Then I saw the baby's head appear.

"Another one. You can..." Belinda was intent on the baby.

Vanessa drew another sobbing breath and pushed. From between her legs the baby spurted out into the water, head, shoulders, arms, torso and tail. All covered with silvery skin like a snapper.

Tears streamed down my face. *Oh thank you, God.*

"Just one more push, and then it's over," Belinda coaxed.

What? There's only one baby. Does she think there's more? Hasn't she been through enough pain?

Vanessa took a ragged breath and pushed one last time. What came out of her looked like a mess of blood, bigger than the baby's head. *What is that? The placenta? Oh.* Then she collapsed against me. There were salt tears on her face, too.

I held Vanessa tightly, as her breathing slowed and she relaxed her grip on my numb hands.

Belinda and Pearl held the baby, severing and tying up the umbilical cord. Vanessa held out her arms. "Give her to me," she commanded.

"Your daughter, Elder Sirena," Pearl said respectfully, as she handed the baby into Vanessa's willing arms. Vanessa cradled our child lovingly and pressed the baby's face to her breast. The baby latched on immediately and started to suck.

Tentatively, I wrapped my arms around Vanessa's, so I was touching our baby, too. *Our baby.* After Marina, even this baby's silvery skin didn't seem so strange. Yet even as I watched, the silver was turning to pink, from the head down. Where the shiny tail had been were two fat, pink legs. Vanessa was now holding what looked like a normal, human baby. My breath caught in my throat.

"What is her name?" Belinda asked.

Heads bobbed above the water again, waiting to hear the name of the newest in their number. Even the dolphins were alert, looking like they were listening. Again, I wondered if all mermaid births were as well attended as this one.

Vanessa's voice came out in a hoarse whisper, so she cleared her throat and tried again. "My daughter's name will be..."

"Vanessa, look," I told her urgently, pointing at the baby.

She gasped and broke off. She tried but couldn't speak.

The mermaids waited, but they didn't realise she'd been shocked into speechlessness. I raised my voice, as loud as I could so they would all hear me above the waves.

"Our son's name will be John Giuseppe."

There was silence. The only sound was the waves breaking on the reef.

The tale will continue in

Ocean's Depths

ABOUT THE AUTHOR

Demelza Carlton has always loved the ocean, but on her first snorkelling trip she found she was afraid of fish.

She has since swum with sea lions, sharks and sea cucumbers and stood on spray drenched cliffs over a seething sea as a seven-metre cyclonic swell surged in, shattering a shipwreck below.

Demelza now lives in Perth, Western Australia, the shark attack capital of the world.

The *Ocean's Gift* series was her first foray into fiction, followed by her suspense thriller *Nightmares* trilogy.

Want to know more? You can follow Demelza on Facebook, Twitter, YouTube or her website, Demelza Carlton's Place at:

www.demelzacarlton.com

Books by Demelza Carlton

Siren of Secrets series

Ocean's Secret (#1)
Ocean's Gift (#2)
Ocean's Infiltrator (#3)

Siren of War series

Ocean's Justice (#1)
Ocean's Widow (#2)
Ocean's Bride (#3)
Ocean's Rise (#4)
Ocean's War (#5)
How To Catch Crabs

Nightmares Trilogy

Nightmares of Caitlin Lockyer (#1)
Necessary Evil of Nathan Miller (#2)
Afterlife of Alana Miller (#3)

Mel Goes to Hell series

The Devil's Work (#1)
See You in Hell (#2)
Mel Goes to Hell (#3)
To Hell and Back (#4)
The Holiday From Hell (#5)
All Hell Breaks Loose (#6)
The Devil Goes to Heaven (#7)

Romance Island Resort series

Maid for the Rock Star (#1)
The Rock Star's Email Order Bride (#2)
The Rock Star's Virginity (#3)
The Rock Star and the Billionaire (#4)
The Rock Star Wants A Wife (#5)
The Rock Star's Wedding (#6)
Maid for the South Pole (#7)
Jailbird Bride (#8)

Romance a Medieval Fairytale series

Enchant: Beauty and the Beast Retold
Dance: Cinderella Retold
Fly: Goose Girl Retold
Revel: Twelve Dancing Princesses Retold
Silence: Little Mermaid Retold
Awaken: Sleeping Beauty Retold
Embellish: Brave Little Tailor Retold
Appease: Princess and the Pea Retold
Blow: Three Little Pigs Retold
Return: Hansel and Gretel Retold
Wish: Aladdin Retold
Melt: Snow Queen Retold
Spin: Rumpelstiltskin Retold
Kiss: Frog Prince Retold
Reflect: Snow White Retold
Roar: Goldilocks Retold
Cobble: Elves and the Shoemaker Retold

www.ingramcontent.com/pod-product-compliance
Lightning Source LLC
Chambersburg PA
CBHW070340170726
48291CB00001B/125